SHOTGUN SEAMSTRESS

zine collection

by Osa Atoe

SHOTGUN SEAMSTRESS
zine collection

by Osa Atoe

Shotgun Seamstress
Zine Collection
by Osa C. Atoe

© Osa Atoe 2012

Layout by Mend My Dress Press

All Rights Reserved. Except as permitted under the U.S. Copyright of 1976, no part of this publication may be reproduced, distributed or transmitted in any form or by any means, or stored in any database or retrieval system, without the prior written permission of the publisher.

Published by Mend My Dress Press, Tacoma, WA
MendMyDress.com

Library of Congress in-catalog-publishing information available on request

Atoe/ Osa
    Shotgun Seamstress Zine Collection, Osa Atoe
    ISBN-13: 978-0-9850131-5-8
    1. Zines   2. Music   3. Art   4. Black History   4. Title

Manufactured in the United States of America

CONTENTS

INTRODUCTION   6

NUMBER 1   9

NUMBER 2   37

NUMBER 3   81

NUMBER 4   121

NUMBER 5   145

NUMBER 6   189

INTRODUCTION

I first encountered *Shotgun Seamstress* not long after the release of its first issue, when I reviewed the zine for *Maximum Rocknroll*. I was immediately excited by Osa's project, as that first issue featured many of the hallmarks of the trailblazing zines written by people of color, women, and freaks in punk that I had long treasured. Like those zines, *Shotgun Seamstress* mixed an unabashed dose of anger, a punk archivist streak, a cool cut 'n' paste aesthetic, and an eye towards Osa's experiences navigating the multiple strands of her identity: Black, punk, feminist, queer, anti-capitalist, music nerd, outsider, artist, etc. I made it a point after that first issue to seek out new issues of *Shotgun Seamstress* whenever they emerged.

Despite this early enthusiasm, I was not fully prepared for what followed from that first issue. Every issue of *Shotgun Seamstress* seems somehow to get better than the one that precedes it. Indeed, not long into its run, the zine takes a leap out from under the shadow of its predecessors; this is not (just) a personal zine, not (just) a music zine, not (just) a political zine, but rather an explosive combination of the best of all of those DIY traditions. Over the issues, Osa's writing gets sharper, the interviews are executed with an increasingly sophisticated sense of purpose and generous sense of humor, and even the visual aspects of the zine seem more vibrant.

In issue #6, Osa announces all too abruptly — at least, that is how it felt to me at the time — that she is no longer going to be producing new issues of *Shotgun Seamstress*. When I first heard this news, I was disappointed; after all, I was a regular reader and devotee! But now, in re-reading the entirety of *Shotgun Seamstress* a year or so after that last issue was published, my disappointment about the zine's demise has turned to unbridled admiration for the trajectory that Osa followed over the course of those six issues.

You are about to experience this trajectory for yourself. As you set out to read (or re-read) *Shotgun Seamstress*, you will come to bear witness to a writer, artist, and self-made historian who follows her own good advice by making art without worrying about industry/institutional standards or punk norms or fretting about the fact that the zine will never provide her with a retirement fund. In the process of reading, you will encounter a writer who is transforming before your very eyes. You will see the anger and alienation apparent in the first issue give spark to the project that brings its author the sassy confidence and verve present by the last. You will witness a fearless punker who has the nerve to hang out with and interview Black punk heroes like Mick Collins or Poly Styrene — and interview them well! — but who self-assuredly knows better than to believe they deserve a pedestal higher than current torchbearers like Adee Roberson or Marilyn of Aye Nako. Perhaps most importantly, you will encounter too many characters to count — both historical and contemporary — who make up the world of Black feminists, artists, punks, queers, and musicians that Osa's writing inhabits. This world will remind you that not only are you not alone but you are also never done learning about the folks who blazed the trail.

And girl, let me tell you, this fanzine is better than school. Can you believe that even as a nerdy brown punk weirdo on the wrong side of 30, I had never heard of the brilliant Alvin Baltrop before reading *Shotgun Seamstress*? That I had never before read an interview with the singer of NYC's NastyFacts? That I was woefully ignorant of feminist DJs like New Orleans' DJ Soul Sister? What's more, I have read and re-read that Mick Collins interview about ten times since I first read it. I fist pump and air drum to the sounds of "Who Are You" at every one of Osa's mentions of the almighty Void. The letters to and from Vaginal Creme Davis bring a tear to my eye and a knowing nod to my skull. The list goes on and on.

Punker, I dare you not to feel inspired by the content of this zine. And in this cruel and fucked up world, inspiration is the name of the game. Osa's hard-won ability to shake off at least some of the pressures of white-male-straight-capitalist standards in order to forge her own way make *Shotgun Seamstress* a mandatory read and an inspiration for those of us trying to do the same.

— Golnar Nikpour, August 2012

Shotgun Seamstress

BANG!

R.I.P. TONI yOUng

A ZINE

BY AND FOR

BLACK PUNKS

CONTENTS

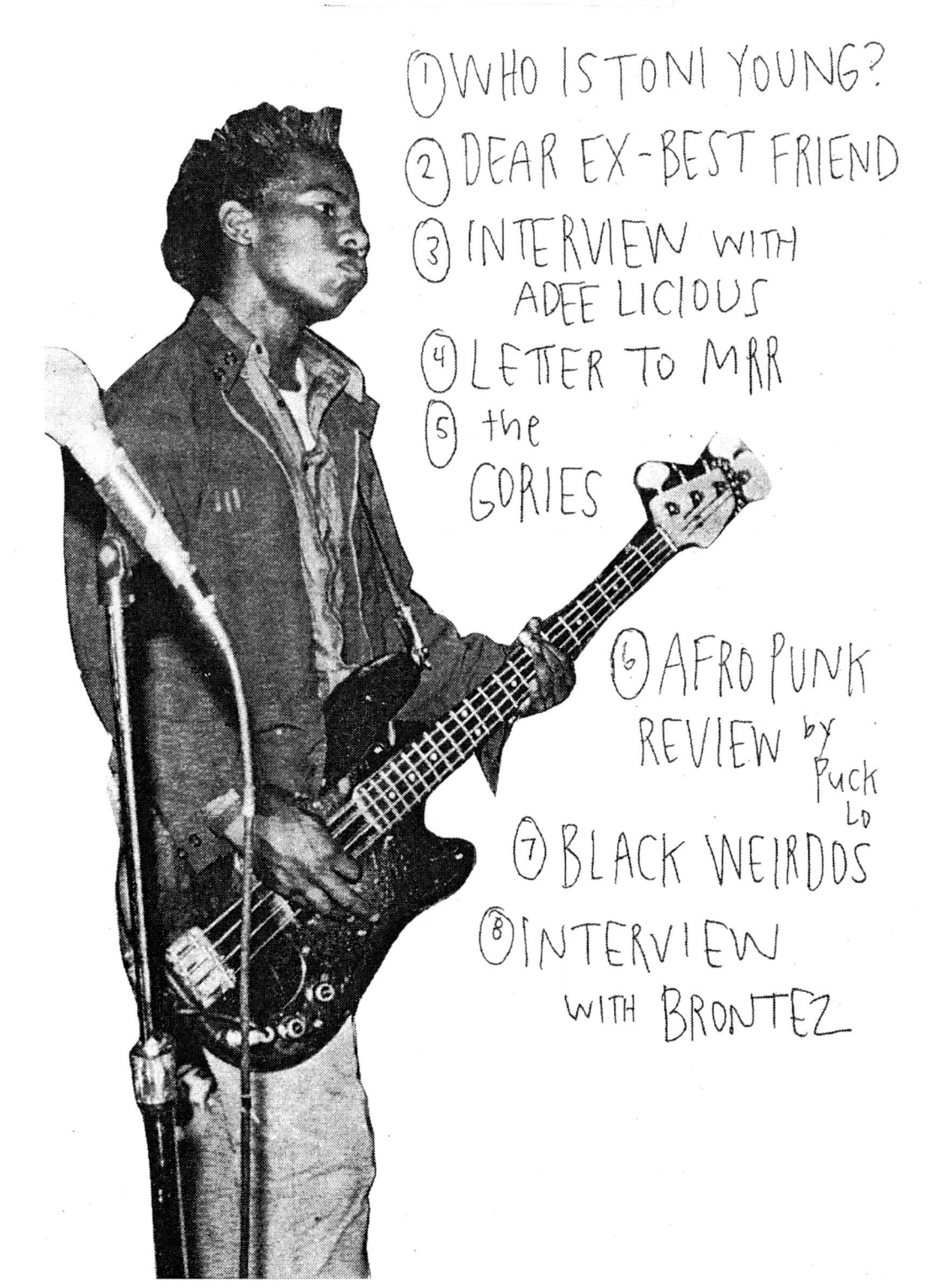

1. WHO IS TONI YOUNG?
2. DEAR EX-BEST FRIEND
3. INTERVIEW WITH ADEE LICIOUS
4. LETTER TO MRR
5. the GORIES
6. AFRO PUNK REVIEW by Puck Lo
7. BLACK WEIRDOS
8. INTERVIEW WITH BRONTEZ

Shotgun Seamstress

AUG 2006

welcome.

for s.n.r

lagos, nigeria 2000

who is Toni Young?

there werent that many girls that hung out. toni was in a band. she's like the first female in a hardcore band. she did a lot for Double O. she set up all these shows out of town. she produced the single.
 —viviene green, friend
  from Banned in DC

toni young was the queen of the early 80s dc hardcore scene. she played bass for Peer Pressure, Dove, and Red C, who has a few songs on that Flex Your Head dischord comp. When i first found out about toni young, i was so excited to find out that a black girl had been so active in punk, playing in bands and putting out records so early on. well, sadly she died of pneumonia in 1986 because she didn't have health insurance. fucked up.
  r.i.p. toni young
   and thanks for getting shit done.

dear ex-best friend

i wanted to share part of a letter i wrote recently because its the best way i can use my own experience to explain (briefly) the way that racism infiltrates personal relationships. in zines by people of color, it seems like its been easier to describe how racism works & manifests itself in less personal situations. early last year i wrote a letter to MRR about being confused with another black kid at a punk show in oakland. i spit that thing out in 10 minutes and didn't care what anyone thought about it. but this stuff is harder to talk about because its harder to see in the first place and its tougher to describe. with the way racism plays itself out these days, it sometimes takes us years to figure out that we are unwittingly participating in an oppressive dynamic with our white best friend, girlfriend, housemate, etc. and when we finally figure it out, what's there to do about it? these are people who we love and who love us, people we've grown incredibly close to. it's heartbreaking situation and there's no one right way to deal with it.

in SUPPORT, a zine about supporting people who have been sexually abused, a woman wrote, "i think in movements that call themselves radical, there are a lot of judgements about women and a total lack of understanding about what real women have to do to make it through the day." when i read that sentence, i couldn't help but re-read it, except this time including the word 'black':

i think that in predominantly white movements, including the punk scene and activist circles, there are lots of judgments and assumptions about black people and a total lack of understanding about what real black people (and specifically black women) have to do to make it through the day.

wouldn't that be even MORE true for us since we're so scarce in these spaces? its been really uncomfortable for me to acknowledge that most of the white friends i've had haven't even really known other black people. they've never had other black friends. they've never been to black folks' houses. perhaps most of their "experience" with black folks has been watchiching us on tv and hearing us on the radio. OF COURSE they have millions of assumptions about us that we will never know because those are the things white people never put words to, at least not while we're around. i wrote this letter in defense of my humanity.

turn....

dear ex-bestfriend,

i've been trying to have this talk with you for the past couple years, but we both know that throughout our friendship, its been so hard for me to talk to you about things you just don't want to talk about. you finally worked on not bursting out in tears upon confrontation, but i still feel like deep down, the same dynamic remains. out of respect for your sensitivity, i put off or avoided saying so much, but now i feel like that's resulted in a pretty hollow friendship.

before when i tried to talk to you about it, you said "i'm really starting to freak out. i feel like our friendship is strong, so i don't know what there could be to talk about." so again, i put things off because i don't ever want to make anyone freak out. but how selfish is it to assume that there can't be anything to discuss just because YOU don't think there is? i'm the one in our friendship that NEVER freaks out. that's just not what i do. i am not a very fragile person, and my eyes do not well up with tears when i am confronted by someone i care about with a difficult discussion.

as a black girl in a sea of white kids, it was easy for me to assume the role of being fiercely independent. it was easy for everyone else, including you, to assume these things about me too. now i realize that i need to make sure my relationships are emotionally reciprocal from now on. i need to make sure that i am demanding as much as i am giving and that i deserve to demand things.

i am a black girl who has built up a thick, strong armor to protect myself from the daily assaults i face. i strive to be responsible and self-reliant every single day. i try not to cop out. i try really hard not to be a burden on other people. but i am still human and i need for people to show me i am special to them. just because i do not verbally demand these things or behave like a basket case does not mean that i do not have emotions or need to be shown as much love as anyone else...

end.

adee licious

adee, 25, is from south florida. in the past few years, she's lived in oakland, new orleans and pensacola. adee's zine, *finger on the trigger*, dealt honestly with what it means to be a black girl in the punk scene and also helped her connect with other people of color isolated in punk scenes all over the country. adee now lives in portland and plays drums in the new bloods.

when did you make your first zine and why?
i think in 2000 or 2001. i didn't know how to play an instrument and i was reading a lot of books at the time, like langston hughes and zora neal hurston, and i'd just went traveling for the first time so i felt like i had a lot to say. when i first started writing a zine, i didn't really think about who i was writing to so much. i wrote short stories and stuff and i was just sending it to my friends. i was reading a bunch of historical fiction and a lot of my zine was reading black literature and then responding to it. i geuss that reading literature is kind of the way i get into radical politics because even though people around me were into radical shit too, they were all white.

why haven't you done a zine in a while?
because i started making more art and playing music and... i got reviews in punk planet and mrr and people would always say "this is really good" but it was always just white people so i was like, "what's the point?" but i did gain a lot of pen pals who were people of color. i do want to do a zine again, but i just started playing more attention to art... it was a lot of little things that made me stop. i got tired of being the "race zine" person. i felt like i was one of the only people at the time, especially in florida, writing that kind of zine.

when and why did you start doing political work outside the punk scene?
first, i started doing work with kids. in pensacola, me and gloria started volunteering at an after school program at a housing project. when i moved to new orleans, i still worked with kids but i also helped organize the INCITE [women of color against violence] conference. honestly, i prefer doing stuff with kids because we just made art and actually had conversations about our lives instead of just stressing out about organizing something. but at least with INCITE i got the experience of what it's like to organize a conference. also, some of the connections i already had with other people of color got stronger through that. working out of the treme [historically black neighborhood in new orelans] was really cool too.

then you worked at an abortion clinic in oakland?
yeah, i found out about the women's choice clinic in oakland from my friends yvette and syd who worked there. yvette used to do this diy women's health tour with a bunch of other girls... i got into women's health because i don't have health insurance. also, it's practical and it's a service you can actually provide to people. i'm not a theory, college person and i don't really care about that stuff, so women's health just works for me. you can also make a lot of money doing it, gain skills, and teach other people the skills you've learned.

what bands have you played in?
bands no one's ever heard of. blood truck, sex jungle and the awful flakes. now i'm in the new bloods.

how'd you start playing drums?
i started playing drums when i was about 21 or 22. i taught myself how. i met this girl at the time who was really chill about playing music. she was like "just try stuff out!" before that, i didn't know i could just play drums in my own weird way before, without "knowing how" to play or getting lessons or something. and i've always mostly been in bands with girls cuz i like girl bands. i love music. it's just another way of making art. it sounds tight and you can make it political if you want.

from finger on the trigger #6

is it political for you?
for me, as far as being a black, queer, girl playing music is political for me because there's not that many girls that are black and queer who are in bands. but in the way that i've been writing songs lately, it doesn't seem like my lyrics are overtly political, except for in a personal way. i've been writing about the experience of moving to different places... just telling stories about change.

hearing and telling stories seem so important to you.
i love stories. i like it when my friends tell stories. i tell the same stories over & over again. i like stories because even when they're fiction, they're still true. they're real life and sometimes they're all crazy and wild and you wish you had been there.

a letter i sent to maximum rock n roll january or february 2005.

dear mrr.

the punk scene is completely useless and totally fucked up. and did i mention racist? yeah, racist too. last night i went to the show at the 40th street warehouse. as soon as i got there, i was told that a friend of mine left the show because two different white people asked her if she was brontez. my friend is black and brontez is black. that's pretty much where any similarities end, but when yr a white punk and you don't know any black people (even though you live in a black neighborhood!) i guess it's all pretty confusing...

so my friend gets back to the show and she's telling me what happened and i say, let's get on stage and make a little announcement. we go up to where the band's about to play and scream "we're not brontez! we don't all look alike! quit asking me if i'm brontez!" for about thirty seconds. at that point, it's all pretty laughable.

literally five minutes later i'm bent over my bag looking for a lighter and i feel someone humping my ass and i figure it's one of my friends. the person is also putting a little kid's firefighter hat on my head at the same time, all gay porn style. (to be clear: brontez is a black queer boy. apparently the only one in the scene...) i turn around and i'm looking at some white dude (complete with dreadlocks) who is not my friend and who looks mortified. he's like "o god, i'm soooo sorry i thought you were someone else." i say, "you thought i was brontez. you thought i was fucking brontez, didn't you." he's asking me if there's anything he can do cuz he's so sorry. (i'm wondering, sorry about what? that he only knows one black person and can't tell the rest of us apart? that he's an idiot? yeah i'm sorry too.) i hit him with the firefighter hat told him he was a fucking idiot, got my friends and left. thanks, everyone, for making me feel completely not at home in my "community." i just moved to oakland, and everywhere i go, people think i'm brontez. the very night i met brontez about two weeks ago, some drunk white punk girl asked me if i was him. in portland, people asked me if i was jamilah. i guess she's this black punk girl in boston. i don't even want to stress the point that none of us look alike because all you white kids look exactly the same and you have no problem figuring out who's who.

i'm not trying to start a dialogue. i'm just calling you out on your hypocrisy because i'm sick of it. the same people who think i'm brontez think it's so fucked up that police always use that "you fit the description" bullshit to racially profile people of color. the same people who think i'm brontez participate and benefit from gentrification, live in formerly all-black neighborhoods but manage not to know black people, not even their neighbors. the white punk scene is so self-serving, self-involved and useless to me. you claim to be a white ally, you claim to be anti-racist. if you're operating out of an

overwhelmingly white scene, what does being a white ally mean? everything you do only benefits other white folks, particularly straight white men. every time a group of folks (typically women and queers) try to make any positive changes in the punk scene, we end up addressing a bunch of white dudes who aren't really listening anyway, and who don't really have to change because they're surrounded by other white people all the time who are exactly the same and who support their half-assed politics and fucked up behavior.

i hate putting all this energy into pointing out to white people how they're fucked up. but i also hate the idea of all of you walking around all smug, thinking you're so radical, so punk, so anti-oppressive, so different from every other dominant culture white person with their head up their ass. it's not fucking true! i've been in so many different predominantly white spaces and it's always the same. and no, i don't have any tips on how you can be a better white ally. i don't care if you never figure it out. i'm done.

The GOriEs

the gories are from detroit, michigan and they put out records and played shows in the mid-80s.

mick collins (left) leads the band with his super rich vocals, wildass guitar playing and sometimes a little harmonica, too.

the front cover of my favorite gories record HOUSEROCKIN shows these black ladies getting SERIOUS on the dacnefloor and the back cover shows the gories playing a show in someone's living room.

mick collins is still around, playing in punk rock bands like the dirtbombs.

Afropunk
The "Rock N Roll Nigger" Experience

TAKING IT ALL BACK
Afropunk: The "Rock n Roll Nigger" Experience
By Puck

Being white in the United States means never having to think about what that means. And most white folks don't. In fact, any frank discussion of race makes many liberal or left-leaning white people immediately nervous or defensive. The U.S. is supposed to be "colorblind," after all. And what better way to prove blindness than by intentionally ignoring something or someone?

James Spooner's documentary *Afropunk: The "Rock and Roll Nigger" Experience* rips the blinders off mercilessly, but with an obvious love for the people, the music, and for some parts of the punk scene such as the DIY ethic. The title "Rock and Roll Nigger" is a reference to a Patti Smith song by the same name in which she compares her struggle as a white feminist in the rock music scene to that of Black people fighting against white oppression. Spooner reclaimed the title in an act of cultural re-appropriation.

Afropunk follows the lives of four Black people involved in the punk rock scene: Tamar Kali, a woman in New York City; Moe Mitchell, singer for the band Cipher from Long Island, New York; Matt Davis, late member from the band Ten Grand from Iowa City, Iowa; and Mariko Jones, editor of the zine Social Inflight in Orange County, California. The film examines how various Black punk rockers from the ages of 15 to 50 years old, in a mostly white punk hardcore scene, deal with issues ranging from how it feels to be the only Black kid at a show, to interracial dating, to feeling unsupported by the Black community because of being punk.

In many ways, *Afropunk* gave much needed recognition and validation to Black punk rockers. One recurring theme in the documentary was challenging the idea that punk music isn't "Black music." Numerous Black punks (separately) argued that rock and roll was actually African music first and pointed to groundbreakers like Chuck Berry, Little Richard, and Jimi Hendrix to illustrate their point. Another insists that facial piercing too is African, going back to "the bush" long before it was "punk."

Often, Spooner's questions—as well as the answers of those interviewed—hit too close to home for comfort. I cringed when I saw brown kids say things that showed how much self-hate or at least lack of self-respect they had internalized and how their white friends seemed to make it worse. I squirmed because those kids were saying things I probably said at one time while trying to grapple with my Chinese heritage and my identity as an anarchist kid. Spooner too commented, "I think a lot of Black people in the scene feel resentful about being the only one in their group of friends who has to think about race. This shows them why it's important."

It was uncanny how people interviewed hundreds of miles and many months apart, but who shared the common experience of being the only Black punk kid in their community, echoed each other's sentiments, sometimes verbatim.

One particularly painful yet funny scene explored how people reacted to seeing another Black person at a show. Several people responded that, although they were quick to seek out fellow punks of color, they had experiences where the other person snubbed them: "I want to go up to them, but I don't want to be like, 'I'm Black, you're Black; we should talk' and come across weird."

"Sometimes I'll get the dis.... Like that person might be Black, but they didn't come here to be Black."

Another common experience for Black punks was being told by their white friends, "You're not really Black." This "safe Black" phenomenon—the idea that Black people who don't act within the allowable parameters of white peoples' stereotypes of them weren't really Black and were thus "safe"—was particularly insulting to Black punks and exposed how deep white supremacist thinking permeates so many of those who have been socialized as white, even the ones who are "open-minded."

Luckily, the film is also rife with examples of Black punks (mostly in their late 20s) who show that self-love, cultural knowledge, creativity, individuality, and dedication to the Black/African struggle can transcend the isolation, alienation, and stagnation of an unsupportive white punk scene. Tamar Kali continues to live and make music on her own terms and challenges the musical sensibilities of her perplexed neighbors. Moe Mitchell, a practitioner of ancient African traditions as well as a driving force in the New York hardcore scene, continues to push boundaries of what's punk and what's Black.

Perhaps the best thing that came from the film is the message board marked "Community" on the *Afropunk* website. The message board is maintained by Spooner and he regularly participates in the discussions, but it's evident that it is the 300-plus registered users, assorted guests, and other curious web surfers who spark the lively debates and find new ways to make punk and race relevant to each other. Topics broached include cultural appropriation, Black skinheads, and biracial identity. There is a section to talk about "the scene," another to discuss politics and a place to recommend books and zines. Black punks in Chicago who met on the message board are now meeting for brunches and setting up shows. There is even talk of putting on a Black punk festival sometime in the future.

But for Spooner, who left the punk scene years before making *Afropunk*, the film was never just about punk. It is a film he made primarily for Black people. Ultimately, *Afropunk* reminds us that in punk rock or anywhere else, it will take people of color organizing to create space for themselves and challenging "whiteness" in order to move toward true equality.

BLACK

FLORYNCE KENNEDY

"i'm just a loud-mouth middle-aged colored lady with a fused spine and three feet of intestines missing and a lot of people think i'm crazy. maybe you do too, but i never stop to wonder why i'm not like other people. the mystery to me is why more people aren't like me."

florynce kennedy was what people call "eccentric". she had weird fashion and basically said whatever she wanted. plus, she was a feminist, which if yr black makes you automatically "eccentric". she was the first black woman to graduate from columbia law school in 1951. she had to threaten to sue the school for discrimination to even get in in the first place. she represented lots of famous black folks like billie holiday & charlie parker and she also represented black panther h. rap brown and the 21 panthers in nyc who were on trial in the late 60s. in 1983 she starred in my favorite movie ever BORN IN FLAMES as zella wiley. in the 60s she had a cable access show called "the flo kennedy show". she died in december 2000 at age 84.

WEIRdOs

SUN RA

"the outer space beings are my brothers. they sent me here. they already know my music."

sun ra was what people just call weird. he was a jazz musician, most famous for the music he made in the 70s, specifically SPACE IS THE PLACE (sun ra was also in a black sci-fi movie of the same name), but sun ra started tying jazz to sciefi/ outer space theories as early as the 50s. he and his arkestra dressed up in pretty amazing, shiny costumes complete with headdresses obviously inspired by egyptian cosmology and outer space. in the 60s and 70s, sun ra started playing free jazz, which took himself & his arkestra to new heights of weirdness. picture twenty black folks in shiny costumes, all in a noise band together talking about outerspace, and somehow tying it all to black liberation. sun ra died in 1993.

BrONTez

brontez, 24, is from alabama but he's been living in the bay area for the past few years. he dances in the band gravy train, just recorded some songs for his solo project, the younger lovers, and writes a zine called fag school.

o: the first time i ever saw you, you were dancing for veronica lip gloss & the evil eyes at a basement show in portland. do you remember that?
b: yeah, and i remember you too.

o: that was a really intense way for me to see one of the first black punk kids i'd seen in like YEARS or something!
b: really?

o: you were like buck naked dancing around in front of all these white people, but not just white people, white portland dykes who'd probably never seen a black man naked ever before.
b: i never used to think about that shit back in the day, but now i kinda think about it more, especially cuz people have talked to me about it.

o: well what do you think?
b: i don't give a fuck. it's punk rock, so...

o: cuz being there, i was really happy to see you and i thought everything was great, but i still had this experience of watching you getting watched by these people, and i was like "this is weird..." especially cuz it was all people i knew. for you it was a bunch of randoms...
b: i harshed a couple of their mellows, i'm sure.

o: and then recently when i saw you dancing for gravy train for the first time, i was really excited seeing how much african dance influenced your performance.
b: dancing with gravy train is what really made me want to go deeper into [african dance] cuz at first i was just dancing at shows, and then as i started dancing more & more, i realized "i want to teach this." and living in oakland at the time, there was a really good community for [african dance] that i didn't really grow up with down south.

o: i'm really excited about what you do because i don't know if its ever been done before. i mean, are there other punk dancers who mainly just dance in bands and are trained to do that, and also incorporate haitian and west african shit?

b: there isn't anyone else, at least that i know of. i like gravy train because it's a punk band, but it's like a caberet show, too... actually now i'm thinking about white people watching you in bands and what they're thinking. cuz i used to go buck, like *a lot*, and there's definitely a different way that [white people] will perceive things... it's only ever white people who come up to me, in most scenarios, after the show and sometimes they'll say things that are really uncomfortable, but then sometimes it'll be just a compliment like "oh i like the way you dance." but some times, there's always some quasi-racial shit attached to it, and it's kinda weird... but in the end, i feel like more positive things have happened than negative things.

o: when did you start thinking about making music solo?
b: i had just been in a bunch of bands, and i was really feeling myself, and i was like "what if i just did it all by myself and didn't have to ask no goddamn body" and it worked out somehow. my friend chris recorded it. it's called the younger lovers. it's delicious. my friend says it sounds like tiger trap.

o: oh really? when you told me it was pop punk, i thought it was gonna sound like the bangs or something. you play drums really loud.
b: i used to listen to the bangs a lot. they were my favorite band.

o: i put a bangs song on your mixtape for you.
b: which song?

o: maggie the cat.
b: oh my god, i love that song! okay, back in the day when i was a young kid living in alabama, i used to call up kill rock stars every day, like just call them and chat and maggie would always talk to me. she even sent me that seven inch for free. and that's before i even did drugs or anything. i don't know how i had the energy to just call up strangers and be like "hey what's up?" i was pretty bored, though.
i was 16 or 17.

o: can you talk about the social lies?
b: the social lies were me and this girl tamika who's actually still my oldest friend from high school. we were the only two black punk kids... probably in all of alabama. i'm gonna claim it: the social lies were the first all black punk band to walk out of alabama. alive, at least.

o: what were the shows like?
b: i go back and listen to the live shows we did and we obviously played with the race thing, and we said things that i would not say today. i was kinda like "woah, i can't believe i said that. i was totally spazzing out." but it was still really funny. everyone always laughed. we had a mostly white audience though.

o: how did you and tamika meet?
b: me & tamika actually hated each other when we first met. she didn't like me so much cuz i was kinda young and goofy. she's three years old than me. she was a senior and i was a sophomore and we didn't get along. admittedly, i was probably more indie rock and she was more hardcore. she was more into filth and stuff, and i was more into sleater-kinney. but we found a drastic middle that i
think really worked. it was still punk as fuck, you know what i mean?

o: how do you feel about that band now?
b: when i think about that band and that being my first experience in punk rock, i think it really set the bar for what i though my experience should be. we pushed a lot of lines. like, i was very gay. i was an out punk queer kid. tamika also listened to lots of bikini kill and stuff like that, and its weird just how that record could open up a dialogue for that kind of stuff. so she was the only punk kid that was really hanging out at my house. otherwise, i would've had to make horrible pop punk music with fuckin lame-ass straight boys if she hadn't been in my life... it feels really weird for me to have a scene that's *totally* white.

o: there's probably more punk kids of color in the bay area than any other place we've lived before, but there still aren't that many. and it takes a minute before you're like, "see, this is why black folks don't want to hang out with a bunch of white people."

b: yeah, it took years for that to kick in too. cuz our generation grew up with this shit about how the world is so colorblind and the older you get, you see that's bullshit. but for white people, it's easier to not think about it. in a place like san francisco, you meet a lot of white people who've never had to think about race personally, but are so opinionated about it! i grew up in an all black community in the south. i was a little black boy country bama and then i got older and became a freak, so naturally you have to hang out with a bunch of white people if you're gonna be punk or whatever. i've walked through all these worlds and race does count for a lot. i see how different people treat you as a black person when you're the only one around. i've noticed a difference when i go into places where i might totally hear a racist joke, but when i got there with you & adee, it was a whole different scene and they were totally afraid to touch it. but whenever you're isolated, the shit people will pull with you is disgusting. i've seen it all my life. it'll be like me by myself trying to defend myself and my entire race against twenty crazy rednecks

asking me these ridiculous questions. it's like, what if i held you and your entire race responsible for everything every white person's ever done to me? like come on. i was talking to this one queen, this mexican boy, and he was trying to tell me that if you're only friends with people because they're the same race as you, you're building the friendship on a negativity, or something. i thought that was total bullshit. punk rock is cool and it's nihilistic, it's free, but it comes with

the same bullshit [as any other white scene]. i know what it's like—you know what it's like—to be isolated in a scene like this. whether its because you're the only queer in town, the only black kid, the only feminist... i know that i've always felt stronger when there are other punk kids of color around me. i always feel stronger when i have my girls with me.

THANKS TO Vaginal Davis FOR PRESENTING HER FABULOUS VIDEOS THIS YEAR AT homo a gogo!

ALSO THANKS:
MOM & DAD, ADEE, BRONTEZ, PUCK, JACOB, HEATHER M., JULIE, ALEX H., CASSIA, CHACH, JACKIE, GLORIA NEGRITA, THE SQUIRRLE SHIP, BOB, JESSE & PAUL KOA.

PLEASE WRITE ME:
SHOTGUN SEAMSTRESS
5225 N. CONCORD AVE.
PORTLAND, OR 97217

This zine was copied at
DITTOS
407 NE MASON ST #6 AT MLK
SUPPORT BLACK BUSINESS!

SHOTGUN SEAMSTRESS
NUMBER 2

everybody say LOVE.

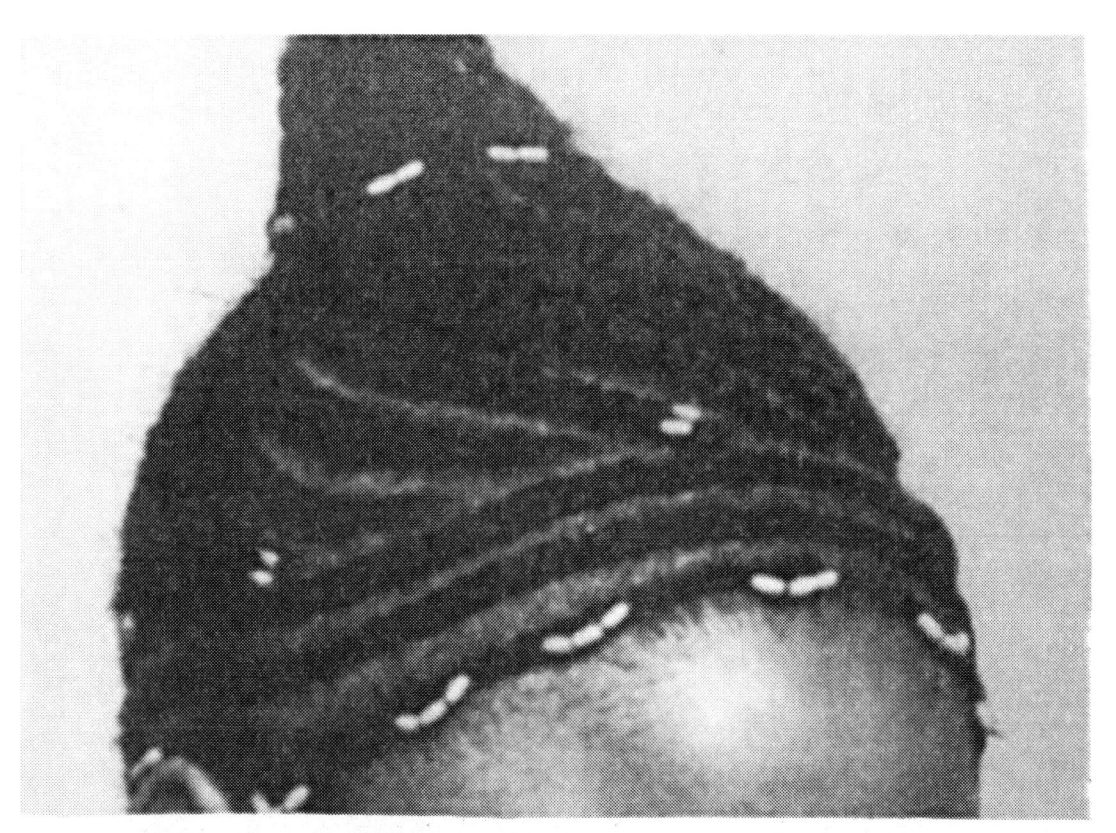

SHOTGUN SEAMSTRESS
NUMBER 2

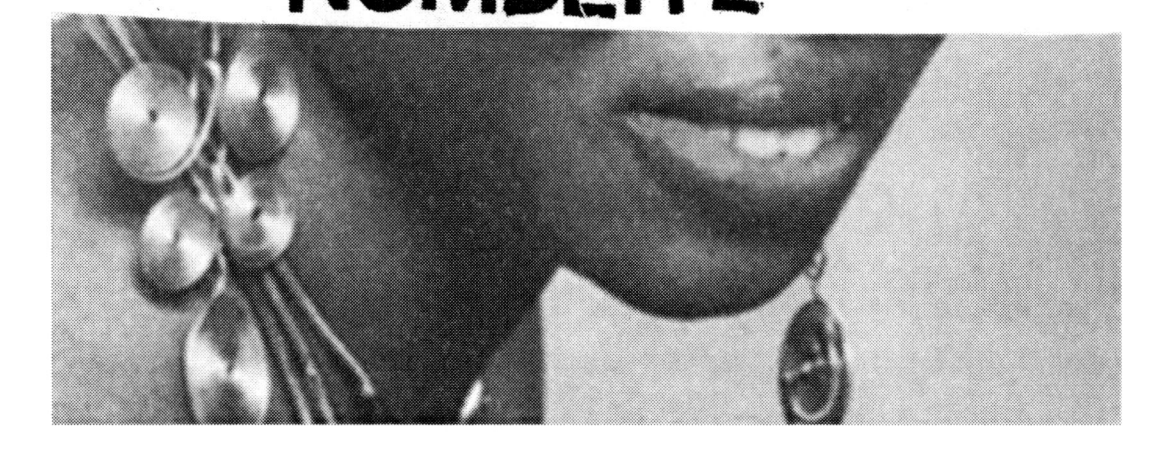

Shotgun Seamstress is a zine by & for Black PUNKS, QUEERS, MISFITS, FEMINISTS, ARTISTS & MUSICIANS, WEIRDOS and the people who support us. This zine is meant to support Black People who exist within predominantly white subcultures, and to encourage the creation of our own.

To SNR

CONTENTS

1. Portland Scene Report

2. black punk zine that never happened / go-go

3. Punk & Black are the same thing?! by Chris Sutton

4. INTERVIEW: Andrea Rhinestone Eagle

5. Books:
   - Lettin it All Hang Out, RuPaul
   - Culture Clash: Dread Meets Punk Rockers, Don Letts

6. Women of Color In Punk Rock
   - open letter by Djay D.
   - resource list

7. I can see beyond this by adee licious

8. INTERVIEW: Magic Johnson

9. why i will be a riot grrl till the day i fucking die by Brontez Purnell

PORTLAND SCENE REPORT

SUMMER 2007

Good thing the summer was fun, cuz it's a shitty winter in Portland, Oregon right now. To everyone's utter shock, Portland was somewhat of a paradise for Brown Punks this summer. NEW BLOODS kicked off the summer with a west coast tour with FINALLY PUNK. That tour turned out to be their last one with fourth bandmate and lover of sea creatures, Veronica Ortuño. But don't worry! The band plans to continue as a three piece.

brown punks on tour!

Those who were lucky got to see San Francisco trio EGGS ON LEGS tear up the basement of Brainstains (back when DJay lived there). When is the last time you saw an all-Asian, all-queer new wave dance band with political lyrics? They also played Storefront in SE a couple weeks later, but the basement show was tha bomb.

HEY, GIRL! also from SF rolled through town as well. I can't remember what house they played at, but it was another chaotic basement show and you couldn't hear the vocals loud enough, but it was still a great show. The drummer, Naomi, does this zine called PUNX IS LADIES and she interviews all these different ladies that play music including her two bandmates Rashida and Rosie who also happen to be women of color. Check out their LP SPILL YOUR GUTS!!!

for punx is ladies write naomiviolet@riseup.net or p.o. box 5356 berkeley, ca 94705

hey girl! from top: naomi, rashida, rosie

42

Tropical treasures ABE VIGODA from LA came through town in July and played a packed and sweaty show in the living room of Dekum Manor along with New Bloods, Hornet Leg and Talbot Tagora from Seattle.

Claudia Meza, renaissance woman of Portland's DIY scene and drummer for oly-to-pdx duo HORNET LEG, was spending her summer on the east coast leaving Chris Sutton to play a series of solo shows. A particularly meaningful show occurred the very day Chris dealt with being racially harrassed by a cop while walking home from a nearby cafe. Again in the living room of Dekum Manor, opening for the Old Haunts, Chris played a half-electric, half-acoustic solo set during which he payed homage to Martin Luther King, Jr., Fred Hampton and all Black Men who have been victims of state sanctioned violence.

Late August saw a benefit for the New Jersey 4 (also known as the Newark 4), four Black Lesbians from Newark, NJ sentenced to prison for defending themselves after a sexist and homophobic attack. For more information go here: http://www.workers.org/2007/us/nj4-0628/
This show also happened to be MAGIC JOHNSON'S portland debut (see MJ interview for more info on them.) New Bloods and Swan Island joined them along with DJs Shedd and JAMILAH to turn In Other Words Feminist Bookstore into a one-night queer punk party for social justice AND to raise $1500 for our sisters behind bars.

A couple of days later, also at In Other Words, as part of B.A.B.E. Fest (Breaking Assumptions and Barriers to Equality), Osa of New Bloods facilitated a workshop on Women of Color in punk rock as well as a discussion for people of color only about our vastly varying experiences with race & racism in punk scenes and all other realms of our lives. The resource list from that workshop is included in this zine.

By the end of the summer, Portland's BROWN UNDERGROUND was one band richer with PURPLE RHINESTONE EAGLE relocating to Portland from West Philly. An interview with their singer/guitarist Andrea is also in this zine.

black punk zine that never happened

SEVERAL YEARS AGO WHEN I LIVED IN WASHINGTON, DC, I GOT THE IDEA TO MAKE A ZINE ABOUT BLACK PUNKS, BUT I NEVER FINISHED IT. I HAD THIS BOOK CALLED <u>BANNED IN DC</u> ABOUT DC'S EARLY-TO-MID 80s PUNK/HARDCORE SCENE, AND IT HAS MORE BLACK PEOPLE IN IT — BOTH IN BANDS AND IN THE AUDIENCE — THAN ANY OTHER PUNK BOOK I'VE EVER SEEN. IN A WAY IT MAKES SENSE BECAUSE OF DC'S HUGE BLACK POPULATION. BUT WHILE I WAS LIVING THERE, THE CITY WAS STILL MAJORITY BLACK, BUT I WAS PRETTY MUCH THE ONLY ONE AROUND AT SHOWS. I THINK MORE BLACK PEOPLE WENT TO SHOWS BECAUSE OF BAD BRAINS. (HR) → JUST THAT ONE BAND PROBABLY MADE ALL OF THE DIFFERENCE IN THE WORLD.

There's this one photo from Banned In DC that shows these two black dudes standing outside the Wilson Center (punk show space), and one of the guys is holding a sign that says "All Ages: PUNK THROWDOWN with Trouble Funk, Government Issue and Grand Mal." I've probably looked at that photo a hundred times imagining what that show must've been like. Government Issue is a white hardcore band and I don't know who Grand Mal is, but Trouble Funk is a black go-go band from Washington, DC (more on go-go later). They played several shows with hardcore bands during the time, including Minor Threat.

Before seeing that picture, I'd never really imagined a punk show looking like that. I started fantasizing about what it must've been like to be a Black Punk in DC in the 80s instead of now. I wanted to make a zine of interviews with all races of people, but especially including black kids that went to shows at the time. I wanted to know the approximate ratio of black people to white people, what it felt like to go see a black band and to hear reggae and/or go-go at a punk show, what the feel of the shows were... In my imagination, it just seemed like so much richer of an experience.

I got intouch with a couple people, but I never did set up any interviews or get anywhere with the project. At that point in my life, I didn't know any other black kids in punk, so it made it so much harder to think about how to frame the things i wanted to communicate. My interest in DC's punk scene in the 80s grew out of a deep feeling of longing for something I wanted but couldn't have. Thinking about communicating that to a white audience felt awkward and uncomfortable to me. So I never finished the zine, but Iwas still left with a million questions that needed answers. For one, how and why did the punk scene in DC turn so white again? It's always interesting when you learn that things haven't always been the way they are now, and that communities/movements of people aren't always making progress.

I mean, who knows, maybe it wasn't all that different back then. Black kids probably still only made up a tiny minority of band & audience members. I know I'm romanticizing a past that I don't know very much about. But that fantasy is just me imagining the possibilities. That's what this is about, is black people expressing, representing and documenting the fullest range of our beings collectively and individually.

Exploring ALL of our possibilities. Instead of allowing the dominant culture to tell us what it means to be black, we can create and recreate what that means all the way to infinity. And we can do it with music and with art.

okay, now back to GO-GO...

When I went to DC as a kid, I remember seeing bucket drummers by METRO escalators or on the Washington Mall by the Smithsonian museums. Mostly it was guys beating those white, 5 gallon industrial buckets with drum sticks. I imagine them beating dozens of different buckets till they found the ones that sounded JUST RIGHT. and they always sounded tight. If i remember correctly, it was kind of modeled after a drum set with one bucket as a snare, the others as toms with different pitches and a bass bucket. genius! I don't even wanna try to explain what a go-go beat is, so if you can go online, go here: http://www.youtube.com/watch?v=3nPKkj8C0Gg and you'll see a video of a guy playing go-go beats on bucket drums! His bass bucket is an upside down garbage can.

One day in 9th grade algebra class, me and my friends Brandis, Atia and Monique all hatched this plan to go to a go-go show in the city. The next day we all returned with the same results. Each of our parents had vetoed that shit before the full request could even leave our lips. It seemed like every night on the news, there was something about another shooting at a go-go show and the police having to break it up. Understandably, my parents didn't want my 14-year-old black ass getting shot by accident.

They'd show footage on the news of black kids at go-gos getting buckwild, cussing and fist fighting. Like I said, I wasn't there, but from the outside it seems to me like another case of the media and the cops uniting to criminalize public gatherings of black people. They hate it when we're out in public having any kind of fun. When we do it, it's loitering. When white people do it, it's the Alberta Street Art Walk or whatever.

Anyway, the 80s were a rough time for black communities considering poverty, crack, homelessness and most social programs and public resources being cut or underfunded

Members of this group were 8-11 years old when they started out. Here they are outside of **junkyard band** the Berry Farms Housing project in Anacostia, SE Washington, DC in July 1986.

thanks to Ronald Reagan. This was post-black power. All of our leaders were dead. There were several major reasons at the time for black communities across the country to be experiencing despair, defeat and a sense of hopelessness. Combined with a lack of resources or opportunity to do anything about the situation, lots of people turned to violence. It is also out of these same circumstances that hip-hop in NYC and go-go in DC began to blow up. We all know the trajectory of hip-hop, but what happened to go-go?

My best friend since elementary school, Koren, moved down to Georgia to live with her dad when we were in 9th or 10th grade. I remember her telling me that when she told her new friends in Georgia about go-go, they told her she was making it up. They'd never heard of it. And we hadn't been thinking about go-go as a local phenomenon. We thought everyone (at least black people) knew about it, but in reality, go-go barely made it out of DC. Even within DC, because of the violence associated with it, go-go music started to be banned at different clubs and events. At least E.U. enjoyed brief national success with "Da Butt" (yep, that's a go-go beat!)

The go-go bands that still play are pretty much funk bands with keyboards, horn sections and heavy go-go percussion. That stuff is cool, but the stuff I'm truly inspired by are the groups of raggely little kids that some of those bands evolved from, banging buckets, pots and pans, and playing toy instruments until they could acquire real ones. That's more DIY than anything I've ever seen in punk. I've heard people say that hip-hop is our punk rock, and maybe it used to be, but I really think **it's GO-GO.**

Everybody put your hands on your TV set, because this is the most important thing you'll ever hear." It may have been the Ecstasy, but I could feel the whole nation leap up from their sofas and place their hands on top of mine on the television screen.

"Now everybody say Love!", I said. "Love!" everyone roared in the audience. "EVERYBODY say love!" "LOVE!" roared the entire nation with one accord. And then the kicker. "'Cause if you can't love your-self--how in the hell you gonna love somebody else--can I get an A-men in here?" It was fun--but it was also true.

RuPaul's re-telling of his appearance on the Geraldo Rivera Show. from LETTIN IT ALL HANG OUT

Punk and Black are the same thing?! By Chris Sutton

Chris Sutton lives in Portland, OR where he plays guitar and sings for Hornet Leg. He is also a member of C.O.C.O., Spider and the Webs, and most recently the Gossip. On top of that, Chris DJs soul records around town and also writes the zine Nigerian Triple Daisy.

Dig it. I'm chillin' in my cold ass house thinkin' about Black Rock n Roll. I was tryin' to think of something relevant for Shotgun Seamstress. Immediately I start thinking of major forces that have influenced me or inspired me (and everybody) in my lifetime. Obvious choices would include Jimi Hendrix, Sly Stone, Phil Lynott, Ike Turner, Mick Collins, Living Colour, Fishbone, 24-7 Spyz, and Bad Brains. Also there's the familiar "roots" historical path that is so often treaded when describing the overwhelmingly overlooked contributions of genius African Americans.

Yes, rock n roll and almost the entire American pop pantheon comes from the blood, sweat and tears of sharecroppers, slaves, and disenfranchised people. "Rock", "Roll","Blues", and even "Punk" are all terms originally co-opted into general culture by black people, usually pertaining to something sexual. Western Culture is obsessed with sexual labels. It needs them to survive. We have to stay within our given brackets and subcultures so we can easily identify each other on the street. As soon as DJ Alan Freed put the terms "Rock" and "Roll" together, white culture could instantly recognize and market it.

Unfortunately for the people who invented the music, humanity only rewards and acknowledges its heroes and artists who are recognized in its own image. For example the estates of Elvis Presley and Bob Dylan are set atop mountains of gold while Larry Williams, Big Mama Thornton, and Leon Bibb remain relatively obscure names even in their own lifetimes, even though they were direct influences on above mentioned deities. If the black populace were the ruling class in the 50's I might be nerding poetic about an obscure rock n' roll musician named Bill Haley[1].

"Blues" is a term corporations decided to pin on "Race" music because the "Race" was creating too many different styles to sweep under a single umbrella. It's hard to tie Skip James in with Sonny Stitt or Marian Anderson[2]. Nowadays, that (or any) term seems like an ideological jail that overwhelms with rigid rules lyric choices and dress. We all know about the thievery of British Invasion excavators. But Jimi came over at the end and destroyed the party. All of the Angloids had to run back into their holes and invent "Progressive" and "Concept" albums and finally embrace their Englishness with vigor (Spend an afternoon with The Kinks discography and they'll take you from Bo Diddley's raunchy "Cadillac" to tea on the village green in a couple of short hours).

All great underground pop music comes from beautiful black people. The Punks were obsessed with Reggae & early Hip-hop, rich influences coming from huge Jamaican communities in London & New York respectively, and later post-punk latched on to the disco styles emanating from the black gay subculture. The Beatles, the Who and the Stones' first records were primarily covers of African American dance hits. The Mods, punk rock's fashionable precursors, based their entire fashion on what Prince Buster or Smokey Robinson was wearing that season. Glam Rock? There is little difference between T.Rex's and The Dolls' guitar riffs and Chuck Berry's about 15 years earlier. Stylistically, Little Richard and Esquivel were exponentially more flamboyant.

So what is there to talk about? Maybe I can offer something personal, an ethnic-eyed view story from the white armpit of the nation (The Northwest). I love rock n roll. I like that it's loud and dirty. In a world where you gotta get in where you fit in (remember my rant about humanity earlier) why would I choose to fully embrace an idiom with so few heroes in my own blended image (Okinawan Hawaiian, Scottish, African & Native American)?

When I was in high school, I'd sit and listen to Iron Maiden and Motley Crue with my friend Gary, ride skateboards and listen to Pharcyde and Digable Planets with my homie Mikey, Go to Nirvana and NOFX shows with Mark, Strum Jane's

[1] Bill Haley of Bill Haley & the Comets, early rock n roll band with famous hit "Rock Around the Clock"
[2] Skip James, blues singer; Sonny Stitt, jazz saxophonist; Marian Anderson, opera singer. All BLACK.

Addiction songs at the park with Justin, and the list goes on and on. I would wear Doc Martins, Punk T-shirts, smoke cloves, and listen to Creedence Clearwater Revival on my headphones. I was approachable enough to be part of the Student Body Committee but I was a little too weird to be understood by most.

I started playing in bands, lots of them, even a crappy lo-fi hip-hop group. But I wanted to rock! That's the music that made me feel good. Guitars, not drum machines were what really got me off (I love drum machines now, tho.) Unfortunately because I lived in a suburb of a city that was actually by all accounts smaller than the suburb itself (Lacey, Washington), nobody looked like me. I couldn't quite picture myself as part of the local culture.

All of my friends were divided by the type of the music that they listened to. My rap friends didn't understand my goth friends and they both made fun of my hesher friends. I was told by my friend Tory that I would be more popular if I dressed like a "Rapper" instead of the "Lollapaloser" that I put my beliefs into. I have too many musical interests, sorry. No, I'm not sorry. Later, being in Olympia, the same town as the International Pop Underground, totally changed my ideas about what music or art was supposed to be. I learned not to label myself.

Black culture is all about what's hot and happening now. Blink for a second and you could get lost in the trend. "White Culture" is generally nostalgic and borrows from the past to be cool today. I mean, that fuckin' band Jet looks like The Stooges had a head on collision with Hanoi Rocks. The Strokes wear the names of past heroes proudly on their fashionably ripped t-shirts. But nobody will ever mistake T-Pain's white T simplicity for Kurtis Blow's futuristic street style. Or Puff Daddy's fade for Rick James' signature braids. Jay-Z wouldn't be caught dead in those little shorts that UTFO used to wear. (However the afro continues to remain cool to this day since its inception in the late sixties, some things are too cool to dismiss). But I like it all! I readily identify with both.

Maybe I don't need to say any of this shit to the average afro-punk. In fact, I feel like the term afro-punk is a little redundant. Punk in the most layman of terms is just black music played fast. I laugh every time I see a racist skinhead hardcore band. Don't they know that their music wouldn't even exist without Ike Turner? The chitlin' circuit that existed in the south in the late 50's/early 60's is very similar to the DIY web that is so frequently trudged by countless bands. At least nowadays you can use the same bathroom as your audience.

John Lee Hooker has an amazing album called "House Rent Party" which is basically a last minute house show that people would put together to get enough money for that's months rent. Sounds familiar. Angry music by and for the disenfranchised populace? Sounds like N.W.A. and Public Enemy to me. Etta James was pretty fuckin' pissed a lot of the time. Who's more fuck you than Nina Simone? Is it too hard to get kinky hair into liberty spikes?

The main message is that sooner or later their isn't gonna be a race issue in underground rock. The information is out. I love reading about mixed race bands from the south that sound like The Cure. Bring it on! In my time in the punk circles, I have outgrown my anxious search for a cultural identity. There have been many people in my life that have taught me indirectly to embrace whatever my heart feels and dig my uniqueness. I love all types of sounds, colors, shapes, and art forms. Every one of the races is beautiful and they all have something to teach us rhythmically, so dig them all!! Being black is the shit tho, for reals.

I would like to cap this article poignantly with an anecdote from the bio-pic "Straight No Chaser" about the great Thelonious Monk. An interviewer from a jazz magazine asks Mr. Monk what artists he favors. Thelonious's reply is, "I love all music". The interviewer then says "What about country music?" No reply, just an annoyed look. I always think about that for some reason.

Oh yeah, I love lists so here's another one.

10 "white" music artists with "black" souls (I think you know what I'm talkin' bout).
1) Talking Heads*
2) David Axelrod
3) B-52's*
4) Johnny Otis
5) Billy Childish
6) Creedence Clearwater Revival
7) INXS (fo reals, dig it!)
8) Quintron
9) Christina Billotte
10) Make-up*
(Steve Gamboa from the Make-up wasn't a white dude, The B-52's have had a brotha playin' drums since the "Love Shack" years, & Talking Heads with
black people = Tom Tom Club)

interview
Andrea Rhinestone Eagle

Andrea moved to Portland from West Philly with her band Purple Rhinestone Eagle last summer. They are a three-piece, all-women psychedelic rock n roll band.

In this interview Andrea talks about her love of the psychedelic and the metaphysical from her standpoint as a queer, mixed-race, feminist in the punk scene.

SS: WHAT ARE THE IDEAS BEHIND THE KIND OF MUSIC PURPLE RHINESTONE EAGLE MAKES?

A: We all have different backgrounds as far as what music scenes we grew up in, but we all have a mutual love for psychedelic and acid rock, stoner metal, garage rock and rock n roll in general. We don't know of a lot of women historically or currently who've played instruments in bands, who've wailed out on the drums or shredded on guitar or bass, so it's really fun for us. Not that we're trying to be this 60s throw back psychedelic band, but a lot of the bands we listen to are from that era and you can definitely hear that currently in the stuff we're making. We're having a lot of fun with it.

SS: WHERE DO BLACK PEOPLE AND PSYCHEDELIA INTERSECT?

A: Up until recently in my life, I didn't know how involved black people were in the psychedelic genre, not just in this country but all over, especially in West Africa in the late 60s and 70s. I'm in love with all the compilations that Luaka Bop and Soul Jazz put out. They are really good resources for finding out obscure black & brown music. Obviously, Jimi Hendrix has always been a huge influence on me. He's one of the most talented people that ever existed musically, I think. Arthur Lee who was in Love is another big one for me. He actually just passed away not too long ago. He was another prodigy, genius type who made really amazing music and who was also another Black Weirdo who, like Jimi Hendrix, was totally rock n roll, but faced some resistance during the era. As far as black women I've been influenced by, unfortunately it hasn't been anyone specifically from rock n roll. But Betty Davis has been a huge influence. She's crazy! She had wild style and a really non-traditional voice. I love Etta James, Chaka Khan, Malcolm Mooney, Sun Ra and Mick Collins, to name a few other black folks in soul and rock n roll.

SS: IS PSYCHEDELIC ROCK RELATED TO YOUR POLITICAL VISION AS FAR AS BEING QUEER & A FEMINIST & A PERSON OF COLOR?

A: I guess I erroneously thought for a long time that that genre, which is so huge it's hard to even categorize it, was apolitical. But as I grow older and listen to the lyrics more deeply and pay attention to what they were playing musically, I realize it was totally revolutionary. Being a person of color in rock n roll, you can't help but make a political statement, just by doing it, in and of itself. I do a lot of reading on chaos theory and especially lately, the concept of criticality. It basically says that when a system becomes highly destabilized, there will be random shifts that suddenly self-organize into higher complexities. That seems to me to describe what's going on now in society in a lot of ways. It's definitely a very unstable world that we live in. But what's going on in Portland right now with people of color making music and art, tha's kind of like a random shift. Maybe not so random. But it's this shift that's happening that's going to help raise the consciousness of punk and DIY communities and potentially larger art and music communities too. I think it'll result in a much more interesting and accessible scene for people like us.

SS: SOMETHING'S DEFINITELY BREWING HERE IN PORTLAND RIGHT NOW...

A: Things are getting witchy, kind of. I think a lot of us are taking a step beyond the material plane in terms of what our needs are as a people and as people of color. I feel like that's where I plug into more, is the metaphysical conversations as opposed to these really dry conversations about capitalism and interlocking oppressions, which are, don't get me wrong, still really important conversations to have. But I've always felt like, "There's something more to it than that." I feel something in the air. Something's shifting. And that feeling is related to this really personal, specific sort of spirituality that I have, and plays a large part in the music we're making. I feel like there's definitely something larger... Earlier we were talking about how much effort we put into finding each other other people of color in punk. We put that intention out there and it's finally coming b back. It took years! It's the real thing. You can't deny that feeling you get, especially when it's being echoed by everyone you know.

SS: HOW DO YOU FEEL ABOUT YOUR RECENT MOVE TO PORTLAND?

A: I think it was definitely one of the best decisions we could have made as a band and also personally. I was a little concerned because it's defintely one of the whitest cities in the country. But honestly, I feel that the friendships I'm starting to have here with other amazing people of color have been way more mutually beneficicial than in any other city I've been in. There's just something going on here that is special. It's definitely still at the beginning stages, but I feel like I'm a part of the beginning of it. It's also easier to live here. It's cheaper and there's a lot of things you can do for yourself like get $15 acupuncupuncture and other things that are really good for dealing with stress, the added stressof being a woman of color. It helps a lot.

SS: DOES IT ALSO HELP THAT YOU'RE A TRIPLE BLACK BELT IN TAE KWON DO?

A: Yeah! You know, I can walk down the streets feeling pretty safe. laughs

SS: SO WHAT ARE YOU EXACTLY?

A: A third degree black belt in Tae Kwon Do.

SS: WHAT'S THAT MEAN EXACTLY?

A: So there are nine degrees of black belt in Tae Kwon Do. And Tae Kwon Do was developed by General Choi Hong Hi, and he was actually my father's instructor. My father had the honor of being taught by the founder of Tae Kwon Do. My dad is a ninth degree black belt.

SS: DO YOU FEEL LIKE THE MUSIC AND MARTIAL ARTS REALMS OF YOUR LIFE SPEAK TO EACH OTHER?

A: Constantly! I can't even really, truthfully divide those two experiences because the first 17 years of my life I did Tae Kwon Do almost every day. And at 16, I started playing guitar so there was a year when they overlapped. Then, music kind of took over my life. But I feel like I picked up the rhythm, the count and the cadence of music through martial arts, and directly through my father as well, as far as the black community he grew up in and the music he was around. He kind of incorporated that into martial arts, too. I think I incorporate martial arts more viscerally into the music I'm making. I mean, obviously I'm not breaking boards when we play sets.[laughs]

SS: WHAT IS YOUR VISION FOR PURPLE RHINESTONE EAGLE AND FOR YOURSELF AS AN ARTIST AND MUSICIAN?

A: I really want to continue writing music with Morgan and Ashley. I would love to put out a 7". I want that to happen so bad! I definitely want to go on tour with them. I want to continue to be this really powerful force. Three is a really powerful number, especially when it's three women. It's intimidating. Anytime I see three women playing music together, I'm like "woah!" It's like thise thing in your chest that happens. I want us to continue to be fierce and get better at our instruments and just really make something happen. For myself, I have this solo project that I'm slowly working on. I really want to continue learning about the technical aspects of music, and learn how to fix my own instruments when they break. And I want to get weird. laughs I want to get really weird. I think we're on our way, though.

Purple Rhinestone Eagle has big plans for 2008. Check them out:
www.myspace.com/purplerhinestoneagle

L to R: Andrea, Morgan and Ashley

BOOKS
LETTIN IT ALL HANGOUT

There is so much you don't know about RuPaul. I didn't really give a shit about RuPaul myself until my ex-housemate, Eve, told me that he had a punk rock past, and was even in new wave/punk bands in the 80s! RuPaul's mainstream success kind of made him invisible to me. Sure, it's always fun to see RuPaul pop up in a B-52s video ("Love Shack") or in a Spike Lee movie ("Crooklyn"), and everyone's heard "Supermodel (You Better Work)" by now, whether they've wanted to or not. But none of that was enough to really peak my interest. Plus, that was all back in the 90s.

But hello! RuPaul is black and gay and has made a living for himself based on the power of his performance as a drag queen. Now, THAT certainly doesn't happen every day. How many famous drag queens of any race can you think of? I can think of two: Divine and Sylvester, and honey, they could only make it so far. So right of the bat, we must see RuPaul as a trailblazer of sorts. Go 'head girl.

RuPaul was born into a family of women in San Diego, Ca on November 17, 1960 (Scorpio!) There is one thing you must understand about RuPaul: He was born to be famous. Celebrity is RuPaul's destiny. When he was born, his mother announced, "His name is RuPaul Andre Charles, and he's gonna be famous, 'cos ain't another motherfucker alive with a name like that." As a baby queen, RuPaul danced and sang along with the Supremes on TV and entertained his mom and his sisters with impersonations of celebrities. He was always very faggy and effeminate, even as a child, and got a lot of shit for it. But RuPaul accepted his fate as a freak/outsider/weirdo from a very early age and played up his uniqueness instead of attempting to fit in with the growd. He grew his hair out into a

huge afro, bleached and dyed it and wore make up and crazy outfits that he sometimes sewed himself. I think it is notable when anyone takes such a stance in life, but it takes an extra dose of courage for a black boy to do it just because there are so many rules around black masculinity and what it means to be a black man. It literally is dangerous-- emotionally, spiritually and physically--to deviate from that. RuPaul speaks directly to this experience several times in his book.

LETTIN IT ALL HANG OUT essentially charts RuPaul's evolution as a performer. He started making a name for himself after he moved to Atlanta in 1976. Apparently Atlanta was a great place to be if you were a freak in the late 70s and early 80s. Coming from California, RuPaul had never seen so many black people in the same place at the same time before. However, it seems that RuPaul's queer friends were still pretty much all white. Anyhow, it was in Atlanta in 1978 that RuPaul's life was changed forever when he saw Crystal Labajia (if ya don't know about her, go find the movie PARIS IS BURNING) performing a Donna Summers selection in a black bustier bikini and black fishnets with big black hair. He couldn't believe

band photo: ruPaul and the U-Hauls

his eyes! He'd never seen such a beautiful, up-to-the-minute black drag queen in his life! After RuPaul dropped out of high school, he began working Atlanta's gay/punk clubs as an MC and developing the persona that the world would come to know and love in a decade's time.

There are two things that are remarkable to me about RuPaul's early drag performance: 1. He was freaky. Gender fuck drag. Terror drag. This was a time when most queens wanted to be pretty like Marilyn Monroe. RuPaul was more like Divine in Pink Flamingos except more androgynous and brown-skinned, with legs a mile long. 2. RuPaul is all about love (like bell hooks! Sorry, I'm a nerd...) RuPaul moved to NYC in the 80s and started working the clubs there. "It was a really dark time in New York... what with the election of Bush, AIDS, and deepening recession, people had just about had it up to here with doom and gloom... I don't do bitchy. I do sassy. I had been doing 'Everybody say love' since Lord knows when. So when I came on the scene with this love message coming from a drag queen that wasn't like 'Bitch! You better get out of my face!' it made an instant connection." The message central to RuPaul's performance is about love and self-acceptance. And who better to make the point than a big old black drag queen? If you're ever having a low self-esteem day, go on YouTube and watch Tammy Faye Baker on the RuPaul Show back when he had his own talk show. I promise you'll feel better.

I could go on and on about how great RuPaul is, but I won't. If you're a Black Weirdo without Black Weirdo friends, this book is a must read. You'll find a friend in RuPaul. He is one of us! RuPaul is a beautiful, sensitive and unique person, using his celebrity to bring self-love and spiritual healing to the masses. There's definitely that 1990s "We are one race, the human race" vibe to the book, but like I said, it was the 90s. We see more clearly now. And anyway, it's way different coming from RuPaul than from some white liberal person who's trying to deny their own racism. RuPaul is my hero!

CULTURE CLASH:
DREAD MEETS PUNK ROCKERS

Don Letts, the son of Jamaican immigrants, was born in Brixton, England in 1956. He is a film maker, infamous for the utterly DIY documentary of London's late 70s punk scene, THE PUNK ROCK MOVIE (featuring the Clash, the Slits, X-Ray Spex, etc.) and for the music videos he made for the Clash, as well as for his latest film DANCEHALL QUEEN, about a woman in Jamaica who decides to enter dancehall contests to make money to support her family. He was the Slits' manager for a while and also ended up on the cover of the Clash's BLACKMARKET CLASH album.

But what Don Letts is really (not so) famous for is bringing reggae to the late 70s London punk scene. He got a gig spinning records at the Roxy, which was THE SPOT at the time. Every British punk band played there (except for the Sex Pistols. Their manager kinda sucked, I guess.) "There were no UK punk records to play," writes Letts, "as none had been made yet. So in between the fast and furious punk sets, I played some serious dub reggae... I played my Dub reggae sounds in between sets by the Clash, the Damned, the Buzzcocks, the Slits, Generation X, the Banshees and many more."

Well people fucking loved it. People on both sides. Punk kids at the Roxy were dancing to Big Youth, Tappa Zukie, King Tubby, and Prince Far I, and smoking spliffs that Don Letts' Rasta buddies rolled and sold at the club. Meanwhile, Bob Marley caught wind of the whole punk thing, dug it, and named one of his records PUNKY REGGAE PARTY. To be sure, the punk kids borrowed more from reggae than reggae took from punk. All of the sudden Letts, with his friends John Lydon, Joe Strummer and Arianna from the Slits could be seen around town in London's best reggae clubs. This "cultural exchange," as Letts calls it,

resulted in bands like the Slits, Public Image Limited and the Clash's later reggae-flavored sound. It also gives us a better frame of reference for bands like the Raincoats. Letts got in on the action, too. Though not much of a musician, he was in a band called Basement 5 for a while. "Basement 5 was the only example in the UK of a black band being influenced by punk rather than the otherway around," writes Letts. "Again it was interesting to see a band doing something that was not classified by their colour or race."

According to Letts, the punk/reggae connection was based in part on politics and identity. Punk grew out of a time when the music and culture of the mainstream were not speaking to the masses, so working class people and other people whose needs weren't being met by the establishment created their own music and culture. (Think back to a time when punk was about critical rebellion instead of conformity.) The same goes

for reggae in Jamaica. Similar to the way that punks went to great lengths to make themselves look fucked up, gross and demented, Rastas were not quite the Untouchables of their society, but they were close. Don Letts, an ex-Rasta, though he still has some long-ass dreadlocks, was drawn to Rastafarianism as a young man. "It railed against the establishment and taught me pride without having to look to the European aesthetic of beauty and values," he writes. The Black Power movement was going strong in the U.S., but didn't necessarily translate adequately to the experience of a young, black firstgeneration kid from Brixton. (Although, one of the funnier moments of the book comes when Letts decides to go to a Black Panther UK meeting, only to pass out during the gathering because he'd had a "too big to handle" spliff before showing up.)

Also similar, the approach to as well as the sound of both reggae and punk music was RAW. Reggae and punk music definitely shared a common thread that both punks and Rastas could identify with.

Don Letts writes from a unique perspective. The beauty of being a Black Punk is that you gain multiple perspectives from walking through so many different worlds. You got your black friends, you got your family (in Don Letts' case they are Jamaican, in my case Nigerian) and then you got your white friends, the punks, the queers. Most people stay pretty comfortable, knowing only one set of people. But we get to hang out with groups that generally never intersect. In some ways, being in so many different places socially is a lonely way to live because at times, there is the feeling that you can only be part of yourself with each group. When I'm with my family, I don't talk about being gay and if I do it's met with some kind of resistance. With white people (punk, queer or otherwise), I don't talk about being black, and if I do, it's met with awkwardness, and who needs that? Not me. You may have read other books about early British punk (and CULTURE CLASH is about much more than that, I promise), but you've never read about it from Don Letts' perspective or the perspective of anyone like him, I bet.

Lastly, CULTURE CLASH helps me to envision a world where we transcend "cultural appropriation" as we have come to know it in this post-colonial reality. Instead of white people continuing to colonize and profit from the art that people of color AND poor people AND women AND queers have invented, maybe things can flow both ways. I love me some Billy Childish and I love the Headcoatees but where's my all-black girl group from Oakland, Detroit or Baltimore doing raw, vintage R&B originals? Why can't it flow both ways? Start makin it flow, kids. WORK.

It's up to you to start taking back what was OURS to begin with.

Although musically PUNK drew more from reggae than reggae drew from punk; REGGAE would benefit from the increased exposure. The "anyone can do it" attitude also worked equally well in both camps. — DON LETTS from Culture Clash: Dread Meets PUNK ROCKERS

and here are BIG YOUTH and JOHN LYDON together in Kingston JAMAICA.

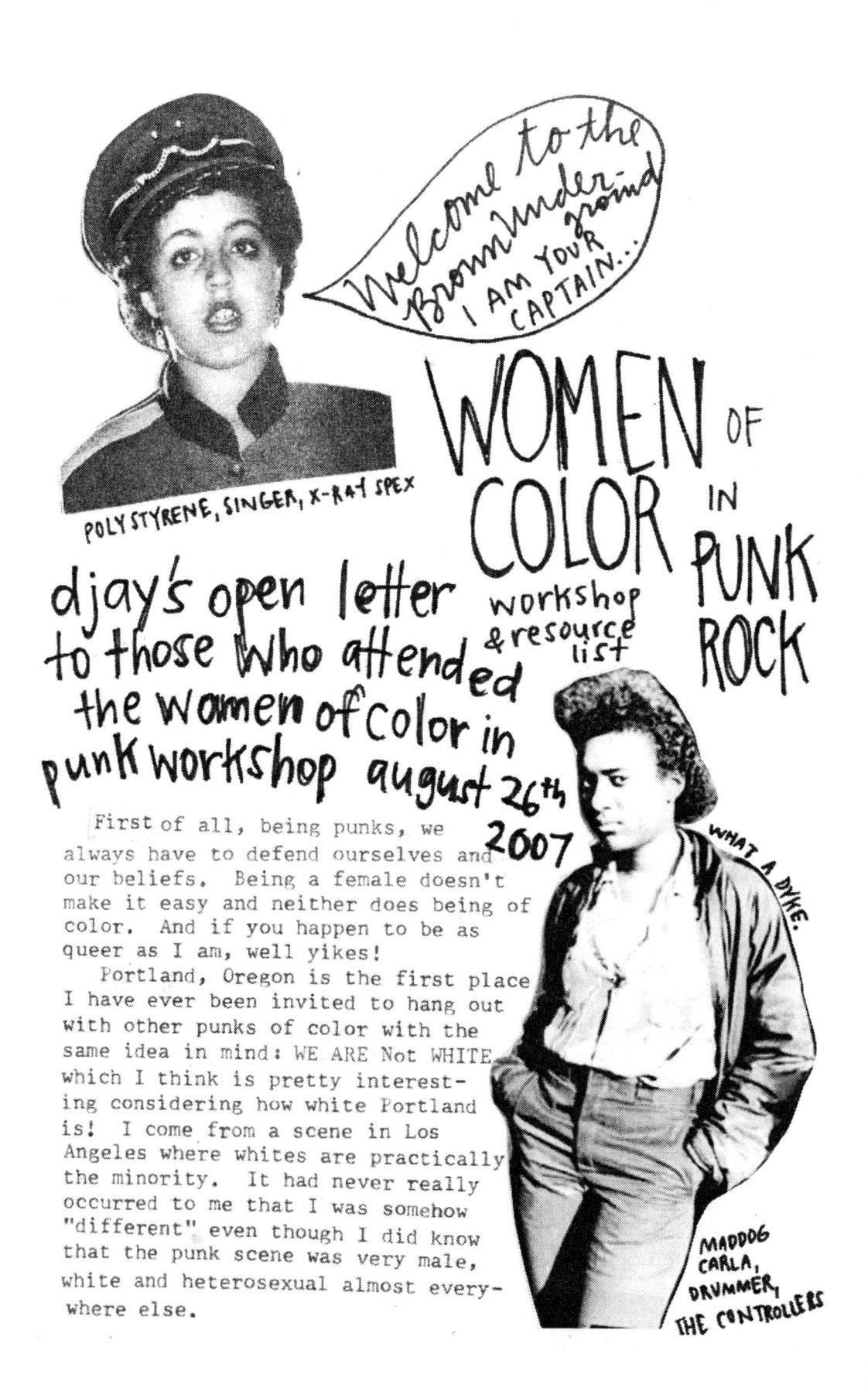

Welcome to the Brown Underground I am your CAPTAIN...

POLY STYRENE, SINGER, X-RAY SPEX

WOMEN OF COLOR IN PUNK ROCK

djay's open letter to those who attended the women of color in punk workshop august 26th 2007

workshop & resource list

WHAT A DYKE.

First of all, being punks, we always have to defend ourselves and our beliefs. Being a female doesn't make it easy and neither does being of color. And if you happen to be as queer as I am, well yikes!

Portland, Oregon is the first place I have ever been invited to hang out with other punks of color with the same idea in mind: WE ARE NOT WHITE, which I think is pretty interesting considering how white Portland is! I come from a scene in Los Angeles where whites are practically the minority. It had never really occurred to me that I was somehow "different" even though I did know that the punk scene was very male, white and heterosexual almost everywhere else.

MADDOG CARLA, DRUMMER, THE CONTROLLERS

One thing that was the same was the lack of females in the scene in LA. At least females who were getting any sort of respect. I think I got a lot of respect because I was down in the pit and I didn't give a fuck. I was just as drunk and tough as the dudes. My friends, on the other hand, were a lot more feminine so the guys treated them like little sissy girls, which they were not. I remember my friends always telling me stuff like, "Djay, kick his ass, he's being a dick!" They had to use me to defend themselves, which I didn't really mind, but was angered by it as well.

August 26, 2007 Osa brought together, by means of B.A.B.E. Fest, a workshop for people of color only entitled, Women of Color in Punk Rock. Wow! Who knew there were so many dating all the way back to the 70's? Truly inspiring on so many levels!

At the workshop, about 25 people were in attendance, mostly female, and all people of color. We gathered at In Other Words Women's Bookstore, very cozy, very appropriate. Osa went through the history and as a group we shared resources, local and non-local, personal stories and explored ideas on how we, as punks of color can create a more positive scene for future punks and for us, who are still in the game. There were all kinds of zines to be had and a resource list was put together and handed out. The workshop lasted for clost to 3 hours, but that was still not enough time to truly discuss and analyze our personal struggles as female punks of color.

I would personally like to thank everyone who came out to the workshop. It's nice to know that I am not alone and neither are you. I am inspired everyday by our meeting and am truly grateful to know you.

Love & Punk,
Djay D.
Music Art Resource Collective
Portland, OR

NENEH CHERRY SINGING WITH THE SURF

1.0 oldbands

Poly Styrene (X-ray Spex)
http://www.terrapin.co.uk/xrayspex

Ikue Mori (DNA)
www.ikuemori.com

Maddog Carla (The Controllers)
http://members.tripod.com/maddogx_78/madbio.html

Taina (Antiproduct)
http://www.myspace.com/antiproductus

Emily's Sassy Lime
www.killrockstars.com/artists/moreartists.php

Azita Youssefi (Scissor Girls)
YouTube: scissor girls on ChicAGoGo

Neneh Cherry (briefly with the Slits)

Vaginal Creme Davis
www.vaginaldavis.com

ESG
http://en.wikipedia.org/wiki/ESG_(band)

Phyllis Forbes (Raooul & Out Hud)
http://www.myspace.com/raooul
http://www.myspace.com/outhud

Nicki Thomas (Fire Party)
www.dischord.com/band/fireparty

Toni Young (Red C, Peer Pressure)
www.dischord.com/band/redc

Alic Bag
www.alicebag.com

Arya (Sta-prest)
http://www.5rc.com/bands/factsheets/sta-prest

Spitboy
http://en.wikipedia.org/wiki/spitboy

Kimya Dawson
www.kimyadawson.com

Leslie Mah & Lynn "Tantrum" Payne of Tribe 8
www.tribe8.com

Yoshimi (Boredoms, OOIOO, Free Kitten)
www.myspace.com/oooiooo

2.0 new bands

Michelle Suarez (Mika Miko-LA)
www.myspace.com/mikamiko

Claudia Meza (Hornet leg-Portland)
www.myspace.com/hornetleg

Condenada (Chicago)
www.myspace.com/condenada

Eggs on Legs (San Francisco)
www.myspace.com/friedeggsonlegs

Hey, Girl! (San Francisco)
www.myspace.com/heygirlband

New Bloods (Portland)
www.myspace.com/thenewbloods

Veronica Ortuño (Finally Punk, The Carrots-Austin, TX)
www.myspace.com/finallypunk

Forever 21 (olympia, WA)
www.myspace.com/jennariotmusic

Magic Johnson (Portland)
www.myspace.com/magicjohnsonmusic

3.0 zines

I dreamed I was Assertive Ed. Celia Perez
Quantify 1-6 ed. Lauren Martin
Evolution of a Race Riot I & II ed. Mimi Nguyen
Fertile La Toyah Jackson Magazine, various video
    zines by Vaginal Davis
        www.vaginaldavis.com/zines.shtml
Finger on the Trigger by Adee Licious
Bamboo Girl ed. Sabrina Margarita Sandata
Mala by Bianca Ortiz
Letters from the Warriors and Breedlove ed. Leah
    Piepzna-Samarasinha
Marimacho by Luna K. Maia
Multikid ed. Jeep, Echo, and others
Sisu ed. Johanna
Greenzine by Christy Road
Negrita by Gloria
Worse Than Queer: An Archive of Writings by Mimi
    Nguyen www.worsethanqueer.com

4.0 distros

Ste. Emilie Skillshare Distro
http://snap.mahost.org/distro

One-Stop Shopping for Mixed-Race Queer Feminist
Cultural and Activist Production
www.theyellowperil.com

other

MARC (Music Arts Resource Center)
Portland, OR
run by DJay
www.myspace.com/marcportland

I CAN SEE WHAT IS BEYOND THIS
I KNOW WHAT THINGS WILL BECOME

TO APPRICIATE WHAT,S IN FRONT OF ME
TO HOLD A HAND TO LEAD THE WAY

ESG

SOMETIMES IT FEELS LIKE THERE
IS SOMETHING IN MY BODY THAT
WILL NOT LET ME ENJOY LIFE.
SOMETHING THAT MAKES ME WANT TO EX
ESCAPE EVERY SITUATION IM IN
EVEN THE GOOD ONES

I THINK MAYBE ITS THE VOIDS
EMPTY SPACES INXMXX**HEART** WHERE
MY MY GRANDPARENTS AND ANCESTORS
MEMORI MEMORIES COULD HAVE BEEN
I AM ALWAYS TRYING TO FILL UP
THOSE VOIDS WITH **WORK** , MEDIOCRE
FRIENDSHIPS AND BLAMING OTHER PEOPLE.

"THERE IS IN EACH OF US AND IN THE OBJECTS
THAT SURROUND US A PLACE OF PRIMAL MEMORY.
I BELIEVE THAT WE HAVE MEMORIES THAT EXTEND
BEYOND WHAT WE HAVE CONSCIOUSLY EXPERIENCED.
THAT WE CARRY WITHIN US ANCESTRAL MEMORY."

—bell hooks

by adee licious

interview

MAGIC JOHNSON

Ana & Mando are best friends. They moved to Portland this summer and formed a band.

Look for them on tour with New Bloods in Spring 2008.
www.myspace.com/magicjohnsonmusic

MANDO WALKS IN WITH A BAG FULL OF RECORDS.

SS: What did you get at the record store?

M: I got Ana the Silver Daggers record since I owed her for her birthday. And I got me Shoplifting and Spider and the webs.

SS: Very fine selections. Okay, Magic Johnson, how did you meet? The short version.

A: Seventh grade.

Both: Fire drill.

A: Out on the field. I turn to Mando and I say [in baby voice] "Do you like south park?"

M: And I said, "Yes." And ever since then, we just got closer and closer.

SS: Why did you move from LA to Portland?

M: I needed a change. I think we both did. We were drunk at this bar and I was like, "Ana I need to go..."

A: I was stagnating big time. I was quite possibly having too much fun seeing other people's bands...

SS: Like who?

A: The regulars were...

M: Abe Vigoda, Mika Miko, Silver Daggers...

A: And whoever came through town, you know?

M: And its cheaper up here. LA was too much.

SS: So how's it different?

M: I feel like you can get a lot more done.

A: I think it's a big deal that we're not living with our parents anymore.

SS: You guys were living with your families before you moved here?

M: Yeah. We were paying rent but it was with our families.

SS: *How old were you when you found out about all the shit that led you to become who you are today, in terms of music*

M: I started listening to HOLE because my cousin who is older than me was really into them, so in first grade I heard Pretty on the Inside and I really liked it. I first heard Huggy Bear when I was about 14. I wasn't out yet, but when I heard "Pansy Twist" and he's yelling "My boyfriend!" it blew me away.
A: When you're a little kid, usually you just listen to pop or whatever's on the radio. So I was really into Mariah Carey and shit, that was my first CD.

SS: *yeah, MARIAH was my girl.*

A: But my dad is kind of an old Mexican hippie, so he was listening to classic rock, like Led Zepplin and I thought "This is cool." And he also had Nirvana and my friends came over and were like, "Your dads cool!" But then in middle school, I started getting into what was really going on. I was listening to KROQ and they'd play Green Day and Hole...

M: And Eve 6! laughs

A: I think it's important to mention that both of us grew up listening to Spanish pop/rock. That's probably the shit we talk about the most now. But then in high school, Mando was into riot grrrl and I got fucked over by some boy and Mando made me a tape and after that,

I was a riot grrl, too!
M: It was a lot of Bikini Kill. And I got really into Babes in Toyland. They're like one of my favorite bands of all time.

SS: *Why did you decide to sing all of your songs in spanish?*

M: A big reason on my part is that Portland's so white, I feel like we need another outlet. Going home, it's so different, like I have to be in Spanish mode again, even though we speak English at home. But the food... and my grandma lives with us and I speak Spanish to her. Over here, I lose it. It's completely gone up here. So singing in Spanish is a great way to keep that going for us while we're here.
A: It's a big part of me and Mando's relationship. We unite in Spanish. We'll be alone, but we're still talking to each other in Spanish. We have each other and that's pretty much it.

SS: *Even in LA?*

A: Somewhat, yeah. Cuz the scene in LA is still predominantly white.
M: But here, it's even more crucial...
A:So there's that. And I went to see... What's that movie? Pan's Labyrinth. When I was watching that, I remember being stoned and being like "Spanish is so beautiful and so a part of me." I felt the movie more because it was in Spanish. And then I heard

Hello Cuca band from Spain and I was like, "Hell yeah, we're gonna do this in Spanish!"

SS: How long have you been playing your instruments?

M: I've been playing guitar since i was 13 or 14 years old.

SS: What's the first song you learned to play?

M: The first real song I learned to play was "plump" by HOLE.

SS: When did you start playing drums, ANA?

A: I messed around on drums a little bit before, but this is the first time I've actually stuck to an instrument. It's been like 3 or 4 months.

SS: Since this is a zine for black people, tell us who are some black artists and musicians that inspire you.

M: I've always loved Stevie Wonder. I love Stevie. Of course Poly from X-Ray Spex. And I've always been inspired by RuPaul.

A: A lot of jazz. Miles Davis was the gateway to jazz for me. One band that I'll probably always listen to and love is the Memphis Jug Band.

SS: What is your vision for MAGIC JOHNSON and what is your vision for yourselves as musicians?

A: Right now. I'm definitely in the middle of trying to figure that out. I know the things I've liked have always been DIY and things that are hands-on visually and aurally too. Things that just sound like people just picked up an instrument and said "Here I go!"

M: And that's kind of what we did. We've never had any formal training onour instruments. We just taught ourselves and our friends have kind of shown us a few things here and there. But I just wanna keep getting better. I've been playing for a long time now, and I feel like I'm not as good as I should be, but then I'll listen to something I've played and think "That's pretty good." I just want to keep getting better and better.

A: I also want our roots to show through more after a while. I want to sound like we're fucking Central American and we're playing punk. And I want to play down there and meet people that are into it, and I wantto inspire others to do it too.

the end

why i will be a ☆RIOTgRRL☆ till the day i fucking die by Brontez

So, there's been much talk of this "Afro-Punk" thing that's going down and I'll surely NOT be the first to say "I'm DOWN." Finally, right? But for right now, the point of this mini-essay is tying my Afro Punk experience and my riot grrl experience together and why it's all very important to me. No probs.

I was kind of a Johnny come Lately to the whole riot grrrl thing. I remember sitting in my algebra class in 10th grade (it was the mid-90's) secretly reading SEVENTEEN magazine. An article on Sleater-Kinney came up and so did an ad for Kill Rock Stars. TOTAL SNOWBALL EFFECT. ABNORMAL OBSESSION. I called and bugged those motherfuckers for YEARS. I had been into the super lame straight boy pop-punk side of punk cause in my town that was all there was. But none of it spoke to me like KRS bands cause like, duh, I was a teenage punk FAG (although at the time, I didn't know that that was the reason--go figure.)

I was in an oppressive climate, Alabama-style. I went to a dumb redneck high school where I was not unusually the only black kid, with a sprinkling of Asians and NO Latinos in the Advanced Placement classes in our military, engineering and old money town of ABSOLUTE HELL. Thirteen to fifteen churches (not the chicken place, but the God place) decorated the road I went to my high school on. Subsequently, my high school was chock full of uptight religious fucking white people (bummer, right?)

Everyday, I had to be the lone black kid defending myself against a white majority of questions--but mostly accusations--about black people. In classes where it was more balanced with black kids, the white kids that would torment me with this bullshit when I was on my own didn't say shit. COWARDS. There was sometimes a white kid on my side, but there were only ever like three altogether that spoke up, but their voices were as unheard as mine!

Since I was in the Advanced Placement classes (which changed my "social sphere" at school and was bullshit-- we did less work than the regular classes and till this day I suck at grammar and spelling) this, along with the fact that I was a flamboyant black punk FREAK,

began to drive this weird social wedge between me and the kids I grew up with, the kids I rode the bus with for up to 2 hours every day. Our part of town (or our part of the cotton field, I should say) provided much of the black population for the school. I didn't understand why I was one of maybe five black kids in these classes when there were up to four bus loads of kids coming from my part of town into the school. Looking back, there were other future poets, writers and comedians on those buses with me, but for some reason I was the "lucky" one. When I asked the question as to why this was happening, I was always met with the same dumb answer from some white person (teacher or student) "They're holding themselves back." If only I had known then what I know now.

Because of this weird social wedge between me and my peers, I had no one to talk to about it really and it was all wearing me down. It started to feel like some weird plan "they" had to fuck with me. I got deeper and deeper into punk and somehow through an act of the GODDESS, I met this other black punk girl at my school named Tameka. At first she HATED me (that natural tension of being the two of maybe five black freaks in our entire school), but then we eventually bonded over our love of rebellion and Bikini Kill.

started a band together called the Social Lies and we started playing out. We met other cool punkers (and racist ones too--sometimes we'd play shows, walk into the place with our equipment, no less, only to have some door guy say "You know what type of show this is, right?") One of the boys we met, Harry from Jarvis, gave me the "Queer Issue" of Maximum RockNRoll 92. Even though it was 1998, I took one look at Vaginal Creme Davis mock-fucking Bruce LaBruce with a strap-on and a light bulb exploded in my lil teen punk fag head. THIS WAS WHAT MY LIFE WAS SUPPOSED TO BE.

I started searching for all the riot grrl zines and writings I could. Through these band lyrics and zines I acquired a "secret language" for what was happening to me in high school and in my life. They explained and deconstructed race and class in ways that weren't taught to me. (Young people are often NEVER taught that in this world, people "trying you" is a life long process. And that honey, THERE IS A FIGHT TO BE HAD.) Those zines let me know that I was not imagining things (as "they" will often tell you) but I was actually being fucked with and I needed to fight back immediately.

The final straw came when this teacher told me that gay people were a genetic mistake. I knew I was a fag and I went home crying and I was so upset I wrote a letter to Kathleen Hanna and SHE FUCKING WROTE ME BACK with advice that was to the effect of, "Girl, keep ya head up!" I knew then, in the 11th grade that I was to be a riot grrl till the day I fucking die.

In some years that followed, I "slowed my roll" a little bit cause I was surrounded by HATERS but thankfully that's over. I see assholes walking around in G.G. Allin t-shirts (thank the goddess he's dead) and skrewdriver t-shirts (contrary to popular belief, that first record BLOWS) and I get hell for sporting my RG pride? I decided that the world (not I) needed to rethink that bullshit.

Though I have to say I would credit my mother for awakening me initially in life to my racial/feminist consciousness, I have to say that I am thankful to those handful of ladies in Olympia (and elsewhere) for keeping the ball rolling in my head.

I often think of my life now as a grown-ass man in SF (which can sometimes feel like the whitest gayborhood EVER) and how sometimes it makes me feel like I'm in high school all over again. Like how sometimes it'll be me at a bar having to endure the comments of some white "punk" (poser) fag in a band t-shirt of a band he doesn't listen to, no less, calling me "the token black guy" in my band. NO LOVE FOR THOSE MOTHERFUCKERS. I always want to slap that bitch and ask him has he been rocking out in punk bands since

he was a teen(the answer 99.9% of the time is "no") and does HE do flawless punk zines like moi? NO HE DOESN'T. I just sit there politely sip my whiskey & ginger ale and when he's done, give him the finger and turn away, my passive way of letting him know I got more punk rock in my tiny black dick than he has in his entire body. (Though admittedly, I usually avoid these situations--getting into verbal spats with jealous bitches is energy consuming and TOTALLY beneath me.)

The shit some of these lame queens talk is soooo tired, I can't keep my eyes open. And the shit they'll say about women (and actually mean it) shocks me. It reaffirms to me while I feel like a total feminist. Near as my junior college classes have taught me, the women's movement opened up hella discussions about gender and sexuality. Other equality movements followed. I always felt an undeniable interlink, and besides we're all usually battling the same jocks, anyway.

This of course does not free me of my internalized misogyny bullshit. I deal with theseissues from time to time and think that every dude (queer, straight, bio and woman-born) has to keep awareness of these things.

A close friend of mine says he hates rants styled like this. He said, "It's like every punk rocker who gets a little space in a zine wants to turn into a politician." Whatever. I assure the world I am NOT a politician. I am simply a man. I'm sitting here right now in the house I grew up in in Alabama. I've had some of my uncle's moonshine, I smoked half a blunt and I want to (fondly) share my love for a scene that (in part) helped me get the fuck out of here.

December 2007

:Thank You:
Mom & Dad, Adee, Brontez, Chris Sutton, Cassia, Andrea, Djay, Ana, Mando, Nikki (thanks so much for letting me use yr computer while i was working on this.), Mimi Nguyen (Race Riot got this shit started!)

SHOTGUN SEAMSTRESS NUMBER 2

5225 N. Concord Ave.
Portland, Oregon 97217

www.myspace.com/29303||4|

This zine was copied at
DITTOS
407 NE MASON ST #6
AT MLK
Support Black Businesses

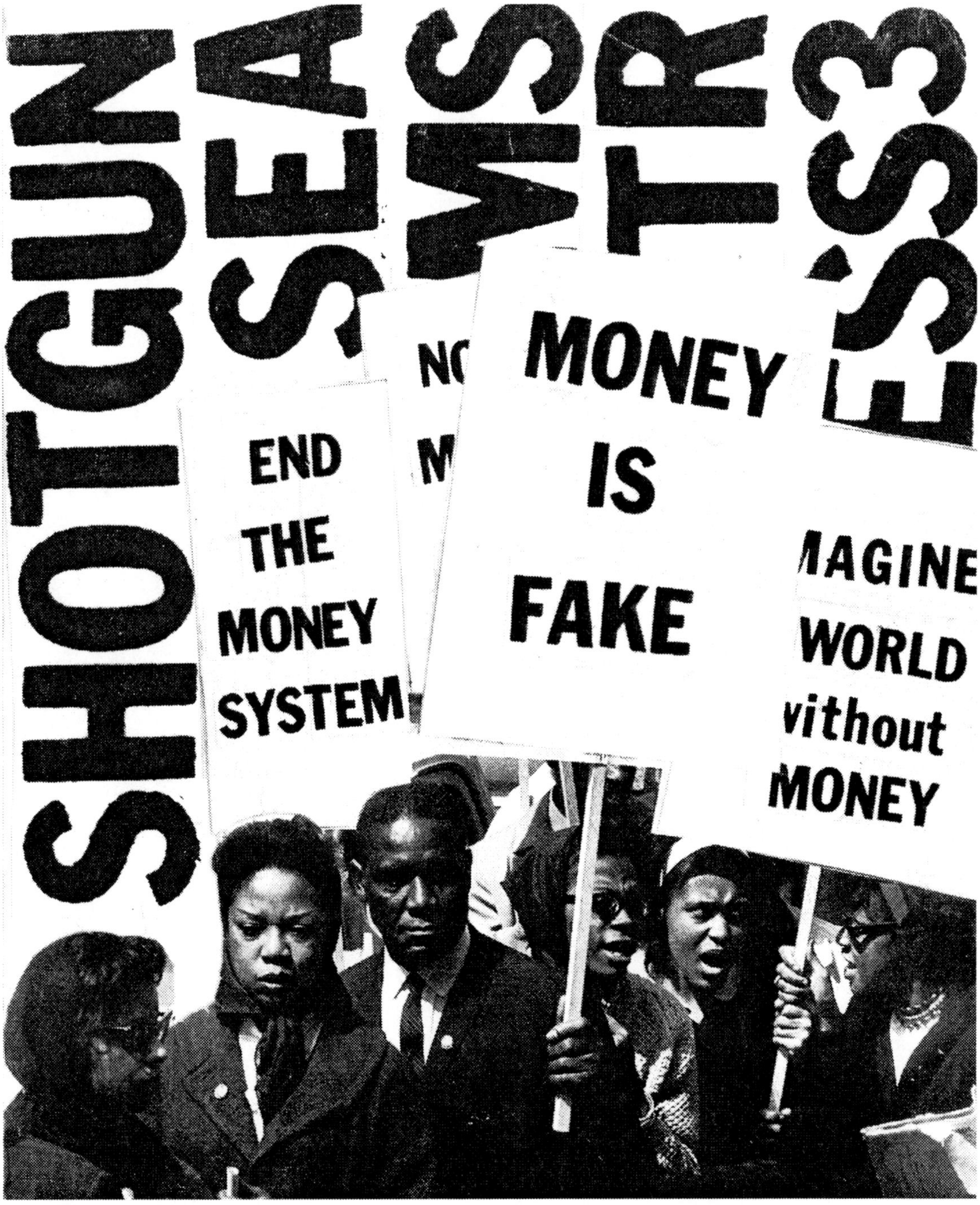

Shotgun Seamstress is a zine by and for Black punks, queers, feminists, artists & musicians.

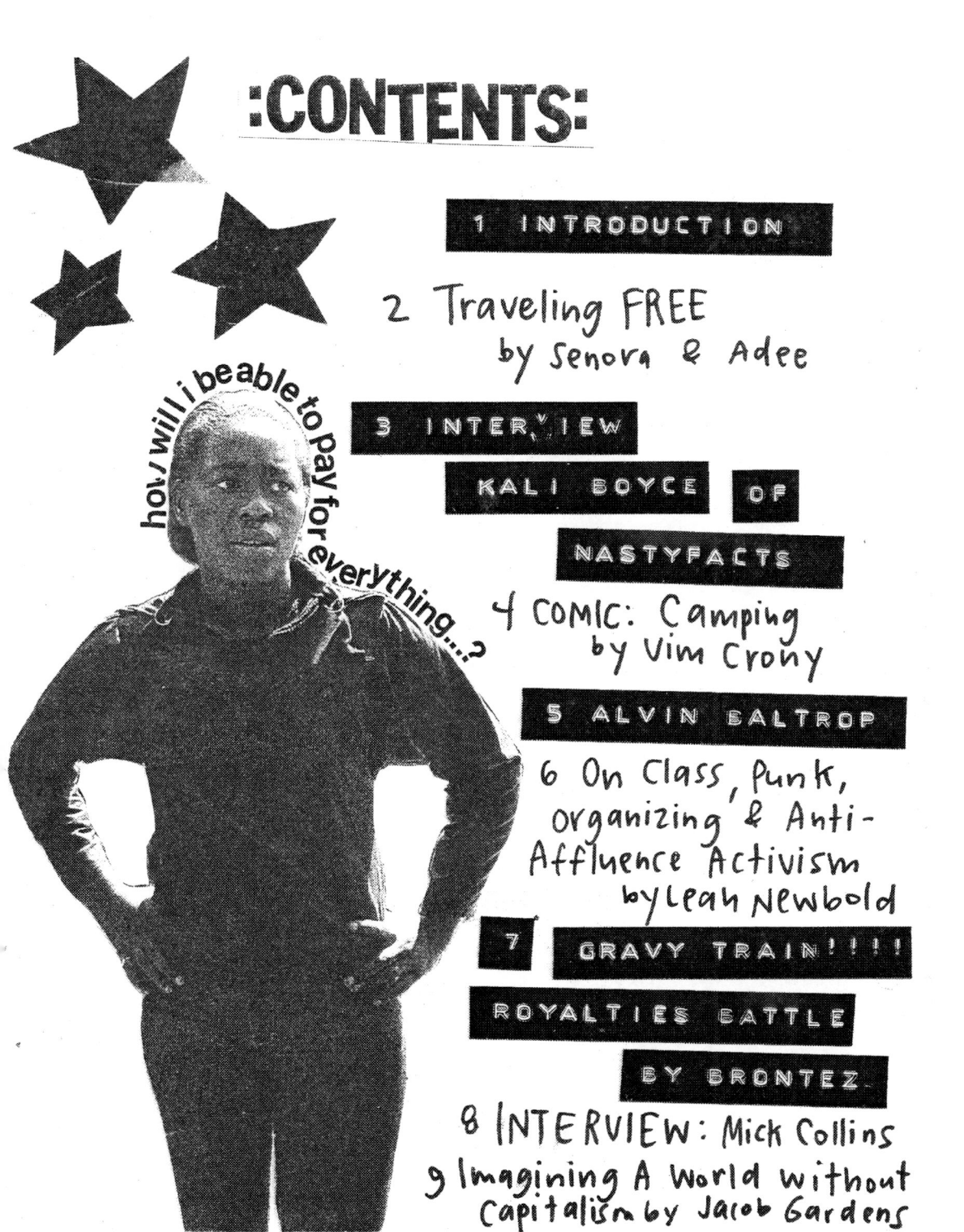

:CONTENTS:

how will i be able to pay for everything...?

1 INTRODUCTION

2 Traveling FREE by Senora & Adee

3 INTERVIEW KALI BOYCE OF NASTYFACTS

4 COMIC: Camping by Vim Crony

5 ALVIN BALTROP

6 On Class, Punk, Organizing & Anti-Affluence Activism by Leah Newbold

7 GRAVY TRAIN!!!! ROYALTIES BATTLE BY BRONTEZ

8 INTERVIEW: Mick Collins

9 Imagining A World without Capitalism by Jacob Gardens

INTRODUCTION

This third issue of SHOTGUN SEAMSTRESS zine gets Black punks, queers, feminists, artists and musicians talking about MONEY. It's the year 2009, we've just elected our first black president, but Black people in America continue to be an economically oppressed group when compared with our white counterparts. Currently, with the recession taking its toll on everyone regardless of race, there is worry that the percentage of unemployed workers will climb into the double digits. Watching the news, I've seen plenty of Black talking heads point out that unemployment in African American communities has already been in the double digits for quite some time.

I've always wondered why more Black folks weren't attracted to punk rock for that very reason. It takes a little bit of the necessity away from money. Punk rock ideally encourages communal living, curbing your consumerism and DIY ethics. It encourages us to live more simply. It teaches us that status shouldn't be tied to the possession of material things, and fuck the idea of status in the first place. It reminds us to value experiences over things.

Of course there are lots or reasons why not everyone can live simply in the purest sense of the term. Maybe you've got kids or you have a disability or you live in a place that's too spread out so you can't bike or walk and you have to drive. Everyone's got rent to pay. There are so many expenses that you just can't escape, and our society is quite unforgiving when it comes to social welfare. Food is expensive, childcare is expensive, transportation (even the bus) is expensive, and healthcare is expensive if you even have it at all.

Everyone needs money. Everyone's life is controlled by money to some degree, and it sucks. It's not fair. We shouldn't have to struggle for our most basic necessities. And if we are constantly worried about how we're going to cover our bills (or how we're going to afford the nicest car, the nicest clothes and shoes, and enough hair appointments to keep our nappy roots from showing through) then there's barely any time and energy left to dream or create. We have so much more potential as a people than our potential to consume, and that's an idea that goes way deeper and way further back than idealistic punk rock ethics.

Talking about MONEY in this zine reminded me of the fact that Black people have always had a knack for creating beautiful, meaningful art with very few financial resources, without art school or private lessons and without fancy equipment. Many of the artists featured in this issue are a testament to that.

In this issue of SHOTGUN SEAMSTRESS, I talk to Black rock-n-roller Mick Collins of the Gories and the Dirtbombs, who has been honing his talent for over 20 years with little or no financial compensation until recently. Two young Black gay women, Senora Grayson and Adee Licious, tell us how they figured out how to travel across the country virtually for free. I also write about Alvin Baltrop, a talented Black photographer from the Bronx who operated with very little money, experienced alienation based on race and class from the art world and ended up dying of cancer after receiving sub par health care. Brontez Purnell, an SS regular, is back with his story of Gravy Train!!!!'s brief battle over royalties. And lastly, new comer Jacob Gardens shares with us his dream of a world without capitalism.

Thanks for reading!
xo ss

February 2009

Traveling FREE

Traveling can be expensive.

In TRAVELING FREE Senora Grayson and Adee Licious tell us how they train-hopped and hitchhiked their way around the country, basically for free.

But just like with anything that's free, there's always a price to pay.

adee

The first time I went train hopping I was almost 19 years old and it was with a white girl who was a Cancer just like me. Her name was Jackie. I wanted to hop trains before my 19th birthday, and Jackie was about to turn 19 too. We started in Lake Worth, Florida and we got a ride to Pensacola, where we hopped a train. It was both of our first time doing it, but we were also with two white dudes who had done it before.

Train manuals kinda give you good information, but they ended up not really helping. We though we were going to Indiana, but we ended up in Kentucky. Our trip was Nasty! We ate fruit cocktails and chili straight outta the can and I just remember my feet were all dirty. There's a picture of me wearing all black, barefoot, with earplugs in (because it got really loud on the trains), eating fruit cocktail out of a can. I'll never do it again! I remember once I brought a hairdryer with me to make sure I could do my hair cuz I had a perm.

i'll never do it again!

Sometimes you have to wait for a train for days. I think we only had to wait for 24 hours in miami, but most of the the time it took much longer than that. We had to hide in train yards from cops and whoever else. Theere were fire ants and we were all getting bit. I got caught once in Georgia. We thought they were cops, but they were these nice people who offered us freezee pops and water. In Kalamath Falls, Oregon there's this infamous dude called Roger the Dodger who checks boxcars.

The things you do to get free shit... It's free, but you pay the price. It takes way longer than other kinds of traveling. When you get picked up by a hitchhiker, they're always a creep, staring at your titties. Every now and then, they'll give you money. My friend Gloria got rich hitchhiking! This one dude gave her one hundred dollars.

It's a beautiful way to travel, though. You get to see parts of the country you'd never get to see driving. We hopped trains to the first zine symposium in Portland. Me, sarah and Alley had an all-girl trip. We had our own box car. It was so fun! We had both sides open and it was so beautiful. We just sat around in our underwear and topless and sewed and stuff.

senora

Me and the girl I was dating at the time always talked about hitchhiking. She made it sound really fun and we didn't have a lot of money at the time.

We started in Olympia, Washington and ended in Arcata, California. We were supposed to hitch all the way back to New Orleans via a rainbow gathering, but Kat got sick, so we had to take greyhound back. All the drivers who picked us up told us we were lucky because we were girls, but I think the fact that I was with a white girl helped too. The majority of the drivers who picked us up never pick up hitchhikers either, they told us, so they had all of these ques ions. They loved it.

Here are some highlights of the trip:
1. some kids in Olympia threw a bottle of piss at us. None of it got on me.
2. someone robbed us in Portland while we were sleeping.
3. we both lost our IDs somewhere along the way
4. we camped in the Redwoods and Moonstone Beach. Very beautiful but very, very cold at night!
5. we ate at taco bell almost every day.
6. one person picked us up in Salem. That's it. We walked most of the way and got dehydrated.
7. swam at Whiskeytown Shasta Trinity near Redd8ing, California and also near an insane asylum. We had the lake all toourselves.

Thinking about it now, I should have been scared shitless. There are a lot of fucked up people out there and we were pretty naive, but my girl-friend looked pretty tough and we both had knives! One guy made us feel a little uneasy because he helped us set up camp and then stayed and talked tous forever! We thought he was gonna come back and murder us in our sleep. He had a creepy vibe. Portland was pretty fucked up too. Everyone we encountered downtown was on crystal or crazy or both and you couldn't trust anyone.

Memorable people:
1. hippie substitute teacher who took us all the way from Portland to Oly. He taught kids about organic farming.
2. Guatemalan truck driver who bought us food and showers. We met him at a truck stop in Oregon, I think. He was worried one of the sleazy drivers would offer us a ride. He was a really sweet guy. He offered to take us all the way to LA.
3. crazy chick who drove us into Arcata. We were driving up a cliff at like 70mph, and all she talked about was drugs, but she took us to her home and let us take showers. A few people even gaveus money.

Kali Boyce
AKA TuffNStuff
OF
NASTYFACTS

Kali Boyce was 12 years old when ze started playing in hir late 70s NYC pop punk band, NASTYFACTS. Ze tells Shotgun Seamstress about life as a queer preteen punk in New York as well as hir current life as a Drag King performer in San Francisco, CA.

SS: WHAT YEAR DID NASTYFACTS FORM?
KB: 1975, I think. I met Brad and Jeff at grade school in Brooklyn Heights. I picked up the bass and began teaching myself how to play. Genji started teaching himself to drum about then too. He got a drum kit AND he had a basement in Park Slope where we hung out and played all the time. Back then we were called Pandemonium (yup) and we were a cover band.

SS: WAS IT YOUR FIRST BAND? HOW OLD WERE YOU AND HOW DID IT COME TOGETHER?
KB: Yes, I was 12 or so. Brad and Jeff used to play with this other kid, a boy of color who had a cute big sis (that I was crushed out on) who, in turn had a boyfriend who played bass in a local band. Everyone used to hang around the guys in the band (well, I liked hanging around the cute big sis). Brad, Jeff and the little brother were forming a band of their own. Suddenly, my big crush and her family moved to another state which left us all sad sacks, y'know? I saw Jeff and Brad in one of the rooms at school, basically just bumming about not having a bassist anymore and, So I said: "Oh yeah, I play bass. I could be in your band." I think I'd maybe held a bass once or twice to try to impress that girl. Anyway, after school that day, I went to my mom and said "I need a bass and an amp, I need to be in this band." And she actually said "OK". She took me down to a pawn shop and we got a used "Harmony" bass and a "Kalamazoo" amp (I still laugh about my first rig!). That was the pretty much the beginning of NastyFacts. Playing loud and fast in Genji's basement was way more fun than kicking it in the projects. I grew up in Fort Green, Brooklyn but I always felt at odds there: I was queer, I was punk, I looked and felt like a strange little boy/grrl. Later in life I found a phrase for it: "Two Spirit". Now I consider myself a "no-op", trans man who performs in boy drag (a natural progression from awkward baby butch punk rocker, yep)!

SS: SO YOU ARE A SELF-TAUGHT MUSICIAN?
KB: My mom and pops were in a swing band together, that's how they met (least that's what I been told). Music was always around when I was growing up, from as far as I can remember. Mom loved calypso music. My dad was from Barbados and played piano (and yes we had a rickety old piano in that teeny apartment in the projects!). Also, my 3 half-sisters were teenagers who loved their Motown so I was surrounded by music all the time, on the radio, on the "record player". Mom was constantly singing and cooking or cleaning and so we all sang. I first played in public at a school concert when I was nine. I played the soprano recorder from 4th grade on. Baroque music believe it or not! So, naturally, I had to REBEL!! Anyway, NastyFacts was pure fun. We started out covering a lot of Kiss songs, which lucky for me, are so easy to play on bass that I started out thinking I was a bad ass because I learned like all their songs in a week! Yeah.

SS: DID YOU WRITE ANY OF THE SONGS? IF SO, WHICH ONES?
KB: I wrote and sang all three of the songs on our first record. But we didn't figure out we needed to write songs for at least another year and a half. There was another local band called the Speedies who thought we were cool for a bunch of kids and gave us some extremely helpful tips really early on - like: if you want to start playing in night clubs you gotta write your own songs. So we all started writing and each of us in the band wrote a song for our first demo. We shopped it to clubs, and started gigging in New York City. Our first show was at CBGB's. And we played Max's Kansas City on the regular! I remember playing shows w/ bands like ESG (from the Bronx) and the Stimulators. I think the clubs would try to book us w/ bands that had something in common w/ us.. The Stimulator had an 11 year old drummer named Harley (who went on to Cromags fame) ESG were peeps of color (and sooo damn cool!). Those were good times! But it was getting a slot opening for the Bad Brains that changed my life! I was 15 or so (the oldest in the band) and we all knew that we wanted to do this (play music) for life.

SS: DID YOU KNOW YOU WERE QUEER THEN? WHEN'D YOU FIGURE IT OUT?
KB: I figured out I liked girls when I was around five years old. But I was one lucky baby dyke: My sisters were teenagers (almost grown) when I was really young. They'd have their friends over, and it was like baby-dyke heaven. While they were sitting around yakking, I'd be hugging on their legs, crawling around and playing with their leg hairs, getting all of the lovings from these cute girls who thought I was just a cute little kid. Meanwhile, I was like "Girls, hmmmm, girls." Yeah, I was about five. But I didn't come out to my family till I was 17, and that was only after I'd moved out to my own space in Greenwich Village. I came out to my closest friends when I was 14 or 15. It didn't really surprise anyone! I'd always been called a "tom-boy", a

NASTYFACTS promo shot

NASTYFACTS

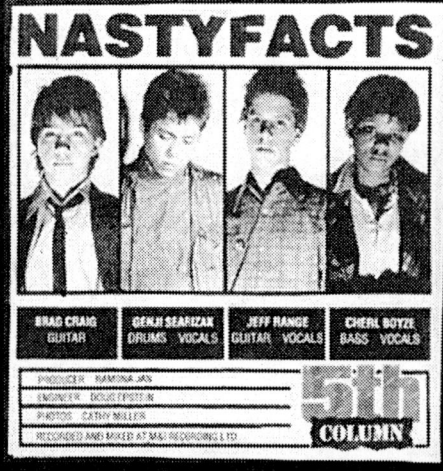

BRAD CRAIG — GUITAR
GENJI SIARIZAK — DRUMS VOCALS
JEFF RANGE — GUITAR VOCALS
CHERL BOYZE — BASS VOCALS

PRODUCER: RAMONA JAN
ENGINEER: DOUG EPSTEIN
PHOTOS: CATHY MILLER
RECORDED AND MIXED AT M&I RECORDING LTD

5th COLUMN

back of Drive MY CAR 7"

jock (cuz I played basketball, tennis, soccer, track) and I was often mistaken for a bio-boy from a very young age so... can you say "baby-butch"? My coming out, it was pretty anti-climactic.

SS: WHAT KIND OF SHOWS DID NASTYFACTS PLAY?
KB: We started out playing house parties and school dances moved on to playing clubs, CBGB's, Max's Kansas City, and other long gone night clubs in Manhattan and Jersey where, apparently, nobody gave a shit that we were waaaay underage! Actually, Peter Crowley (Max's Kansas City) and Hilly [Kristal, founder of club] at CBGB's treated us like we were their spawn. They booked us monthly and paid us right! And offered advice about stuff and thangs in the N.Y. scene. What a way to grow up, huh?

SS: WHAT DID THE MONEY YOU MADE GO TO?
KB: We got paid, usually a percentage of the door price. We also sold T shirts and, of course, our ep (it had to be re-issued after we sold out the first run). The first thing I remember buying w/money from our gigs was a sound system for our rehearsal space. We were stoked and, actually, that lead me into audio engineering which I'm still into today!

SS: WHO PUT OUT YOUR FIRST 7 INCH?
KB: A cat named Jim Reynolds approached us about putting out a record. He owned an indie label called Jimboco. So our 7 inch EP single, with three songs on it was born. All three songs (Drive My Car, Crazy 'Bout You and Gotta Get to You) were my originals that I wrote in my room on a piece of crap guitar that only had 3 strings (I shit you not). That's me singing lead vocals, with Genji howling on back up vocals.

SS: DO YOU HAVE A JOB RIGHT NOW? WHAT IS IT?
KB: I perform as a Drag King called "TuffNStuff" playing slide on the resonator guitar and doing basically what ever songs I feel like, in a "Delta Blue-esque" style. I do some originals, some old punk covers, some classic blues like Lead Belly and Skip James. I play all kinds of music because I love all kinds of music and I have big fun doing it! Check me out at: KingTuffNStuff.com or myspace.com/kingtuffnstuff. I am also an Audio Engineer (which I got into back in the day when NastyFacts bought a sound system). I freelance doing pre and post production audio for indie films and videos as well as live sound reinforcement in the Bay Area (I did post for a while in L.A. (for really bad horror flicks). I much prefer living in San Francisco, and I've been getting my original music (I also build 'beats', trip hop style) into indie films for the past 8 years or so. I've got tracks and/or incidental music in "By Hook or By Crook", "Live Nude Girls Unite" and "Sugar High, Glitter City" to name a few of my faves!

SS: WHEN YOU WERE JUST STARTING OUT, DID YOU BELIEVE THAT YOU COULD MAKE PLAYING AND PERFORMING MUSIC YOUR JOB?
KB: Yes, and I still do. When we started playing clubs, we all decided that's what we wanted to do for life. Making music keeps me happy! I will never quit!

CAMPING

The Cheesecake Philosophy
By Nim Crony 2009

Casey has a dilemma -
I can't believe rent is due already!? I'm working way too hard and I don't feel like I'm really getting ANYWHERE...
DAMN IT!
This isn't living!
IS IT?
Arghh, now I have a headache!

What do you think, Cheesecake?
purr
purr
purr
Well, considering all the energy you're putting into some shit job that doesn't really mean anything- I'd say some decisions need to be made. You've got the ability and skill to fucking make your own way in life! Of course it's going to take dedication and of course it will be difficult. That's LIVING - That's PUNK! Make your own Path in life and don't settle for working for someone who honestly doesn't give a fuck about who you are or what you believe in. And as a young punk of color, there is a choice for you to make--- TO BECOME AWARE OF HOW AWESOME YOU ARE AND RUN YOUR OWN BUSINESS
(YOUR OWN LIFE)
You know, if you could talk I bet you'd have some RAD things to say!
meow.
FOR REAL

On Class, Punk, Organizing and Anti-Affluence Activism

by Leah Newbold

I feel like I owe a lot to punk rock, since it was one of the first things to politicize me. Picking up those old people of color punk zines like *Race Riot* and *How to Stage A Coup* was the first time I was kinda like....okay...I'm not on my own. There are other peeps who go through the same stuff as me and I don't need to feel like I'm just a complete drama queen. Racism, classism and homophobia are real and we can name them and talk about them and we can fight fear and shame with fierce words and hold.each.other.down community. In other words, we can participate in power...we who live and breathe shit can reveal shit, fight, shape and be proud of our realities.

Needless to say, it pissed me off to realize that though punk is powerful, it is like everything else...a microcosm of society, and all that oppressive shit that happens outside also happens within. In the punk scene, in the queer community, in community organizing, in activism, among people of colour (and all these communities have been linked for me) there has been racism, there has been queerphobia, transphobia and abelism and there has been CLASSISM. Goddamn there has seriously been classism.

So...steppin into punk from what I come from. So...what I come from—lemme situate myself cuz I think that's the first thing. In terms of class, I grew up mostly workin class with particular middle class privileges. My mom was a grade school teacher sometimes single parenting and my daddy is a first generation Black West Indian so most of the 80s he spent unemployed despite his university degree before getting a steady job in a grocery store...all the while both of them sending money home to help out his family in the West Indies. Aside from that there were some factors that compounded our families' class situation to do with addiction and illness....which is the case for a lot of people. On the other hand I've had the privilege to attend university, to access health care based on my parents having status and health benefits and to benefit from support from middle class family members on my mama's side. I also come from pride and from my daddy's ON criticisms of labour injustice, slave mentality and migrant exploitation.

So fast forward to punk and steppin into the scene there have always been a few things that just haven't sat right with me. And most of those things fit into three bigger phenomenon which is basically "slummin it", ad-buster style anti-capitalism (which I also call judgy judgy stushy stushy), and the model-minority-work-for-free-ethic of the activist world. I could go on about these three things forever.

Let's start with the first one. So one of the weird things about punk is that it's cool to be poor. It's cool to live in rapidly gentrifying neighborhoods of colour, it's cool to be on welfare, it's cool to eat food out tha garbage and it's cool to wear tore-up clothes. Which...cool—let's challenge each other about consumerism, about food and housing access and about what defines success and appearing successful. Now what I feel is *not* cool is doing a, b, c and d while accessing your trust fund, without talking about your class privilege, while carrying out oppressive attitudes and behaviours towards working class people and all the while not interacting with working class people cuz they are excluded from the scene/the movement. My main point here is that there's nothing inherently cool about struggling and poverty, it only seems cool when you don't really live it. What might be cooler is honesty about who you are, where you come from and what participating in community solidarity might look like. Don't get swallowed up in guilt about gentrification—let people who's neighbourhoods are being swallowed up be the visionaries of an anti-gentrification movement and show support—offer your neighbors to help out with childcare at least rather than trying articulate their experience for them.

And stop judging working class people. STUSHY STUSHY. This is my big critique of a certain type of punk endorsed anti-capitalism. Consumer consciousness is a really inequitable and classist way to try and challenge capitalism, i.e.: judging people for shopping at Walmart and eating McDonalds is not an effective way to challenge capitalism. It's really good if you feel like you are punk and vegan and you have ideals like you love animals and you don't want to support the exploitative labour practices of multinational corporations but check this—not everyone can afford your ideals. When we were growing up we wore pants from Walmart and ate McDonalds cuz dem pants cost $4.99. I believe in challenging exploitative labour practices but who should bare the judgment—poor people or people who actually own capital? I love animals but I also love other Black people—Black people who harvest Dole bananas and grind sugar cane... Let's get serious y'all.

And this third thing. Let me start by saying that part of the irony of classism is that poor people work like hell. My dad has done shift work/on-and-off night shift for the past 16 years. He works as hard or harder than any doctor or lawyer and ten times harder than a multinational CEO, I can guarantee you that. He doesn't get praise for this, he is tired and he is sick from this. He believes in freedom, he believes in fairness and liberation. But he is not an activist. What I'm saying is that we cannot expect to include working class people in community organizing movements while expecting that people do work for free cuz it's "for the cause" and cuz we "don't believe in capitalism". Not believing in something doesn't stop it from being a reality for those who are directly affected. Working class people don't have time or money and—like everyone else—need to feed families and hold down lives. It is classist to pay people late, to expect people to work for free, to expect people to work free overtime etc. cuz it's "for the revolution". It is not revolutionary to reproduce oppressive patterns by expecting people of colour to have a model minority work ethic and take one for the team. We need to seriously examine what the goals of our movements are and where our movements and communities are exclusionary.

So...I'm pissed. But with love. Cuz I love punk rock and I love feeling that I am part of communities that believe in and will fight for liberation. I just feel like we have some shit to work out. Part of what I owe to punk rock is helping me not to feel shame in where I come from and who I am and at times it has been amazingly affirming. So it just sucks that punk ethics continue to shame working class peeps because of a lack of perspective and lack of self-interrogation. Working class experiences are built into punk and the stories that it tells way back into culcha reggae and I think for that reason we owe punk the integrity to own up to our own stories too.

Leah's playlist of Reggae songs

THE MAYTONES
"Money Worries"

TANYA STEPHENS
"Warn Dem"

ETANA
"I Am Not Afraid"

HARRY BELAFONTE
"Banana Boat Song"

BALTIMORE
"If I Were A Rich Girl"

DENNIS BROWN
"Money In My Pocket"

QUEEN IFRICA
"Rise Ghetto YOuth"

about STRUGGING with MONEY

THE MAYTONES

"Money Troubles"

"Youths Dem Cold"

LADY SAW

JACOB MILLER

"Ease My Mind"

"Tenement Yard"

TRACY CHAPMAN

"Talkin Bout a Revolution"

FREDDY McGREGOR

"To Be Poor Is a Crime"

BABY CHAM

"Ghetto Story"

ALVIN BALTROP

1948-2004

"You must be a real sewer rat, that you crawl around at night and photograph things like this. So I I have to consider you a real sewer rat type of person, and I don't know if I like you."

At the age of 26, Alvin Baltrop began photographing what was going on at Manhattan's West Side piers. The area, full of abandoned warehouses and dilapidated industrial piers, became a temporary home for queer teenage runaways and a cruising spot for gay men. It was a place that was under the radar. People went there to do drugs, muggings were common and so, unfortunately, were rape, murder and suicide. Baltrop's camera captured gay public sex, the public art of muralist Tava, various unknown graffiti artists, as well as pieces by David Wojnarowicz, who also visited the piers. Baltrop documented homelessness, death and the stark decay of run-down warehouses with depth and grace.

Of course, not everyone saw it that way. The mainstream art world, even the gay portion of it, couldn't see the value in Baltrop's work. Hostile reactions to his pictures were common. One curator he showed his portfolio to likened Baltrop to a sewer rat because of the content of his photos. Most art gallery owners and academic art critics could only see dirty homeless fags fucking in an abandoned warehouse, and stopped there.

According to his close friend and assistant, Randal Wilcox, gay art galleries were the most unreceptive to the late photographer's work.

"Al Baltrop endured constant racism from gay curators, gallery owners and other members of the 'gay community' until his death. Many of these people doubted that Baltrop shot his own photographs; some implied or directly told him that he stole the work of a white photographer. Other people who were willing to accept the photographs treated Al as though he was an idiot savant. Other people stole photographs from him."

It didn't take long for Baltrop to get the picture. He subsequently withdrew from the art world and focused more of his energy on photography. As a result of his experiences, his work received very little attention during his lifetime. He had a few small shows in New York, one at the Glines, a gay non-profit, and another exhibit at the East Village gay bar where he sometimes worked as a bouncer. After his death, his work received a bit more attention. Since 2004, his work has been show internationally. In February 20008, ARTFORUM published an article on Baltrop including several reprints of his photographs. Most recently the Whitney agreed to purchase one of his photographs for their permanent collection.

So, Alvin Baltrop definitely wasn't in it for money or recognition. Conclusion? The man loved photography and he loved the people and places he photographed. Baltrop began taking pictures in junior high school and continued while he was in the military, taking scandalous photos of his friends in the navy. After he left the navy, he worked as a street vendor, a jewelry designer, and a printer. At one point, in order to spend more time at the piers, he quit his job as a cab driver and became a self-employed mover. He would live out of his van parked nearby the stoop he inhabited while he stayed at the piers for days at a time. His life seemed to revolve around his art.

"I learned photography from some unusual people," said Baltrop about the beginnings of his career. "Old photographers who are dead now, who'd say 'bring your camera, kid, and we'll go out shooting.'"

In the navy, he was a medic, serving during the Vietnam War. They called him W.D. for "witch doctor." He didn't have all of the supplies he needed to do his art, so he made them himself.

"I built my developing trays out of medic trays in sick bay; I built my own enlarger. I took notes about exposures, practiced techniques and just kept going." Later, when he began taking pictures at the piers, he used make-shift harnesses to hang from the ceilings of warehouses, where he watched and waited for hours to capture the moments that made up life on the West Side piers.

Baltrop didn't come to the piers as an outsider, like some kind of white guy anthropologist living in the Amazonian jungle amongst "the natives." Baltrop, originally from the Bronx, was part of the community there. Baltrop took thousands of photographs at the West Side piers between 1975 and 1986. He sat at the same stoop everyday at 89 East Second Street and was friends with the folks at the piers. He exposed himself to his subjects as much as they exposed themselves to him. In fact, friends and neighbors noted, he was one of them. Baltrop knew the story behind every face he photographed.

"These two kids here [having sex in a photograph], their fathers found out they were gay and threw them out of the house...At one point the piers were full of kids who had been thrown out." Baltrop continued, "This guy [pointing to another model in a photograph] was a banker and this one worked in soap operas. This guy was a part-time minister. This guy was a security man. I knew these people," he said. "They'd see me everyday. Some people took of their clothes and *demanded* to be photographed."

Baltrop always gave credit to his girlfriend at the time, Alice, for encouraging his photography work and pushing him to get better. In his personal life, Baltrop had long-term relationships with men and women but never really put a label on his sexuality. He disliked the word "bisexual" because, according to his friend Randal Wilcox, Baltrop felt it was too politically correct and sounded fake. He preferred being called "gay" to being called "bisexual."

Alvin Baltrop was an afrocentric brotha, "a tall, funky, elegant mix of Africana and military," as a friend once described him. Before cancer took its toll on the photographer, he was a big guy. He often wore kufis and dashikis, big jewelry and carried a large cane.

Baltrop discovered he had cancer in the late 1990s. On top of dealing with his illness, life added insult to injury when economic issues and hovering vultures from the art world came into play. Baltrop could not afford health insurance and ultimately did not receive adequate care for his condition. He ended up dying in 2004 due to substandard treatment at a veteran's hospital.

According to Wilcox, during the fall and winter of 2003 as he was dying in various hospitals, a gay filmmaker decided to pay Alvin Baltrop a visit. The filmmaker came to ask Baltrop to give away the rights to all of his photographs. Now why on earth would anyone do that? Did he think Baltrop was stupid? Did he think he could be easily taken advantage of because he was Black and poor? Or ill? Or both? Either way, the request was insulting. This particular filmmaker had a history of taking advantage of terminally ill people.

"He used to work for ABC," said Wilcox, "and he was able to have the first televised interview of a person with AIDS in the early 80s. He fired the guy he scheduled to interview because he looked 'too healthy,' and hunted and put the most sickly person he could find in front of a camera, so he could basically say, 'This is a gay person. This is a gay person with AIDS.' What is the gay equivalent of an 'Uncle Tom'?"

If Baltrop's photographs had little value to those people during his life, why would they then begin to have value after his death? Why is a Black, poor, queer artist's work only valuable after he is dead?

"The losers who rejected him or would have rejected him had they known him are now trying to canonize him as some kind of 'hero,'" fumed Wilcox. "In short, now that Al is dead, they are willing to accept him. This is appalling."

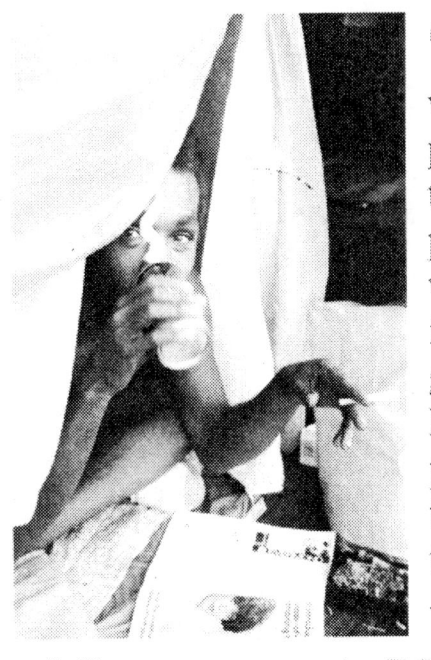

"The guy in the tent was slightly mentally unbalanced, possibly schizophrenic. In addition to hustling, he'd also dance for people on the streets for money, wearing elaborate costumes he made for himself out of rags. Anyway, the guy he's talking to was kicked out of his home because he was gay. In the photo, the hustler/dancer is telling the guy about safe places to stay at the piers, where to bathe, etc."
—Randal Wilcox

It is appalling.

However, there are those of us who see the work of Alvin Baltrop and immediately understand the language he speaks with his photos. Why does so much art have to be filtered through the doors of white-owned, high-brow galleries before it makes it to the general public? Who are the people who decide what art gets seen and what art doesn't, and what is their agenda? Asking these questions makes me appreciate the dozens of DIY art shows I've been to over the years in friends' houses and in bookstores, record stores and coffee shops. The whole point is to share art that we'd never otherwise see unless we choose to take control of the whole process and do it ourselves.

Alvin's story reconfirms my belief that people of color and queer people desperately need our own independent media to cover our own work. We also need to make it a point to work within communities who take racism, classism, sexism, transphobia, homophobia and other forms of bigotry seriously. Mainstream white-owned media won't cover our art unless it matches up with their stereotypes of us, i.e. nothing too gay, too weird or too complex. When they do cover our work, they don't do it justice or they try to whitewash it. Wilcox has always sent an assortment of photographs to the few publications that have been interested in covering Baltrop's work. Even though Baltrop photographed plenty of people of color, the vast majority of magazines are much more likely to publish the photos he took of white males.

We can see by the decisions Alvin Baltrop made throughout his life that he didn't make art because he wanted to be famous or get rich. When I ask to see the creation of more Black media for Black art and more queer media for queer art, I'm not necessarily hoping that more Black & queer artists get famous. I'm hoping that more Black artists receive support and affirmation so that they are able to thrive as artists while they are alive.

Besides being beautiful pieces of art, Baltrop's pier photographs help us piece together our queer history.

The piers brimmed with activity during the time period after the Stonewall riots and before the AIDS epidemic ravaged gay communities in New York and across the country. Ultimately, it was AIDS that helped bring an end to the glory days of the West Side piers. The disease wiped out numbers of people who used to visit them regularly. New York City officials eventually used AIDS as an excuse to demolish the site by claiming that doing so would stop the spread of the disease.

The West Side pier photographs are Baltrop's main body of work, although he photographed many different people and places over the course of his career. He could only afford to print a small number of the pictures he took, leaving thousands of unprinted negatives that have yet to be seen by the world.

"One of the many, many reasons why the pier photographs are extraordinary and important," says Wilcox, "is that Al documented a certain group of gay people in a specific place at a specific time in a way that didn't glorify, demonize, exaggerate or stereotype, ultimately showing [his subjects] as being human beings."

Each of Baltrop's photos resonates gentle humanity, even the ones of dead bodies and broken buildings. His gaze is understanding instead of judgmental, which is exactly how you have to look at his photographs in order to appreciate them.

Alvin Baltrop died on February 1st, 2004 though the spirit of his art lives on. May his soul rest in peace.

it doesn't make any sense

In the wake of this bail-out business, don't you wonder where all of this extra money is coming from? Where will the money for OBAMA's $825 billion dollar stimulus plan come from? If the U.S. government is already trillions of dollars in debt, what is the source of this extra money? How come debt never seems to matter? No matter how much debt an individual or institution has, it never seems to curb their ability to spend more. The average American with a credit file has $16,635 worth of debt, excluding mortgages. Personal bankruptcies surged to more than 1 million filings in the U.S. in 2008, the most since the rewrite of bankruptcy laws took effect in 2005. So how are all of the items paid for that now-bankrupt consumers bought on credit? How does this all work? It seems so fake! It's all a game. Our economy is fake.
MONEY IS FAKE!

MONEY IS FAKE

All the Not-So-Sweet Stuff
Gravy Train!!!!'s brief battle over royalties
by Brontez Purnell

Disclaimer: This was years ago and I'm over it. Long story short, there was basically a battle in Gravy Train!!!! over royalties.

We had just finished recording ALL THE SWEET STUFF and we were deciding what record credit goes where. Me and Funx (Carolina) wanted the royalties to be split four ways. Chunx and Hunx (Heather and Seth) had a problem with that. Both of them never gave clear arguments for why they felt that way. The only reason they ever really gave was that the girl I replaced, Drunx, had left the band with a fourth of the royalties on HELLO DOCTOR, GT's vbest-selling record, eventhough she hadn't written any of the songs on it and that had really burned them. There was the record before ATSS we did called ARE YOU WIGGLIN? On that record, when we decided royalties, I got 20% (I'd written one song, "Hump Lights") as most of the songs had been written before I was in the band. Funx got some percentage between 10-20 because she didn't write songs but she did play keyboard on all the tracks.

Despite all of the excuses Hunx and Chunx gave as to why it should be split that way(some of which I later agreed with), I took it really personally. I felt like a second wife with a bogus pre-nup. When ALL THE SWEET STUFF came out, I felt confident that it'd be split four ways. Hunx had said tome that everyone had put in an equal amount of effort on the record, so when we asked for it to be split four ways, I didn't understand the hesitation on Hunx and Chunx part. They tried to scapegoat Drunx again, but I felt like that wasn't an effective argument since I actually wrote songs in the band (danced harder too). There was the matter of Funx not writing songs, but I didn't know what the deal was. Chunx could only play some sparse notes here and there and give ideas. She needed Funx to turn her ideas into workable songs.

When it was decided that this was going to be an issue, things turned ugly. I felt that GT songs were pretty easy to execute pop songs with some pretty flimsy 2-3 part structures. I felt like if this was the precedent, all someone would have to do is write a 3 second keyboard hook and a lil guitar part, call it a song and then dominate the songlist onthe record with their "effort." This aspect wouldn't have been so troubling for me if not for the fact that I always felt like Chunx and Hunx never included me in their songwriting process as much as I included them in mine.

It turned really ugly. I wrote the band the most ego-destroying email I could with what I felt were some really good points that were unfortunately wrapped up in too many paranoid accusations to be effective. It was really the wrong way to go about it, but then there's this other part of me that feels like even if i had been polite about it, it wouldn't have mattered and things wuold have stayed the same and I would've only been silent, hostile and resentful. I really do feel in life that there are times where you're better of dropping the bomb. There was a point where Hunx got upset with me and said I was being greedy and only concrned with money, but I don't think that's true. Honey, I have NEVER expected to get rich off of a Gravy Train record. I always felt like me asking for a fourth was more of a symbolic gesture type thing. I mean, I was never gonna see a cent from the records that people actually bought and I didn't give a fuck. I just wanted credit. There was also the fact that I didn't really do any of the tour planning, merch, etc. Most of that was handled by Hunx.

I got so crazy about the royalty credit because I felt like it was weird coming into a band where so much had already been established. When I was told that I wasn't going to have a fourth, I felt like I was being slighted out of the only part of the process I could really contribute to. My personal aesthetics don't really match the Gravy Train one, so I could never contribute record art and I don't even have a credit card so there was no way I could help with tour as far as renting vans. Merch and show money was always split equally (made more from that than I would've made from flimsy roaylties anyway.) But I can't shake the fact that that scenario really bugged me. We all argued about it and then just stopped talking about it altogether. It was never really resolved I also felt that it was one of those things we probably were nevergoing to reach 100% consensus on. One positive thing that came out of it was the situation prompted me to start the Younger Lovers—I wanted to learn to do thiings for myself.

I urge all people in bands to talk about shit like this and settle on something. Get over it, quit or SOMETHING, but just talk about it, decide on something and move past it because talking about money and creative control with people can get pretty fucking boring.

Mick Collins

of the Dirtbombs & the Gories talks to Shotgun Seamstress about being a Black Punk in Detroit before the dawn of hip hop and about where he thinks the pressure on Black people to conform comes from.

SS: WHAT WAS THE FIRST TOUR YOU EVER WENT ON?
MC: That would be The Gories. We did three shows in the Ozarks with Untamed Youth and Cornell Jackson. We played St. Louis, Columbia and one other city I can't recall.

SS: WHAT WERE THE SHOWS LIKE?
MC: They were actually really good. I was surprised that they did very well at all. People kinda knew who we were cuz by that time, word about us had already started getting around and stuff. And then we were on the bill with Cornell Jackson... Basically it was a bill of curiosities. Also Kansas City is the home of the Untamed Youth, so people came out to see them and they stayed to see us and Cornell Jackson.

SS: COOL. SO DID YOU HAVE TO WORK WHEN YOU WERE IN THE GORIES?
MC: Yeah, I did. I had a job doing IT. Network Admin.

SS: LIKE COMPUTER STUFF? IS THAT WHAT YOU STILL DO?
MC: No. I haven't had a 9-5 job since 1994.

SS: SO WHEN YOU WENT ON TOUR WITH THE GORIES, Y'ALL WERE ABLE TO BREAK EVEN?
MC: I don't recall us breaking even on that, but at this point I don't even remember.

SS: BUT WHEN DID IT CHANGE OVER TO WHEN YOU DIDN'T HAVE TO WORRY ABOUT THAT ANYMORE?
MC: Well, I started playing music professionally in 1980 and the first year I was ever able to pay all of my bills through just making music was 2003.

SS: DANG.
MC: Yeah, it only took 23 years.

SS: WHEN YOU WERE A LITTLE KID, DID YOU JUST WANT TO BE A MUSICIAN OR DID YOU THINK YOU WERE GOING TO HAVE TO HAVE A REGULAR JOB?
MC: When I was a kid, I really wanted to be an astronaut. Music didn't enter into it. I wanted to be an astronaut.

SS: DID YOU HAVE THE KIND OF PARENTS THAT WERE LIKE "YOU GOTTA DO SOMETHING PRACTICAL AND MUSIC CAN BE YOUR HOBBY!"?
MC: Mm hmm. Oh yeah.

SS: DID THEY EXPECT YOU TO GO TO COLLEGE AND STUFF?
MC: They did, and I ended up in broadcasting school. I figured if I couldn't make music, I could at least play it [on the radio]. I graduated from Spence Howard School of Broadcasting, here in Michigan. They basically teach you how to be a radio or TV personality.

SS: SO DID YOU GRADUATE?
MC: I did.

SS: DID YOU EVER USE IT?
MC: No. I worked in radio twice: once before I went to Spence Howard and once after I graduated, and the job after, my being at Spence Howard was not a requirement. By that point, it was enough that I was me.

SS: SO WHAT WERE YOUR EXPECTATIONS GROWING UP? BECAUSE IT SEEMS LIKE MOST PEOPLE IN GENERAL, BUT ESPECIALLY BLACK PEOPLE FEEL LIKE THEY'RE NOT GONNA BE ABLE TO MAKE IT DOING ART, OR MAKE A LIVING OFF OF IT.
MC: Right. I think that being in Detroit probably helped with that because there was nothing else to do. One of the reasons people are always hearing about bands coming from Detroit is because we were really bored here. There's nothing going on, so we had to make our own entertainment. And it helped that, at least till around 1983, the radio was really open to that sort of thing. You could hear local bands on the radio. You could hear independent bands and imports on the radio in Detroit. The first time I heard Dead Kennedys was on the radio.

The week "Too Drunk to Fuck" came out, I happened to tune in. Till this day, I don't own any Ramones records because they were always on the radio. They were just around. The cost of living is also really low here. A person can do what they want in terms of making art and not have to worry about starving because it doesn't cost anything to live here.

SS: YEAH, THAT'S PRETTY MUCH HOW PORTLAND IS. THAT'S PRETTY MUCH THE ONLY PERK OF LIVING THERE. HAS THERE BEEN A GENTRIFICATION BOOM IN DETROIT?
MC: No. They tried, but it doesn't really work because the amount of investment needed is so high, that no one can mount it. So they try and try but it doesn't work because no one wants to move here. So, the good part is that the cost of living is really, really low. There was a program where you could buy a beat down old house for about a hundred bucks. You had to bring it up to code, but you owned it for a hundred bucks. You can buy a livable house in Detroit for five grand, but it's in a really shitty hood. So while the property rates are staggeringly low, it's because the neighborhoods are staggeringly shitty.

SS: SO WHEN YOU WERE GROWING UP, A BUNCH OF KIDS YOU KNEW STARTED BANDS TO FIGHT THE BOREDOM?
MC: Mm hmm. Yeah. I often get asked by European magazines why is a Black guy in a punk rock band. And my answer is always the same: I'm not the only Black guy who was ever in a punk rock band [in Detroit]. I'm just the only one still in one after 20 years.

SS: YEAH, SO WHO WERE THE OTHER ONES?
MC: Well, hip-hop killed punk rock in Detroit.

SS: KILLED IT?
MC: Killed it. Because at that time, punk rock in Detroit was about to get totally taken over by frustrated Black teenagers. There was a show called MV3 that played new wave videos. We'd used to watch it every day when we'd come home from school. It was like American Band Stand for freaks. We were sitting there, my two close friends and I, on my sofa watching MV3, totally vegging out, and they showed the video from "Buffalo Girls" by Malcolm McLaren. We sat there, and none of us moved. We looked at each other, and we got up and we walked to the record store. And when we got to the record store, there was already a line stretching out around the corner and everyone was there trying to buy the "Buffalo Girls" 12". They had just seen it on TV and everyone was buying it. And just like that, punk rock was killed in this town because people realized really fast that a turntable is 60 bux while a guitar is 300.

SS: WHO WERE THE OTHER BLACK KIDS IN PUNK BANDS BEFORE THAT HAPPENED?
MC: Seemed like every neighborhood had at least one teenage punk band that had all Black kids. You could go three or four blocks in any direction and you could hear them blasting away, beating on boxes if there weren't drums. It was amazing. I would love someone to take the time to track them down. These dudes are all in their 40s now and they don't have any of those recordings. I'm pretty anal about that stuff, so I have a lot of stuff that I did. The first band I was in that was like that was called the U Boats. I played organ in that band. But I don't have any of the recordings from that.

SS: IN THE LAST ISSUE OF SS I WROTE ABOUT BEING FROM DC AND HOW THERE WERE MORE BLACK KIDS IN PUNK THEN PROBABLY BECAUSE BAD BRAINS EXISTED. IT'S WEIRD BECAUSE YOU ASSUME THAT AS TIME PASSES, PROGRESS GETS MADE AND THAT PUNK WOULD BE MORE RACIALLY DIVERSE INSTEAD OF LESS SO, BUT IT SEEMS LIKE IT WENT BACKWARDS. SO YOU'RE SAYING THAT HIP-HOP HAD A LOT TO DO WITH THAT? WHAT'S YOUR OPINION?

MC: Hip-hop set both Black and white music back quite a number of years, specifically "Planet Rock." I always maintain that "Planet Rock" set Black music back 20 years. And then 20 years later, suddenly without fail we're finally getting actual soul music again. "Planet Rock" rock ground everything to a halt while everyone tried to sound like "Planet Rock" for two decades. Not that there's anything wrong with "Planet Rock". I've got nothing against Afrika Baambataa.

> hip-hop set both Black and white music back quite a number of years, specifically "PLaNeT rOck"

SS: NO, THAT STUFF IS COOL. BUT I WONDER IF SOMEHOW AROUND THAT TIME, THE MESSAGE GOT SENT OUT THAT THERE IS ONLY ONE KIND OF MUSIC FOR US TO PLAY INSTEAD OF A VARIETY OF STYLES. AND AS A YOUNGER PERSON LOOKING BACK ON THAT HISTORY, I JUST WONDER HOW THINGS GOT MORE NARROWED DOWN, MORE RESTRICTING INSTEAD OF LESS SO.

Adee: Well, it seems like that just has to do with what got put out on the radio and whoever's controlling that. Because if that's the one kind of music that gets put out there...

SS: DO YOU FEEL LIKE IN THE LATE 70S, RIGHT BEFORE HIP-HOP HIT THERE WERE FEWER BOUNDARIES BETWEEN WHAT'S CONSIDERED WHITE MUSIC AND WHAT'S CONSIDERED BLACK MUSIC?

MC: Oh yeah. Things were really starting to happen between the late 70s and around '82 or '83. There almost weren't any boundaries anymore, especially in England which is an island so they literally have nowhere to go. Once they turned inward to see what else could be done, the place just exploded. That's one of the things I liked about the punk rock and

new wave stuff coming out of England. There were absolutely no boundaries between "white music" and "Black music." We were talking earlier before the tape player was on about Don Letts and the Basement 5. Perfect example. They were a Black band that played punk rock, as opposed to a punk band playing Black music.

SS: HE CLAIMS THEY WERE THE ONLY EXAMPLE OF THAT HAPPENING.
MC: Nah.

SS: WELL, I DUNNO MAYBE THAT'S HIM TRYING TO BLOW HIMSELF UP. [We're all laughing right here.]

Adee: Oh, he was feelin himself in that book.

SS: I KNOW, "I DID THIS FIRST..." [more laughs] **BUT STILL, I DO THINK IT'S TRUE THAT THERE'S ALWAYS GONNA BE MORE EXAMPLES OF WHITE BANDS BEING INFLUENCED BY BLACK MUSIC THAN THE OTHER WAY AROUND. TODAY, I FEEL LIKE THERE ARE MORE EXAMPLES OF WHITE PEOPLE WHO RAP AND PLAY REGGAE AND WHATNOT, AND THERE ARE MORE CONFINES FOR BLACK ARTISTS AND I'M STILL ALWAYS TRYING TO FIGURE OUT WHERE THAT'S COMING FROM.**
MC: I think it's coming from Black people. [Me & Adee got real quiet when he said that.]

Adee: I feel like one of the only reasons I know about Black music other than what's marketed to the mainstream is because I had to dig for it. I had to meet a bunch of other people with similar interests and be kind of obsessed with music to find stuff. Being able to buy records and borrow records from people. And I think that not everyone has that option. I think that if people heard it, they'd be psyched. Like if my little sister heard the stuff I listen to, I think shed' be excited about it but she can't hear it because it's not being put out there. My brother is 12 years old and anytime I let him listen to punk stuff, he's so excited. We play music together when I go to visit him. But I feel like if he's just watching TV, he'll never found out about it.

MC: There's a lot of pressure from the media, but I think there's a lot of inside cultural pressure too. They always say about Japanese culture that the nail that sticks up gets hammered down. The same is equally true about Black American culture. There is a great deal of pressure to conform. And part of that pressure to conform is enforced by the media. I mean, how many times are you going to turn on BET or whatever and see Black people doing anything besides rap?

Adee: Or anything challenging that's just different.

MC: You're never gonna read about it. You're never gonna see it. If you listen to Black media outlets, you're never gonna see the crazy people. You're never gonna see the fringe artists.

SS: WELL, WHY DO YOU THINK THAT IS?
MC: I don't know why that is.

Adee: I know why that shit is! [we're all laughing again]

SS: WHY, ADEE.
Adee: That shit would be too crazy for people! People would be too scared. Why would you put on TV Black people doing all these things, representing all of these different possibilities? It would freak people out! I think if you presented all of these possibilities it would freak people out. It's a historical thing that's always happened. Just like how you [Osa] were talking to me about the Reconstruction period in the U.S. between when Black people were freed and the rise of Jim Crow. Black people just flourished during that time. Started Black neighborhoods, there were Black doctors and artists. Once that window is open, things can go crazy and the media just works to keep things in order because if people can see those options, they're just going to change so many things and people don't want that to happen.

SS: DANG, JUST JUMP RIGHT IN. NOW IT'S AN INTERVIEW WITH ADEE. [laugh laugh laugh] **BUT YOU'RE RIGHT, GIRL.**

Adee: Well, It pisses me off because if people could see all the options, they'd be going buckwild right now, doing all kinds of shit.

MC: Well there's the internet now that's opened things up. Now, people are spoiled for choice.

SS: WELL THIS IS A LOT. WE JUST GOT REALLY DEEP.
MC: I feel like we're just getting warmed up. [all laughing] I could keep going!

and we did...

ESG drummer snared in $13G MTA scandal

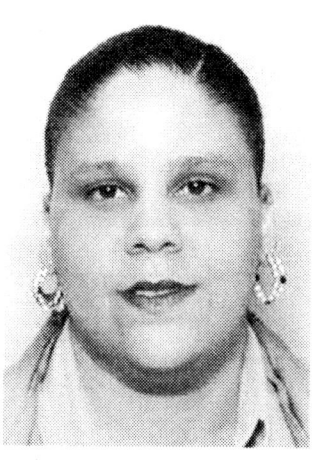

May 10, 2007
New York Daily News

It was a picture-perfect bust.

Valerie Scroggins, the drummer for acclaimed **art-funk ensemble ESG**, autographed CDs and posed for photos with fans during a concert tour in Europe last year.

But one of the fans turned out to be an investigator for the Metropolitan Transportation Authority, and Scroggins, an NYC Transit bus driver receiving workers' compensation for shoulder injuries, was nabbed.

Scroggins, 44, was **indicted yesterday** by a Brooklyn grand jury on charges of taking more than $13,000 in workers' compensation, Brooklyn District Attorney Charles Hynes said.

Three other transit workers also were charged and are awaiting indictment for allegedly receiving compensation for injuries they never sustained or grossly exaggerated, Hynes said.

"They all signed documents that said they were unable to work," said Hynes, playing a video of a concert featuring Scroggins whipping through the drums. "She told us she was unable to work between September 2006 and January. But she was playing around Europe with a rock band."

But Scroggins' lawyer, Stacey Richman, said three doctors verified in documents that she was unable to drive a bus.

"The injured arm is actually lame on the tape," she said. **"It actually is injured.** It wouldn't be prudent for someone who can't properly operate a bus to operate a bus."

A Europe-based investigator caught Scroggins in concerts with ESG, a band formed by Scroggins and her sisters in 1978, in Amsterdam and Dublin last fall, Hynes said.

"Afterwards, she signed her CD and posed for our investigator.

She's pretty good!" Hynes said.

Also charged yesterday were: Louis Guadagni, 54, a train operator who collected $7,660 for back and leg injuries even though he could carry a keg of beer and commute 40 miles to another job; bus driver Steven Sanfilippo, 54, who took $23,275 for a neck and back injury but worked as a real estate agent, and Ricardo Yolas, 53, a car inspector who took $20,800 for a back injury even though he ran a cleaning business in the Poconos, according to Hynes.

IMAGINING A WORLD WITHOUT CAPITALISM

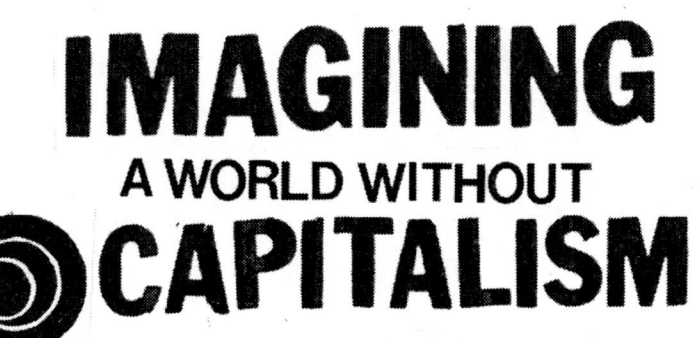

by JACOB GARDENS

I want to unlearn the lies that capitalism has taught me, but that is not an easy task. Because we live in a world where the majority of its citizens value people who have money and devalue people who don't, it becomes hard not to see yourself through the eyes of others. As a visible, queer, Black person, I feel that my self esteem and self worth is called into question every day. I must daily remind myself that just because I am a working class college student who doesn't have a lot of money doesn't mean I am worthless or should buy into the idea that I need to pursue making a lot of money in order to be happy.

Since the beginning of American history, there has always been an unfair distribution of wealth and power. The Merriam-Webster online dictionary gives the following definition of capitalsim: "An economic system characterized by private or corporate ownderhip of capital goods, by investments that are determined by private decision, and by prices, and the distribution of goods that are determined mainly by competition in a free market."

There are a few words that really stick out in the above definition.o In a capitalist country we are taught to compete with one another on so many levels. Not only are we taught to compete with one another for a job, we also compete with others for education, friends, even love. Through the course of our lives we are taught that competition is healthy and that there are always winners and losers. We begin to see the people who have less than us in our lives as responsible for their condition. Capitalism makes it okay for some people to be poor and others to be rich. The ideology of capitalism teaches us that we are essentially responsible for the bad things that happen to us, like poverty and oppression. Capitalism and capitalist advocates urge us to believe that if we work hard enough, we can overcome any obstacle and be rich and happy like all the people who are satisfied and not complaining.

Sometimes it becomes depressing to think of how many people center their lives around amaking money. In her book, **Rock My Soul, Black People and Self Esteem**, author bell hooks talks about the ways in which people, but especially Black people have been conditioned to value themselves according to how much they have. She states, "A few years ago, I began to think about the place of love in African-American life, to look critically at the way success for Black people has been increasingly measured by a limited yardstick, one that primarily looks at material wealth and acquisition as the sole sign of well being."

In this new millennium that we are now living in, I think it is important to try and imagine a world where people love themselves and one another not because of how much money they make but because they are simply humans deserving of love. I want to live in a world and a country where things like food, education and beauty are free and available for everyone to have and enjoy.

check out Jacob's video art & music: www.myspace.com/jacobgarden

thank you ★

to everyone who contributed to this issue of SHOTGUN SEAMSTRESS:

Jacob Gardens
Brontez Purnell
Leah Newbold
Donovan Vim Crony
Senora Grayson &
Adee Licious

and to everyone who helped make this zine possible including: Mom & Dad, Randal Wilcox, Mick Collins, Kali Boyce, Vaginal Davis, Brett Lyman, Bryan from AfroPunk, Jason Paroxysm, Bea!

Shotgun Seamstress #1-3 available through Learning to Leave a Paper Trail zine distro

~~http://papertrail.com~~
http://papertraildistro.com

shotgunseamstress@gmail.com
www.myspace.com/shotgunseamstress

3
SHOTGUN SMSTRSS

Shotgun Seamstress zine No. 4

SISTER OUTSIDER ART

This zine is about art by black queers, black feminist punks and other black folks I admire. This is **VAGINAL CREME DAVIS** our sister/mother outsider.

Shotgun Seamstress is a zine by and for black punks, feminits, queers, artists & musicians. Usually I focus a lot on music, but in this issue I focus on visual art.

March 2010

"Sister Outsider," the title of feminist writer Audre Lorde's book of essays, refers to the experience of being part of a community, but also separate, on the margins. Outsider art is the creative work of self-taught artists that exists largely outside of the mainstream art world. Put the two together & what do you get?

Contents

1. Interview with James Spooner
2. Letter to Vaginal Creme Davis
3. FOLK/PUNK: the Art of Adee Roberson
4. Kalup Linzy
5. Silence = Death: video performance artist Jacob Gardens
6. Madivinez by Lenelle Moïse

the artwork on this page is by Adee Roberson.

James Spooner is the filmmaker responsible for the documentary AFROPUNK, that had a huge roll in bringing all the brown punk babies across the nation (& world!) a little closer together. He's an ex-vegan/hardcore, straight, biracial dude and him & his lady are expecting a Baby! This interview was done via iChat because this is the future.

SS: Talk about the punk scene you came out of and how you were involved.

JS: I got into the punk scene when I was 13. I lived in Apple Valley, California, this crappy racist town with very few punks. Ironically, the first punk kid I met was a black kid named Travis. He was instantly the coolest kid in school to me and I wanted to know what he was about. He introduced me to a bunch of bands and we started one of our own. Long story short, it was a lame scene and we were a bunch of dummies. Thanks to my mom we moved to NY that's when I got into real punk/hardcore. About a year later I started doing going to shows out side of NYC because I was getting into DIY and ABC NO RIO was the only real place doing it. Also, I eventually started my own record label and zine. Put out four 7inches. It started to get big and I couldn't handle the responsibility at 17 so I quit.

SS: What was your zine called? What was it about?

JS: It evolved. At first it was called "Blinded By Lies blinded by Draino." It was a vegan zine. Then in the second issue, I decided to do some other stuff. The second one was called "Kidney room." I talked about animal rights, feminism, masculinity, and scene politics to some degree. It started getting some praise; good reviews in MRR and Heart Attack. A lot of the popularity came from these patches I made. The most popular one said "It's ok not to drink milk."

JAMES

SS: Do you still have copies of it?

JS: Yeah, over the years kids have sent them back to me so I have most of them. The last one was called "What little boys are made of." That one was way more personal. Dealt with sex, gender politics, being a boy growing into being a man. This one I gave a way free and did semi anonymously.

SS: Anonymous because it was so personal?

JS: Well cause it told intimate details of womens lives. Women I was involved with. So I didn't want to put them on blast. That did backfire on me. Its hard to be anonymous in such a small scene.

SS: You're talking about the scene you moved to in NYC?

JS: Well this was in Ohio. I moved and traveled a lot. You know, punk rock stuff.

SS: Yep. So before you made "AfroPunk" did you have any expectations of the impact it would have?

JS: Never. I thought I'd show it three times and keep it moving.

SS: How does the AfroPunk scene, especially the one in NY, compare to your experience with punk?

JS: There are a lot more black kids at the AfroPunk shows. Honestly, at this point I don't know how "punk" you could call AfroPunk. I mean, it's way bigger than I ever hoped it would be. I don't go to shows with stages taller than me or bouncers keeping audience members from the band. So although I'm happy black bands are getting shine, I don't really enjoy those kind of big shows. We also never had all ages shows until after it got corporate. NY sucks for all ages venues.

SS: I'm glad to hear you say that because even though I think AfroPunk is really important in the way that it made room for black kids who don't only listen to hip hop and r&b and don't wish to be pigeon holed, the result of AfroPunk wasn't exactly punk the way a lot of us have experienced it. But at the same time, I'm wondering if a sub-scene might come out of the larger AfroPunk thing...

JS: There will always be a reaction. I mean here is the thing. The kids have to control things, otherwise its not punk rock. I was 25 when I started AfroPunk. My partner was 32. He is now 40 and running the show on his own. It can never be the same as the 5 dollar all ages shows with bands who don't care about money cause their parents pay for everything. So, Jenelle Monea is important to the black community in general

SPOONER

but will do nothing for the punk scene. Except maybe get kids into the scene who then find underground bands. Like Nirvana might have done for your generation and I don't know ... Jane's Addiction might have done for mine.

SS: How old are you? I don't think I'm that much younger than you.

JS: I just realized I'm 33. My birthday was like 15 days ago, but I never said it out loud.

SS: I'm 30!

JS: Oh, your 30. No wonder you're doing a paper zine.

SS: Yeah I guess. There's some young kids out there still doing paper zines though. And all the time, younger kids on AfroPunk send me messages like "How do you make a zine?" cuz they wanna do it too. That's what I'm saying about maybe a more DIY scene will eventually come out of the whole AfroPunk movement.

JS: That's cool. Yeah, I mean AfroPunk is at this point of entry for a lot of black people, children & adults. And that's okay.

SS: So I read you were a sculpture student before you made AfroPunk and that you never took any film classes before you made the documentary.

JS: I wasn't a student. I just made sculptures. I've never been much for formal education. Maybe that's why I'm still broke but you know, punk rockers are always reinventing the wheel.

SS: Did you make any movies before AfroPunk? Like even shorts?

JS: Nope.

SS: Ever seen Don Letts' "Punk Movie"?

JS: Of course. Someone had a tape of it when I was 14. It would have really helped me out to know that was a black dude directing it.

SS: I haven't seen the whole thing myself. But his approach is the same as yours, you know?

JS: Yeah, I met him once. He seems like a right place at the right time, living off the legacy kinda dude. But he still keeps making work.

SS: So when did you find out he was a black guy?

JS: When I was making AfroPunk.

SS: No way!

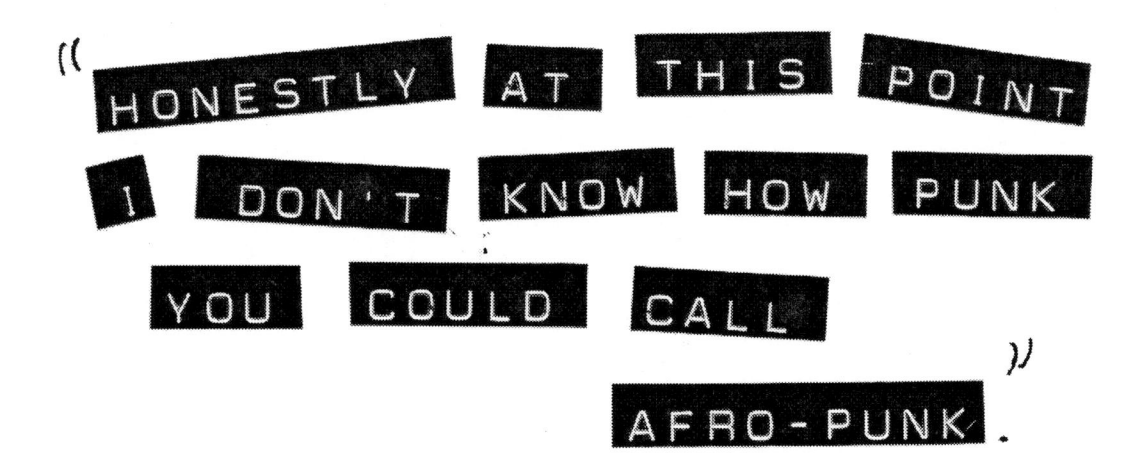

((HONESTLY AT THIS POINT I DON'T KNOW HOW PUNK YOU COULD CALL AFRO-PUNK)).

JS: I never even heard of him till i was doing the research. I mean that tape my friend showed me was pretty shitty quality. Trying to read the credits was pointless.

SS: I kinda like that feeling though. I didn't know that Poly Styrene (of X-ray Spex) was half black for a long ass time. I just didn't realize it and no one ever told me.

JS: Oh yeah, I would love to talk to her. She is some kind of Hare Krishna or something.

SS: Yeah a lot of those people from that scene got super religious after their punk days...

JS: Addicts.

SS: Yeah?

JS: Don't know how much of it has to do with punk as it does with drugs. Addicts gotta be hooked on something. But she for sure got cuter as she got older.

SS: I know she looks good. I saw this semi-recent picture of her and she's got this little perm now.

JS: Yeah she was in DPN's last punk movie "Punk Attitude".

SS: I haven't seen it yet. So are there any other artists in your family?

JS: My mom was an art teacher when I was young before moving on to special ed. My eldest brother whom I didn't meet till I was in my mid 20's is an artist too but he lives in Barbados so he is more of a craftsman. Island culture in a lot of ways doesn't allow for the privilege of making traditional art. He has to make a living but I can tell he is an artist. He makes his own clothes and can build anything.

SS: So your family was pretty supportive of you making art?

JS: My mom always admired me. She is one of those "My son can do no wrong" types. My dad always wondered where the money was. But once he saw me in Ebony magazine or one of those black mags, he was cool. Getting in the New York Times was a big legitimizer.

SS: Is your dad black?

JS: Yeah dad's black, mom's white.

SS: You were in Ebony? I wanna get in Essence one day!

JS: I can't remember. It think it might have been Essence. I was in all of them at one point or the other. At least a mention if not an article. The mentions are harder to keep up with.

SS: That's awesome. So what do you think about the idea that the creation of art is a liberating activity for black people?

JS: I think it's liberating for all people. The thing is, I don't think young black artists ever have the dilemma of "What to paint". You know a lot of young artist are talented but there themes are bullshit. Pretentious. Pointless. The best art comes from pain. And yes, white people have pain. But its easier for us to tap into the obvious and have it be moving. But when an artist, any artist, moves past the surface and deals with personal pain, that's when art becomes important. So yeah privilege like anything else is the thing that separates white artists from everyone else.

SS: Ok. What's the weirdest dream you've had lately?

JS: Oh, you'll have to ask me in the morning.

SS: Do you usually remember your dreams?

JS: Yeah but if I don't say them out loud they are gone. They are usually gone shortly after that anyway.

SS: Do you feel like there's any connection between your dreams and the art you make?

JS: Not really. Unless you can call my baby art. I dream about her all the time now.

SS: You're a dad!

JS: I will be in august.

SS: Congratulations!

JS: You gotta check out my blog popnbottles.com. It's the thing I'm most excited about these days.

SS: That's super exciting. Thanks for doing this interview!

JS: For sure. Tell people to be my friend on Facebook, read my blog and ride bikes.

dear miss davis

I hope this letter finds you well and I hope you are loving your life in Berlin. Even though we've been in touch before, I've never had the chance to tell you how I found out about you and how your work makes me feel. The first time I got to see you perform was in 2006 or 2007 in Olympia, Washington at HOMOAGOGO, but I'd probably known about you since 2000. I want to say that your being one of the many names listed off in that Le Tigre song "Hot Topic" brought you to my attention, but I have a feeling I'd heard of you before that. The point is, you weren't anything more than a name and maybe a picture or two off the Internet for me for years. But I held onto your name, keeping it safe in my memory for so long because you were the only queer black punk I knew

con't →

miss daVis says...

"It's the person who doesn't fit in who eventually makes the greatest achievement, who has the outsider's view of culture that really sticks."

...vaginal creme davis...

letter con't...

of that I could trace back to the earlier days of punk rock. Even though I hadn't seen a single video zine, paper zine or performance, just to know you existed was really important to me. You showed a bunch of videos at HOMO-AGOGO and the one I remember the most is the one where you and your friend, Glennda Orgasm, walk to the streets of New York in drag, interviewing women about this self-help book →

called "10 Things Women Do to Ruin Their Lives" (or something close to that.) The video is called "One Man Ladies" and I remember loving it so much because it's cool to see male-socialized people relating to their own femininity. When you were interviewing those women, I loved the way you related to their experiences and admitted making some of the same mistakes. Yeah, the whole thing was fun and funny but it still rang true. It feels really important that you speak from a "grey area" or a perspective that isn't really established in our society, even if it is a lonely place to speak from. Both times I saw you, I remember you referring to the lonliness you experience as a black, queer, intersex, feminist drag queen artist & performer... who is also, on top of all that, broke. You make it seem like you're joking when you talk about it, but we all know you're not. I've always wondered about the way you talk about lonliness and isolation so publicly, in that funny-but-I'm serious way, especially after the last time I got to see you in Berlin. For us, the same identities that can be a source of struggle can also be a source of pride, and I really see how you communicate that in your performance. Anyway, I have to go now. Thanks for being a pioneer and a BAD ASS. Love, ~~█████~~

FOLK/PUNK

the art of adee roberson

Not folk-punk, like the genre of music. It's more like the work of folk-artist Nellie Mae Rowe channeled through a black punk girl who listens to the Raincoats while she draws.

When I met Adee, she was making this cool looking new wave-inspired art with photocopies of tigers' heads and screen prints of wild horses sitting on top of florescent colored backgrounds of stripes and geometric shapes. Her pieces looked great and were really inspiring to me. She is a completely self-taught artist with so much fearless, stubborn ambition. She made me feel like if I had art in my heart, I should quit making excuses about how I can't do it cuz I'm not good enough, and just spit it out.

While she was living in New Orleans, Adee put on a hugely successful benefit DIY art show featuring art by herself and her friends. She was definitely taking it to the next level, but at the same time, I think she was looking to breath more meaning into her work. Adee had always been politically active, volunteering at women's health organizations and helping to organize the 2004 INCITE Conference (Women of Color Against Violence) in New Orleans. She finds great inspiration in history, particularly obscure Black history. She taught me about Queen Nanny and the Maroons of Jamaica, escaped slaves who banded together as early the 1500s and created their own free societies. She had been living in New Orleans for almost two years and was just beginning to be inspired by the celebratory sequins of Mardis Gras as well as Haitian-Voudou sequins art that she had been researching. Soon enough, sequins began to show up in her pieces as an homage to these art forms.

Along with photocopying, screening and painting, Adee would also use fabric in her art. Adee is the original shotgun seamstress, sewing together outfits, all cute, short and tight in just a few minutes flat. She brought her love of sewing to the canvas, stitching pretty pieces of cloth onto her paintings. Almost everything Adee used in her artwork was found or stolen.

Adee's art always had a lot of warmth to it. For a while, she was obsessed with the color peach. Everything she made had a peach background. Adee is originally from South Florida and before she moved to New Orleans, she lived in Pensacola, Florida a small town right on the Gulf of Mexico. Pensacola has some of the most beautiful beaches you've ever seen, with none of the super-commercialized boardwalk action to ruin it. White sands and warm, clear, green-blue water. You can see the influence of the beach in Adee's art. The water. She is a Cancer with a Pisces moon (both water signs). Her grandmother is Jamaican, so Adee always identified really strongly with the imagery of islands: palm trees, coconuts, pineapples, mangoes, water.

When I think about water, I think about the moon, dreams, the subconscious, the feeling of drifting and renewal. I would say that Adee's art is equally inspired by the intensity of Black people's experiences in this continent since we were brought her as slaves, as well as by the desire

to transcend the oppressive nature of that experience through fantasy, dreams, beauty, visions of love and the reclamation of our humanity. She believes, as I do, that the creation of art has been a liberating activity for Black people, and that there is no reason that the creation of art by oppressed peoples should not be considered a political act in and of itself.

Around the same time as the peach obsession, Adee started drawing these weird flowers with long, spiny petals. Each flower had about a dozen skinny, seemingly fragile petals twisting in the imaginary winds inside of her paintings. She also became very focused on family in her art. She included enlarged photocopied photographs of the women in her family: her mother, her sister, her grandmother and her aunts when they were young, with permed hair curled into mushroom-esque styles and with big 80s glasses. These photos would be set on top of her peach backgrounds, with those strange and beautiful flowers spinning around her auntie's heads.

GLassEs

The drawing of spiny flowers lead to lines. Lines and lines and lines. It kinda started tripping me out how many lines the girl was drawing. However, the drawing of these lines proved to be therapeutic for Adee. She talked to a friend who was an art therapist and they told her what the drawing of those lines actually meant. I won't tell you what the therapist told her because Adee would kill me if I did! But she told Adee to keep drawing the lines as much as she wanted or needed to. There was obviously something Adee's subconscious was trying to work out through the drawing of those lines. Now, there were no more flowers, just millions of tiny lines, lines, lines that eventually would create these seemingly three dimensional landscapes.

FRiEnds

In the winter of 2007, Adee spent a month in Providence, Rhodes Island completing an art residency at AS220. Adee spent thirty days living rent-free, making art and researching other artists. That's when she found out about Nellie Mae Rowe, a black lady folk artist (see next page for more info on her), who also used a lot of line work in her art. It was as if Adee had put herself through DIY art school. You could really tell the difference in her artwork after she returned. There was more confidence in it, it was neater and more refined in a way, but hadn't lost any of it's folk arty rawness. She designed the screen that our band New Bloods used to make our t-shirts, which were a huge hit in Portland, Oregon for about fifteen minutes. The screen was absolutely beautiful: carefully traced kitty cats (Adee's newest obsession) surrounded by all of those swirling lines and lines and lines with "New Bloods" lettered neatly near the top.

Adee's art has been such and inspiration to me, not to mention her zines and her music. Currently she is spending six months in Jamaica, once again at an art residency. Traveling to Jamaica has been a life-long dream of Adee's, and I can't wait to see how this experience impacts her life and her work.

Written February 2009

To see new art by Adee & to read her own thoughts & ideas on her work visit pineappleblack.blogspot.com

I found out about KALUP LINZY last spring when I was in New York. He had an exhibit at Studio Museum in Harlem that consisted mostly of hilarious low-budget video shorts. First of all, Kalup Linzy always performs in drag in his videos, and he's a BLACK GAY MAN, but his movies are about as serious a commentary on race, sexuality or gender as any of John Waters' early movies are. Linzy is clearly just trying to have fun while being openly QUEER in his art.

My favorite drag queens are the messy ones with their beards shitty wigs and their refusal to make their penises invisible. Kalup Linzy rocks this powerful version of femininity (& masculinity) in some of his videos. In others, like "Key to Our Heart," which is a spoof on a classic, old-school black & white movie, he's done up more like a high-class, middle aged woman. His stuff is pretty raw as far as video production goes, and his aesthetic seems shaped by such down-to-earth influences as drag conversations, performances, phone conversations, soap operas,

KALUP LINZY

Old talkies, and Whitney Houston. Seriously, "Melody Set Me Free" uses as many clips from Whitney Houston's self titled debut as he could possibly fit in a 10 minute time span. That video, by the way, is about a young woman, Patience O'Brien (played by Linzy) who decides to run off to HOLLYWOOD to try to become famous despite her mother's wishes. Aside from his music video shorts, he has videos featuring original songs and, if I remember correctly, he had a little bit of visual art on display, but his videos definitely left the biggest impression on me.

SILENCE = DEATH

VIDEO PERFORMANCE ARTIST

JACOB GARDENS

Jacob Gardens is 24 years old from Flint Michigan who has recently moved to San Francisco. Earlier this year, he made his very first video performance art piece called "A Child of Oshun." In this interview, Jacob talks to Shotgun Seamstress about overcoming his initial fear of putting himself out there as an artist. He also discusses his queer, feminist and punk rock roots, his love for Yoko Ono, and how his belief in the occult influences his work.

SS: Well first, for those who haven't seen it, what is your first piece of video art about?

JG: I have been deeply inspired by various queer coming out stories. I wanted to make a short skit or performance piece about coming out as gay.

SS: Which queer coming out stories have you been inspired by? Whose stories were they?

JG: There is a really great book that I read a while back which is called *Gay Soul* and it is edited by Mark Thompson. He interviewed sixteen gay men and asked them various questions about coming out and life in general.

SS: In "A Child of Oshun," you play all of the different characters in the video. You play yourself, your mother and Oshun. Did you feel like playing women in your video was an outlet for your gender expression, or were you just having fun, or both?

JG: Kate Bornstein really did a great job of breaking down the difference between gender and sex for me in her book titled, *My Gender workbook*. I read her book when I was like fifteen and I was really starting to get into gender outlaws like the early all-girl Portland band the Third Sex or one of my favorite heroines, Patti Smith. Kate Bornstein writes about gender in a really practical, easy to understand way. In my piece I didn't really use a very noticeable voice change for the characters because I wanted to point out again that gender is a performance not something that is stagnant or finite. Kinsey said that our sexualities are on a continuum, he gave evidence of this in his bell curve study or something but I really agree with him on that and just because I am gay doesn't mean that I don't find women sexually attractive or that I could never have sex with a woman at some point in my life. I never have had sex with a woman and I really don't feel or see a need to because I love making love to men and having sex with men, but in all of my performance art and solo music I really would like to touch on issues of race, gender and sexuality and how these things can be so easily changed, even the color of our skin can be changed now and a perfect example of this would be Michael Jackson.

SS: Haha! Or the fact that skin bleaching creams are really popular in Nigeria. Sad but true. I wanted to talk to you about music. I love the music you used in your video. I'm a big fan of Yoko Ono's music and what Black punk kid didn't feel like they died and went to heaven after hearing ESG for the first time?

JG: I love ESG!

SS: Are you a fan of Yoko Ono's performance art? Would you count her as an influence? If so, how?

JG: Yoko Ono is one more artist who I can honestly say changed my life. Many people scrutinize homosexual men for having a "girly" voice and encourage us to "man" up, whatever that means. Yoko helped me to see that it isn't my job to make everyone fall in love with my voice. Tons of people, (especially heterosexual white men) are obsessed with disrespecting Yoko based on their relative "fact" that she cant sing and that she has a horrible voice. Not too many people are aware that before she met John she was a working feminist performance artist and one of the few feminist performance artists of color in the decade she started working in. I appreciate all of Yoko's art not only her music. I only have owned three of her albums, however I first fell in love with Yoko's performance art pictures from her cut piece. The talented and wonderful feminist visual artist Judy Chicago, did a tribute to her and other women artists in her exhibition titled, "The Dinner Piece." In Judy Chicago's piece every feminist artist that has been excluded and somewhat erased from art history is given a place at her table. I never has seen the actual dinner piece exhibit, but I have seen pictures of it and they are breath taking.

SS: What are some of the obstacles you had to overcome in order to put yourself out there and start making your own art?

JG: I'm currently still in college pursuing my BA in theater performance/ Women's gender studies and minoring in French/ Spanish. For a long time I thought that in order for me to perform, I had to have a BA or a BFA to be taken seriously. After our talks and thinking it over, I realized that I just needed to go ahead and make performance art and who cares if anyone takes it seriously or likes it. I've done very little live performance in my life, but I'm only twenty three so I guess there's still time. The biggest obstacle I have had has been myself and MTV for making music and performance look really hard, intimidating and costly. I have had to tell a lot of demons in my "mind" that I am good enough and smart enough to be seen and heard. I've had to remind myself that my ideas are not dumb but based in years of study that has not only come from an actual college setting but also from real live environments.

SS: This is why I wanted to talk to you even though you're not an "established artist." I feel like the hardest part is just getting started, you know?

JG: Yes, I do know what you mean, and I thank you for recognizing artists who are just starting out. Many people don't or won't.

SS: So tell us about those "real live environments" that taught you what you needed to know to make art.

JG: The first time I ever performed something that I had written was in 2004 in Philadelphia at this punk place called the CODE space. It was a short skit/workshop on guerrilla theater and street theater. Also I have just read many books on various subjects and had the privilege to talk to so many beautiful inspiring people who have taught me so many things. I really like the idea of oral learning.

So many authors have inspired me and helped me learn, too many to name. But as far as authors who have shaped my political views and worldviews I would have to say bell hooks, Luisah Teish, Andrew Holleran and other queer and feminist authors have really helped me.

JAcoB GArdEns

SS: Luisah Teish*! I'm so glad you mentioned her because I wanted to ask you about your interested in the occult.

JG: I recently took a class with Luisah Teish in the bay area at this store called Ancient ways located in Oakland. The class was great and everyone should go visit Ancient ways if you are ever in Oakland CA. I have always loved the occult and witches and witchcraft. I like the idea of being able to change your life through the use of prayer, candles or incantations and affirmations.

SS: In your video, you reference the goddess Oshun. Why did you make that choice and how did you first get in touch with Afro-centric spiritualities?

JG: Oshun is an orisha of beauty and power. If by chance another young gay black kid watches my video and has Christian parents who reject him or her because of their queerness, I want them to know there are other options as far as deities or spirit guides go. The story of Jesus is not the only story that a person can find strength and comfort in and I wanted to relate that in my video. I first learned about Santeria and Vodoun when I was about eighteen and walked into my first botanica in Philly.

SS: Why'd you go to the botanica in the first place? What were you looking for?

JG: I had been to various occult shops before but I had never been to a shop that instructed people in the tradition of Santeria. When it comes to my spiritual beliefs I label myself an eclectic witch. I have not been initiated in Santeria or Vodun but I appreciate the religion.

SS: So you used to be a punk kid. Does your background in punk have anything to do with your present artistic aspirations?

JG: My background in punk was very brief but also very life saving. When I found punk groups such as Blatz or Bikini Kill I finally found an outlet for my anger at a society that wanted to make me feel inferior for being black, poor, and queer. Unfortunately, I found the punk scene too white dominated and felt that I wasn't always safe or welcomed at shows or punk spaces.

SS: What community did you turn to instead?

JG: Thankfully, I found visionaries such as Marlon Riggs, Audre Lorde and many other queer black writers and thinkers that spoke to me in a way that an angry white kid with a guitar just couldn't. I also am so thankful that I found you and other punk black and brown kids of color who have basically healed me in so many ways.

SS: I'm grateful to have met you too. I can't wait to see how your art grows and changes as you continue to make it.

* Luisah Teish is a black feminist witch who was born and raised in New Orleans, Louisiana. She is the author of the book *Jambalaya: The Natural Women's Book of Personal Charms and Practical Rituals*.

141

Madivinez
a poem by Lenelle Moïse

mommi
in the apartment i share
with the woman
i love, we have
a bright yellow bookcase.
used
as an arts altar. we shelve
crayons, watercolors, ink, paper
and glue for collages. i keep
my haitian kreyol-english dictionary
behind the colored pencils.

its red cover taunts me, daily.
i am often too afraid
to open it. i pick it up
once—
when i first got it—hungry
for familiar
words that could make me
feel home. i tried
to look up "lesbian"
but the little red book denied
my existence.

i called you, remember?

mommi how do you
say lesbian in kreyol?
oh, you said, you say madivinez
but it's not a positive word.

it's vulgar
no one wants to be
called madivinez.

it's like saying dyke.

but how can cruelty sound
so beautiful? madivinez.
sounds so glamorous. something
i want to be. madivinez.
my divine?
sounds so holy.

i thank you & hang up the phone
to repeat my vulgar
gift word
as i write it
into the dictionary,
next to ke, kreyol
for heart

glamorous, holy, haitian
dyke heart.
something i want to be.

©2007 by Lenelle Moïse

(Thank You:)

Senora, Takiaya, Candice, Bea, Brontez, the City of New Orleans, Mom & Dad, Nathan Jessee, everyone who's read this zine & passed it on, everyone who's written me a positive letter and all of the artists who are a part of this issue.

(write me:)

1228 N. Broad Ave.
New Orleans LA 70119
shotgunseamstress@gmail.com

colums for Maximum Rock N Roll at
www.shotgunseamstress.blogspot.com

☆ next issue... back to the basics!!

SHOTGUN 5 SEAMSTRESS

dj soul sister

ESG

ZINE & Record reviews

cOMicS

KickTEase

Shotgun Seamstress is a zine by & for black punks, queers, feminists, artist & musicians.

August 2010

Contents

1. I'm obsessed with ESG
2. Q&A with Marilyn of Aye Nako
3. This is a public hair announcement!
4. Interview: DJ Soul Sister
5. Interview: Kicktease
6. CAMPING
7. DIY or DIE
8. DEATH is nothing to be afraid of.
9. Record Reviews
10. Zine Reviews

I'm obsessed with ESG

ESG exists in a nameless space, between genres. If I had to put a label on them, I'd probably call them R&B or funk even though they sound nothing like any of the other groups that are typically associated with those genres. Then again, musically, they could also be lumped into a group with the other bass-driven dance music that came out of the late 70s and early 80s NYC No Wave scene, like "Burning Spear" era Sonic Youth or the band A Certain Ratio. I've always thought of those groups as white punks/experimentalists who were enamored with "black music" and playing their own dirty, tripped-out version of it. Weirder, noisier, sloppier, more primal.

But ESG isn't influenced by black music, they *are* black music. ESG, originally Emerald Sapphire Gold, was a band comprised of four sisters, plus their friend Tito, who lived in the South Bronx in the mid-70s. They were inspired to play music and had a mother who encouraged and supported their talents. To make a long story short, ESG entered a neighborhood talent show and didn't win, but got the recognition they needed to start being an active band that played shows around NYC.

ESG got attached to the punk scene because they opened for A Certain Ratio one night and this guy from the UK who ran Factory Records (Joy Division's label) was really impressed by them and asked them to record a single. I've always found it really fascinating and attractive that a band like ESG found themselves in the company of a bunch of white weirdo art punk bands. They were also big in the dance club and hip-hop scenes. Sampling has always been a controversial issue for the band, mostly, it seems, because of the issue of financial compensation. A hip-hop group could sample an ESG and blow up while ESG themselves existed for the most part in obscurity. They even wrote a song addressing the issue called "Sample Credits Don't Pay the Bills."

I don't want to make it seem like ESG is this forgotten band that never enjoyed the success they deserve. Sure, I believe they deserve more recognition, but the band also made a series of decisions based on their values that possibly put a cap on their level of success. They'd been approached by major labels and turned down their offers due to their desire to retain complete artistic control of their music and their image. They've even self-released some of their own music over the years.

The thing with ESG is that their sound is so simple, I wonder why it's so rare. I haven't listened to much of ESG's newer recordings, but their older stuff like "Moody" and "Come Away" feature the simplest, funkiest, spaced-out bass lines, dancey drums and sassy vocals. The tambourine in "Dance" makes me lose my mind every time I hear it. There are only two notes in the bassline for "My Love for You," which drives home the age-old lesson that in music, less is often more and that you don't need to know a lot of fancy technical tricks to make a good song.

Having said that, I would also like to acknowledge the genius that is the drum work of Valarie Scroggins. Wow! It's only because she's such a good drummer that their bassist can play the simplest part and still have it sound amazing. I really believe that Valarie's drums are the backbone of the whole group.

After I found out about ESG, I would scour the used Soul and R&B LPs in numerous record stores looking for another stripped down, experimental, female-fronted band where all of the members played all of their own instruments and wrote all of their own songs. Why is it so hard to find? Perhaps my criteria is too high? Is it so wrong to expect artists to stretch the boundaries of R&B (or punk or whatever), or to challenge the idea of what "black music" is or can be? In most genres, it's so much easier to find a pretty lady in a dress and make up singing songs that someone else wrote for her. I wanna see a butch looking woman beating the skins while her best friend plays bass and sings and gets all gross & sweaty. Why is that such a rare sight to behold?

There really isn't another band like ESG. While digging through record bins, I did happen upon this record by a band called Carleen and the Groovers. They're a James Brown-sounding funk band lead by a female drummer named Carleen and they've got a four-song EP reissue out on Now-Again Records. Not nearly as original as ESG but pretty cute and sassy in it's own way. They've got a song called "Hot Pants" and their most popular song at the time was "Can We Rap?"

Q&A with Marilyn of Aye Nako

Since this interview, Marilyn moved to Brooklyn and her band, previously called Fleabag, has changed back to its old name, Aye Nako.

ss: i don't know you that well, but when i met you a couple years ago in bloomington, you seemed kinda shy. then when i saw you this past summer in new orleans, you were singing your guts out. do you identify as a shy person? if so, how do you find the courage to perform your songs so confidently in front of other people?

m: i do identify as shy, but i know i shouldn't say that if i wish to improve on my social well-being. i love making music too much to stay reserved for, at least, that part of my life. my shyness is something i've always struggled with and playing music has certainly helped an incredible amount to get me to open up. although painful at first, i try to make eye contact with the audience and talk in between songs to feel a little more connected and at ease.

ss: you are a killer guitar player. how'd you learn to play?

m: aw thanks. when i first found out about the internet in my early teens, aside from pretending to be a well-hung 18 year-old male babe in chatrooms, i'd spend hours at a time searching for bands that women were in. i had to be one of them. bored and lonely, i taught myself how to play guitar when I was 15. i didn't go out. i didn't have friends. so, i dedicated my waking life neglecting homework to play video games and guitar. in the beginning, i learned songs that i was really into and then that sprouted into creating original songs.

ss: how do you go about writing songs? do you write your lyrics first or last or is different every time?

m: most times, a guitar riff will come about and i mess around with that til i find something i want to keep. next, comes a vocal melody "ba da da..." and then actual words come out and sooner or later, there's a new song. the lyrics are always the hardest step because i become so critical of myself.

ss: fleabag's songs are addictive, much like candy or chapstick. how do you do it?

m: it's natural? i'm no good at writing metal, thrashy, rock 'n roll or more obscure songs. I think i get it from listening to a lot of catchy, pop songs.

ss: name some bands you play with in SF or oakland. do you feel like fleabag is a part of any certain scene?

m: we've played with songs for moms, onion flavored rings, trouble, sourpatch (san jose). I don't feel that fleabag is part of any particular scene because a lot of times we don't even get asked to play shows in which it seems like we'd fit in so perfectly. we're not quite on peoples' radar (or gaydar.) but the word is spreading.

ss: how do you feel about your experience as a queer, mixed-race punk in the bay area punk scene?

m: I really like Oakland. This is the first place I've lived where I can look around at a show or party or other event where I'm not the only brown person or the only queer person. in the Midwest, I had no black friends and could count the number of lesbians I knew on one hand but living here, it's not an issue. It feels so good to see people and become friends with people who look like me. even outside of punk, every visit to my bank is a relief because all the employees are women of color.

ss: fleabag plays a wonderful cover of "divine hammer." did you ever get to see the breeders live?

m: no! I've never seen them!

ss: what music have you been obsessing over lately?

m: bettie serveert, songs for moms, the supremes, "learned to surf" by superchunk, "empire state of mind" by jay z + alicia keys, "sweet lovin' man" and "strange powers" by magnetic fields.

ss: read any good zines lately?

m: I haven't read many zines lately, but I came across Prescription For Change: Community Response to Substance Use in the bathroom at my house. Baitline is a monthly, queer personal and regular ads, announcements, and other stuff zine with wonderful drawings. Also, one of my roommates writes Toothworm.

ss: what does the future hold for fleabag?

m: these days have us busy working on a whole new batch of songs that sound and feel different than our previous songs. there's talk about recording them for an album and possibly going on a spring break tour with sourpatch. who knows!?

This is a public HAIR announcement!

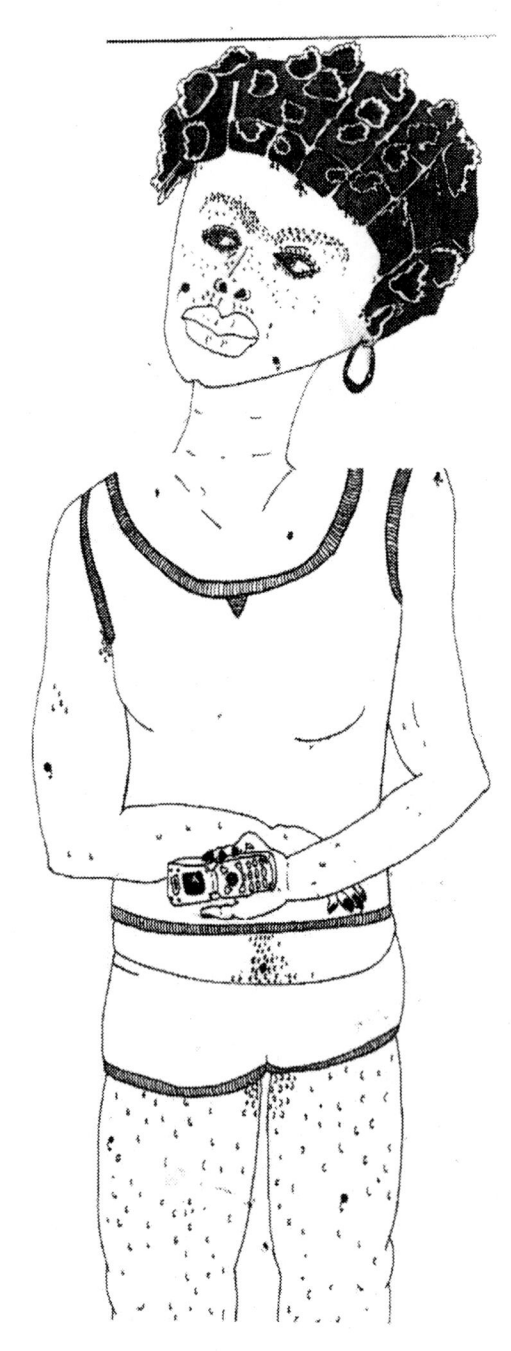

drawing by Natalie Woodlock

I'm hairy. Fuck you.

I only started shaving my legs in 9th grade because Michael Jean-Pierre (the dude with the hottest eyes and an ass you could set a drink on) touched my leg and complained about my unshaven, bushy man leg hair. Ever since that moment, I have been absolutely paranoid about shaving my legs. My hair is course and nappy. It isn't cute and straight and blond like white girls'. Shaving my legs gives me razor burn and shaving my armpits gives me a rash and ingrown hairs. I'm suffering through this shit for what now? Fuck a bunch of shaving.

Once it gets cold in Chicago, I stop shaving through the winter. My pits grow nappy and bushy and I don't give a shit. But the reason I don't give a shit is because it's all covered up. I am so self conscious of my nappy pit hair and my bushy leg hair because society tells me that it isn't...right. Well you know what society? Fuck a bunch of you.

At work, I am paranoid of going natural because it comes off as unprofessional and unclean to show up unshaven. Dudes get to come to work with unruly beards and disgusting back and neck hair, but that shit is totally acceptable. I show up in a sleeveless shirt and a pencil skirt with a few scraggly hairs and I'm called to the office for looking unprofessional. FUCK YOU

My mom has hurtsutism and is constantly picking at her jaw and plucking the hairs under her neck. Why is it such a big fucking deal for a woman to have a few fucking whiskers under her chin?! Now she has scarring that she's even more self conscious about. I have so many friends who spend thousands of dollars getting hair BURNED OFF OF THEIR BODIES. That hurts my heart. The amount of pain that we put ourselves through daily just to be aesthetically pleasing to society. FUCK YOU.

My pube area is curly and unruly and I don't give a shit. If you are down there and worrying about the amount of hair I have around my pussy, or how coarse it is, then you don't deserve the privilege of being down there. I am of Afro-Caribbean decent and my hair is fucking nappy. The curtains match the drapes - DEAL WITH IT. I have scars under my arms from painful shaving episodes, and my armpit hairs aren't "cute" or straight. It's natural and it's REAL. I refuse to suffer through painful shaving and discolored armpits to please some motherfucker for the 30 seconds it takes him/her to get off. FUCK YOU.

I admit that I have been envious of beautiful straight pit hair that most white people have. It took me a long time to come to terms with my beautiful, nappy hair – from the top of my dreadlocked head to the nappy hairs on my feet.

It has gotten to the point where there are some women that BLEACH THEIR ASSHOLE HAIR. I mean, really? The newest atrocity is called "vadazzling." Yes, this is exactly what it sounds like. Now not only are women waxing and ripping hair out of the pussy area, they are now decorating their vaginas with JEWELS. Can we stop and think about how ridiculous this has gotten? What's next, sewing that shit shut? Stuffing bags of potpourri in your pussy so that it keeps that ever so fresh flowery smell?! Dangling car fresheners from your navel ring?!

So I've taken it upon myself to protest shaving my body hair. I need to stop mutilating my body just to please you.

It's hair. WHO GIVES A FUCK?!

Kisha is a fat, black, nappy headed punk who lives in a house in Southside Chicago. She loves riot grrrl, d-beat, punk, and early 90s r 'n b jams. She writes the zines *Terrible, Horrible, No Good, Very Bad Life*, *I Could Live in Hope: Sexual Abuse and Survival*, and *Ft. Mortgage: Punks Buying a House!* Todayneverhappened@gmail.com

DJ SOUL SISTER

This is what happens when two music nerds get together. The longest interview in Shotgun Seamstress history! We discuss woman-positive dance parties, R&B, go-go and punk rock. Soul power!

SS: How was Jazz Fest?

DJ: Jazz Fest was a blast! I got to interview George Clinton on Friday and then I did a benefit that night, and then this past Saturday, I did my regular gig at Mimi's but I also played at Jazz Fest that night.

SS: I saw your interview with George Clinton online already! It's already up there.

DJ: I wouldn't want to say that that was the highlight of Jazz Fest, but it was definitely a great experience.

SS: Seems like this is the kind of place George Clinton would like to play. I mean, New Orleans.

DJ: He loves Tipitina's. He was saying in the interview that Tiptina's is one of the plast places left in the country where you can play all night long. Like at House of Blues, they're tyring to get you off stage and maintain their costs. And New York doesn't have a curfew but it's just like House of Blues, where they're rushing you off stage...

SS: This is an all-night town, for sure. Well, I wanted to tell you that I found out about you through going to your dance nights at Mimi's and I'm in love with the stuff you play, specifically that mid-80s, post-disco stuff that reminds me of being kid. I have no idea what it's called besides R&B. Like "Rock Steady" by The Whispers or "Object of My Desire" by Starpoint, but the lesser known songs that were never hits that fit into that style. It's a really nostalgic kind of music to me and I love that you play it. Is there a name for it?

DJ: Well, thank you. The name of the dance party is Hustle, and I started off doing a radio show on WWOZ and the whole thing there is having a hardcore knowledge of music. Now, my thing is funk and WWOZ is a non-commercial station so I can't go playing the same stuff that's on WLYD [local mainstream R&B station]. I've gotta do it OZ-style, meaning the stuff that isn't on the Top 10. So that R&B stuff that you're talking about? There's a name of that genre of early to mid-80s R&B underground dance music, and that's called "Boogie." I mean, that's what we call it now but, you know, when it came out it was just funk or R&B.

SS: I guess I'm just differentiating it from other 80s R&B that were ballads.

DJ: Right. See me and my friend like to come up with all these little names like "rare groove," "boogie" and all of these things, but it's all after the fact. On a Saturday night I'll playing this rare record and there's always some old-school cat calling me up saying, "I saw them back in the day!" [Laughs] There's nothing new under the sun. The songs you mentioned, I remember. They were hits, but I like to focus on the underground stuff.

SS: Of course! I love that you play the kind of music that I remember hearing while I was growing up but the more hidden stuff that I've never heard till now.

DJ: Yeah, and some of its new to me, too. I'm 35, so it's not like I was out at the club when these songs came out. I was like eight years old! But I love the music.

SS: The other thing I like about your night at Mimi's is that you draw a very, very

diverse crowd. Much more so than other parties I've been to in town.

DJ: Well, I do that on purpose. I almost prefer to call myself a party promoter rather than a DJ. I chose Mimi's because the place was right. It's got an underground vibe. It feels welcoming to different kinds of people and it's in line with what I'm about, which is being different. And I'm glad that people are catching on to that. I talk to other DJs about how it's not just about showing up and playing records. It's about the music and the space and about the way you promote your show.

SS: It's really cool to know that it's all really well thought-out. So, back to this thing with names. I wanted to ask you about the name of your radio show, "Rare Groove" and what it means and where it came from.

DJ: Rare grove is a term that was started in the 80s, I believe in England. It was just a catch-all term for funk soul music in the late 70s and early 80s.

SS: Yeah, I've even heard you play Afro-Beat and Latin stuff, so it's kind of a multi-genre umbrella, right?

DJ: Right, but the underground stuff. I mean, I'm not a record snob. I don't turn up my nose at mainstream stuff, but I just loved the music so much, I wanted to dig deeper. So "rare groove" is the term for the obscure stuff. It's a new term, it wasn't called that back then.

SS: Okay. So when did the radio show start?

DJ: I started at WWOZ in 1994.

SS: And that's before you were DJing around town?

DJ: Yes, but this is a difficult question because when I was in 8th grade, I used to watch Yo! MTV Raps and I loved it, and this guy told me I looked like Spinderella the DJ from Salt N' Pepa and I really liked what she was doing because I'd always been collecting records since I was little. So, asked my dad to buy me DJ equipment back then. I was in 8th grade, or a freshman in high school. He bought me everything I needed: turntables, a mixer, everything. But the thing is, he bought me the wrong turntables. DJ turn tables are direct drive and regular turntables are belt-driven and he bought me the kind the kind that are meant for home use, with the belt so you can't move the plate around. So I never ended up DJing at that point, but then WWOZ happened when I was a freshman in college. Sometime in high school, I was listening to a show called "The Kitchen Sink" and the DJ was playing all this old James Brown funk sort of stuff. He put on a record and said, "All the young kids leave the room, this music is for the grown folks." And that made me mad! I wrote him a letter saying, "I like James Brown, too!" I never sent it to him and I wish I still had it cuz it was a long kind of rant letter [laughs]. Anyway, when I was in college, I decided to start volunteering at the station, but never intended to be on the air. I was there so much, that they started having me do voice overs and things. I became friends with a woman who was doing a soul show, and when she left town, they gave me her slot. That was in 1994. And then after a few years of doing the radio show, a girlfriend of mine said, "You need to do it live." And the thing is, I'd always wanted to do it live, but I didn't know how to DJ. My friend was like, "My boyfriend will teach you." I also didn't have a sound system but my friend said she could get it for me. I didn't have a way to promote, but she was like, "I'll promote it for you." So she was the reason I am doing this today because she really pushed me. Her name was Sarah Fritz, and that was in 1997.

SS: So were you mostly DJing house parties at the time?

DJ: No, actually I was DJing at this spot called Caddyshack, it was on Poydras Street. Now it's Cornolia's Sushi Restaurant. It was a place where a a lot of good DJs who are still around started doing their thing. It was one of the big party spots and I had Wednesday nights. We called it "On the One Wednesdays." That's where it started. So wanting do live stuff started first, then the WWOZ show, and then I finally started playing live after that. And it was always about the funk. It was never about playing what someone else told me to play. I never knew that that's what DJs were supposed to do, but I didn't really understand that. I just did it my way because that's all I knew.

SS: So you played what you were into versus what people were requesting or what was trendy at the time?

DJ: Well, I was ignorant. I wasn't brought up in DJ culture, I was brought up in live music culture. If someone requested something and I didn't have it, well that was that. If someone requested something that I didn't like, I was kind of like, "Well, why would I play that?" I had no idea that DJs were there to play the current trends because I was brought up in the live culture of music. You don't go up to a band and say, "Hey can you play this? I wanna hear this." So my style was based as much on ignorance as anything else because I didn't know... I was true to myself because what else could I do? If someone had told me, "Hey, Melissa, you need to play to the crowd," it might have been different, but I didn't have anyone to tell me that. I was just true to myself.

SS: Which in the end, is probably the best thing because that attitude or perspective can only bring a more unique style to your DJing.

DJ: And that's the way it should be.

SS: My girlfriend was telling me about these all-female DJ nights you used to have. What were they called and how did that come about?

DJ: They're called the Chocolate Kitty parties and I do intend to have another one this year. Normally I have it in the spring, but I haven't had the chance to do one this year. It started the Mardi Gras after Katrina. I was doing my thing, and then there was this other DJ playing called DJ Ladyfingers... The name came from the comment that [former Mayor] Ray Nagin said about New Orleans being a "chocolate city." So it was four female DJs and I just wanted to put something together to support women DJing and to throw a fun party. It grew from four the first year to seven or eight last year, and all underground style DJs. I plan to do that next year again and it'll be the fifth year of the Chocolate Kitty party.

SS: You say that you throw the party to support other women who are DJ. Why do you think that kind of support is necessary based on your experience as a female DJ?

DJ: Well, my intention is to give women, especially who are spinning at the underground level, the support that I did not have. I feel lucky to have a platform, so if I put other women on, then that helps everybody. It's to through a fun party, sure, but it's really for support. It's to show people that there are women out there who are really doing it. The one thing I hate as a promoter that I see other promoters doing... This city is full of male promoters and they have these flyers with these really risque, scantily clad women on them and not everyone wants to go to a party that's promoted like that. That's ridiculous. That's some man's fantasy. The point of my parties is to have fun and the all-women DJ party isn't a new concept, but it's not promoted as, "Yeah, sexy women DJs." I've had male party promoters call me and say, "Hey we want to do a party like yours but maybe can you guys dress in sexy outfits," or whatever. Hell no. Hell no.

SS: They ask you to dress sexy?

DJ: Yeah, and I tell them that if they want to call the other women and ask them and they agree then that's on them, but there's no way in hell that I'm down for something like that. That goes against everything I stand for. It's all about the way you do it. I have my Booty Patrol dancers and yeah they're cute and kinda sexy, but it's a woman power thing. It's not done in that hypersexualized way. So yeah, I'm very conscious in everything I do of women being comfortable. It's what inspired me to do that night at Mimi's. I was DJing a night and it was just so uncomfortable for women and I thought to myself, "This can't be my only option for night life." I've actually been thinking and hoping for years that a young woman would come up and be into the music that I do, because I'm ready to pass the torch to someone else. But it's work. You have to love music and love DJ culture...

SS: Well, that's the thing is I did want to ask you about being involved with DJ culture and how that feels because I find it kind of intimidating. Just the sheer amount of shopping & digging you guys do, and then all of the unspoken rules about what you should and shouldn't play, like how some people are against DJs playing tracks off of compilations...

DJ: There are no rules, you know. Play what you like. And as far as compilations, I used to think like that and then Katrina happened. And I told *Wax Poetics* [magazine] that at the end of the day, I don't care what it comes off of, it's about the music. Because you have a whole lot of people here who have lost everything and I'm not going to judge people who don't have the original record. People think I'm against digital mixing and I'm not, it's just not what I do. As far as being a woman and a black woman, it's like anything. People won't believe you and they're going to try to discredit you... I mean, once a guy said about me that I get all of my credit because I'm a woman, and something to look at. I was just looking through records at the record store recently and this guy looked at me and said, "What you know about some vinyl?" And I looked up at the record store owner and said, "Not too much," and kept on digging [laughs]. You're going to always get that. In *Wax Poetics* I told a story about how I was going to Guitar Center to buy some gear, and the clerk asked, "Is this is for your son?" and I'm thinking, "I don't even have any kids! It's for me!"

SS: Guitar Center is the worst! I was talking to Brice [mutual friend, DJ Brice Nice] last night and he told me you're kind of into punk rock.

DJ: Oh wow, yeah.

SS: Yeah?

DJ: Totally. When I was younger... And when I say "younger," I mean seven, eight or nine years old, I was a strange kid. I was into hardcore like Black Flag and Minor Threat and, you know, the stuff people know like The Clash. And I used to listen religiously to WTUL [Tulane college radio] on Friday nights. WTUL probably inspired me just as much, if not more than WWOZ. So anyway, on Friday night there was a hardcore show from midnight to 2am. And then after that there was a Rock & Soul show. But I just like both musics. It just turned out that way. [laughs]

SS: That's so cool. So what is your attraction to the underground versus anything else? It seems like from an early age, it was natural for you.

DJ: I really don't know, but I feel lucky that I got that gene or whatever it is. [laughs] It's not like I got it really from my parents. I was an only child...

SS: Me too!

DJ: I don't know how that happened. I really haven't a clue.

SS: I guess I'm asking you this question because I wonder the same thing about myself. I remember before I was into punk rock, I was into hip-hop and I was always looking for the stuff that they weren't playing on the radio, like when I was around 14 years old or so, staying up really late on a Sunday night trying to catch the radio show that played all the underground stuff.

DJ: I can't even say... You know, I don't know where that comes from. There were a lot of different people in my life, like this next door neighbor when I was a kid. I remember she had gotten the first B-52s record. She was like 14 and I was like 8 and she was like, "Check out this record!" Have you ever seen the cover of that record?

SS: Yeah, the yellow one?

DJ: Yeah! And I just remember seeing the ladies on there with the crazy high hair and thinking it was cool. And I really liked the music. But I don't know where I get that from...

SS: So speaking of being into punk, I wanted to ask you about ESG. You play them sometimes, don't you?

DJ: Yeah, sometimes.

SS: To me, they're kind of a punk-funk crossover band and after I found out about them, I was always looking high and low for other bands with black women who played instruments and wrote their own songs. Have you run into any others?

DJ: Well, I'm going to name a band and you're going to laugh at me when I say this, but they were a group that was really powerful to me when I was younger, but the disco group A Taste of Honey, with their hit "Boogie Oogie Oogie," was lead by a female guitarist and a female bassist. I remember seeing them and being like, "Wow!" And they wrote their own songs as well. There's Teena Marie, too. As far as on the underground tip... Oh gee...

SS: You gotta think really hard, huh? [we both laugh]

DJ: I'll have to think some more on that, because it's mainly vocalists but it's hard to think of musicians. There were some singer songwriters, like Linda Lewis who was from England in the 70s. But women playing instruments... That's much harder to think of.

SS: You're also a Chuck Brown fan, right?

DJ: Oh, yes.

SS: I grew up outside of DC and got to see some go-go shows and bucket drummers and whatnot growing up. How'd you find out about it?

DJ: Well, I started hearing about go-go when I was young because there was a radio station around here called WAIL and there was a DJ on there called Slick Leo and people called him the Grandmaster Flash of New Orleans because he had his own radio program, he had a live dance show and someone told me about these huge parties he used to throw in the Superdome. He was huge. And he played DC go-go. In the early 80s the label was TTED and DETT and they had Trouble Funk and that stuff that came to New Orleans through Slick Leo. If you're into go-go in New Orleans, he is the reason why. I even took a trip to DC to go see it for myself and I was astounded because down here, people like Trouble Funk because that's what was big back in the early 80s through Slick Leo. Now, in DC if you say Trouble Funk they will laugh at you. It's sort of like if someone comes down here and they wanna go to a second line—like, a tourist—and all they know is the Dirty Dozen Brass Band and they're looking for them, "Where's the Dirty Dozen Brass Band?" We're gonna look at them and say, "Dirty Dozen? They haven't been around in years! It's about Rebirth Brass Band and Hot 8, etc." So the big band in DC is Rare Essence. And they laughed at me when I started talking about Trouble Funk cuz they're old! But down here, we don't know who Rare Essence is.

SS: Well, it's good that go-go made it down here, because I always got the impression that go-go never really never made it that far.

DJ: Well, it really didn't.

SS: What's your opinion on that? It came out around the same time as hip-hop but never really made it as far...

DJ: Exactly. And the story was that go-go was thought to be bigger and that it was going to take over and that hip-hop was a joke. I actually read an article about this, but I can't remember it exactly. My opinion today would be that in go-go there aren't many original songs, it's mostly covers. But I'd say one thing that really helped out hip-hop was just the NYC scene in general. Punk kids going to hip-hop shows and bringing it back to their own neighborhoods. Debbie Harry borrowing from hip-hop and taking it into the mainstream. There was more crossover which is how ESG and the whole post-punk thing could happen. In DC, you hear from Ian McKaye that they were scared to death...

SS: They were scared? I thought Minor Threat played with go-go bands.

DJ: I talked to Ian McKaye once and he said that if you were white you'd never go to a go-go show. And the drug culture surrounding go-go, from what I understand, was a little deeper... I mean PCP was so big. I have a go-go record from the 80s and the label is called Love Boat Records and "love boat" was what they called PCP. [laughs] So, you know, mainstream people weren't trying to hear that stuff. Island Record bought TTED records out and there was a movie by the label called "Good to Go" from 1986 or '87. It's been renamed now, but it was a very violent movie and people in go-go hated it because it portrayed their scene really badly and gave more attention to the violence than the music itself. So that one effort at trying to bring go-go to the mainstream pretty much killed it, so much so that the go-go community didn't even want to have anything to do with it. I think I have it on VHS. Art Garfunkel [of Simon and Garfunkel?!?] is the star of the movie. [laughs]

SS: Uh, I don't even know what to say about that. He seems like the least likely person in the world to be in that role.

DJ: But yeah, they tried to make it happen. And then EU had "Da Butt." But then from what I hear, EU got backlash in the local community because they were too mainstream.

SS: And that was like the only national go-go hit except for that one Amerie song that had that backtrack with the go-go beat.

DJ: Which, interestingly enough, that drumbeat came from a Meters song! From New Orleans!

SS: Wow, crazy. I had no idea. I mean, it doesn't sound like a straight-up go-go beat to me, but it's really reminiscent of it and I was glad that people were talking about go-go again. So, I'm all outta questions! But what's in store for you in the future, Soul Sister?

DJ: Well, I'm always working on more underground DJ nights. I'll probably have another one of my Right On 80s parties at One Eyed Jacks over the summer. And you know with 80s night, it's kind of always the same, like they forget that black people had 80s hits, too. So I decided to take over One Eyed Jacks and do my Right On 80s party where you'll hear stuff like Atlantic Star, the Gapp Band, Doug E Fresh, Zapp, you know things like that. That's 80s music, too! And that's all I'll play. And those parties have been pretty popular.

SS: You know, people are still talking about the Prince vs. Michael Jackson party you did. You gonna do another one?

DJ: You know what? I'll tell you what I will do because you know, now that Michael is gone and I can't do Prince vs. Michael anymore.

SS: Why not? What do you mean?

DJ: Because there's no battle! Before, I did MJ vs. Prince party, I just did an all-Prince party and that was the year after Prince played at Essence Festival. And then I did the Michael vs. Prince party and now I might go back and do another all-Prince party. But no more MJ vs. Prince party. Rest in peace, Michael... And who else could you put Prince up against? Nobody! [laughs]

KICKTEASE

This interview took place on the steps of Lee Circle right after Kicktease played a show at the Circle Bar. The band talks about the scene in Baton Rogue, their home town & their experience as an all-girl punk band in the South.

This interview took place on the steps of Lee Circle, right outside of the Circle Bar on Saturday January 23rd at about 1am, so I guess technically it was Sunday. Normally, Kicktease is a three piece punk band, but that night they added Shivers, who played organ on three or four songs during the set. Alan is Alicia's boyfriend who played drums for Kicktease once when their regular drummer, Mary Beth, couldn't make it. Alicia plays guitar and Jacinta sings.

SS: Okay, so first question: Where did you find Shivers?

Alicia: We found her on the streets, really! (all laugh and start talking over each other)

Shivers: I met these girls through my friend Hank. They lived on Government Street.

SS: So are you guys, like, an official band in this formation, or...?

Shivers: Right now it's a "project."

Alicia: It evolves, it changes...

Jacinta: I love changing things. It makes it interesting, it makes things different and I thoroughly enjoy it. I really do. It's something different for Kicktease.

Alan: It's like Dr. Jekyll and Mr. Hyde!

SS: It really is! Me and my friend were just talking about how it's like listening to a Bad Brains record, or like for people who actually got to see them, and how they go from punk to reggae in a split second, it's like two different bands in one! Ok, what's the scene like in Baton Rouge? (everyone starts talking at once again)

Shivers: There are people who love to play music and are sincere about it, and I'm not hatin' on Baton Rouge, but when I go to a show, no one's rockin' out, there's too many hipsters. New Orleans is the place to go for a good show. It's about the people who are at your show, it's about the energy you get from the people. You don't get that kind of energy in Baton Rouge.

Alicia: I don't think anyone in Baton Rouge really goes to shows to hear music. They basically just go to get drunk and have a good time. You're considered a good time if you are good sociable drunks, I think.

SS: You think it's because it's a college town?

Alicia: It's a *small* town.

Shivers: The house shows are good. You get the energy that you need from house shows.

Alicia: The house shows are rockin'. I don't know what it is about Baton Rouge. I hate to use the word, but it's just kind of clique-ish.

Jacnta: It's like high school all over again. It's about how you dress, it's not about character...

Alicia: It's definitely not about creativity... I dunno, Baton Rouge, you tell me! What's up with the scene there? Because we would love to be a part of it. Honestly, Osa, we would love to play in Baton Rouge, but it's... We've played the Spanish Moon how many times? Like three or four times and people enjoyed Kicktease, but it wasn't like New Orleans. People aren't just gonna go out and see bands, they're gonna see their friends who happen to play music, so it's not about pursuing anything more than that: Hanging out and drinking, watching your friends do stuff.

Jacinta: There is some support, but it's not the kind you get in New Orleans.

Alicia: I'm sure it's the same stuff that goes on in New Orleans, but with a greater number of people, there are more people that will be interested in what you're doing.

Jacinta: Our fans were here tonight! Our two fans! (everyone laughs) They were being so nice! They were like, "We love Kicktease!" I cry for everything and almost started crying when I saw them there!

Alicia: I think a lot of it has to do with Osa. She definitely gives us support and has really hooked us up down here.

SS: Aw you guys! So were the three of you friends before you started the band?

Alicia: Jacinta and I met through the Internet and then we met Mary Beth through my friend who was in a band with her. We met in 2008, and there was instant connection. We did a Food Not Bombs acoustic performance of Noisettes songs and Bloc Party.

Alan: We raised like $500 and two trash cans full of food.

Alicia: And I met Shivers when our boyfriends were living in the same house.

SS: That's kind of a cool way to meet.

Shivers: I remember coming over to that house on Government Street and listening to you play and Jacinta was singing, and, you know, it encouraged me to keep doing what I was doing.

Alicia: Awesome!

Jacinta: Yeeeah!

Alicia: I like the idea of just pickin' up girls... (laughs)

SS: Ok, have any of you seen the movie Afro-Punk and what did you think?

Alicia: Yes, I saw it! There was a girl, her name was Mi..

SS: Oh, Mariko?

Alicia: She had total self-hate all over herself. It was really painful to watch only because I experienced that when I was younger, and I think everyone goes through that. Black kids especially, but everybody, for various reasons. I first heard about the movie when I was 17 at FAMU. I heard about it on the Internet, of course, and I couldn't find it until four years later. It's a great movie as an introduction to these issues that black punks may face. There are a lot of things that weren't covered in it, but maybe those ideas just aren't as accessible, I guess. As an introduction to those issues, it's a good movie, but it could go further.

Alan: In most things like that, you can always afford to go further. I think what that movie accomplishes is that it brings up stuff that most people in the punk scene would never even consider. And that is the crux issue of any punk scene, is the issue of identity, like finding yourself and stamping out all of the misconceptions that you've been poisoned with, and finding what your essence is here on earth and what you're going to do it. [Alicia] showed the movie to me, and I showed it to a lot of people. I was living with a house full of dudes at the time and everybody benefited from seeing it. Of course it could've been way more in depth, it could've been twice as long, but at least it served the purpose of introducing people to a layer of this thing we all want to partake in.

SS: Afro-Punk was filmed almost a decade ago. Do you feel like the experiences reflected in that movie are dated? Do they still ring true for you?

Alicia: It definitely matched my experience, but personally, it was stuff that happened in the past for me because it just reflected on that young, pre-teen age when you're insecure about everything and everything feels like a struggle. But that's a timeless feeling, so it's not dated at all. Everyone has had that feeling and will have that feeling.

Jacinta: Anyone who is not of Caucasian decent who is born into the punk scene or the rock scene or whatever you want to call it, they will get that feeling of insecurity. They will be belittled. I went through it in elementary school, in middle school, in high school. I was picked on almost every single day for who I was because I looked up to my brothers and all they listened to was hardcore and metal, and that's all I knew. But then I was like, "Maybe I should listen to the Cranberries just so I'll be accepted." I didn't really like them too much, but I grew to like them because I wanted to be a part of that normal scene.

SS: See that's so weird because in the 90s, for me listening to the Cranberries, people were like "You're listening to white music!" It wasn't that acceptable for black kids to listen to alternative back then because it wasn't "black music."

Jacinta: Till this day, my brother tells me, "Don't tell people that you followed me."

Mary Beth

And I'm like, "You are who I followed!" Because he thinks that I went astray, but it's not astray. Punk music, rock music, is beautiful.

Alicia: It's really interesting how young kids, for their lack of experience, they know well what the boundaries are: black, white, girl, boy, smart, not smart. They know those boundaries.

Alicia: It's really interesting how young kids, for their lack of experience, they know well what the boundaries are: black, white, girl, boy, smart, not smart. They know those boundaries.

Jacinta: I was always like, "What are you talking about?" I was the one crying in the bathroom. I didn't understand it until I reached high school. I didn't realize there were things that I was supposed to be. I grew up on country music. It took me a long time to understand that there are these boxes you're supposed to fit into.

SS: Where are your parents' from?

Jacinta: My mom's from Trinidad & Tobago and my dad's from Venezuela. Their wedding song was Anne Murray "This Dance." (laughs) That was their wedding song, and I didn't know any different. When I got to high school, I realized the separation. But the way things are now for me, this is normal.

Alan: And that's a good thing you can say that, especially here in the South of the U.S. because there are still so many places in the world where this is all really abnormal.

Alicia: I think a really good example of that was the release of that game Left for Dead. People were claiming the game was unrealistic, not because you're chasing zombies down in this post-apocalyptic world, but because the black girl in the video game has a Depeche Mode shirt on and she's from the south. So unrealistic! This was a recent thing, where people who probably consider themselves progressive say these things and don't really know that there's anything wrong with it.

SS: Ok, I just found out about Valley Girl Intelligensia*, that radio show on KLSU? Do you know the girl who does that?

Alicia: Yeah, she's really great. Her name is Meredith.

Alan: She's been a mainstay for a while up there and Kicktease has actually played live on her show before.

Alicia: We did an interview and played a demo. She's probably the greatest support we've had from Baton Rouge.

Alan: Her show is bad ass too. Her show is one of the best on KSLU.

SS: So it's the year 2010, y'all. Do you feel like women, queer people and people of color still need extra support or do you feel like the playing field is leveling out at all?

Alicia: Anyone who says that race and gender doesn't matter anymore and that they're not impressed with females and minorities doing things, I have to say that you're probably a little bit blind and part of the privileged class.

Alicia: I think it's good to see it to be aware of it, but you don't have to be bogged down by it.

Jacinta: I don't want to be bogged down by it, and I'm thankful that Mary Beth is with us still and that she's not afraid to be in a band with two black girls who love this music. She's a beautiful woman and she plays drums like a pro.

Alicia: She has big booty beats! (laughs)

Mary Beth: Playing with all women is awesome, but what I hear more than anything is, [in dude voice] "Aw, three chicks! Aw, that's awesome!" (laughs) I don't like that too much.

Alicia: I've noticed that a lot of girls just feel like they're not an expert at what they do. They're not that confident. I'm like that too sometimes.

Jacinta: We're all like that!

Alicia: Yeah, we all have these insecurities about the things we do.

Alan: I think that particular reason is what makes it still relevant that y'all are women and y'all are women of color making this music. There still is something very powerful about it. We still live day to day with people feeling insecure automatically with whatever little slot they were born into. And as a dude, there still is something powerful and enthralling about seeing women play music. There's something very beautiful and seductive about it too. Seeing women totally in control and being themselves and not compromising any part of their identity... There's still something very powerful and moving about that, and as crazy as it is that there's still dudes out there who are like, "Hey! Chick band!" Under that surface layer of "Wow, y'all are chicks!" is something moving, enthralling and relevant about women making noise.

SS: Yeah, I guess I can see how that's just some dudes' trifling way of expressing what you just said so articulately.

Alicia: I would love for more female musicians to realize that. There are so many girls I know who play piano or play acoustic guitar and are like, "I just like to do it in my room. I don't think I could ever go on stage. I don't think that's the place for me." But it's a place for anyone.

Mary Beth: I've gotten some really good comments from other girls saying it makes them want to play music and that feels really good.

Jacinta: I just have to say, I love my band. I love playing with all women. Every time I go to band practice, every single time, I feel so thankful and so lucky.

*Valley Girl Intelligensia is a radio show on KLSU (college radio for Lousiana State U) that plays riot girl, queer core, girl art punk, etc. You can listen online here: http://www.klsuradio.fm/valley-girl-intelligentsia/

CAMPING

The Jam

CREATED BY VIM CRONY

MEANWHILE...
A.T.H.
"AMENDED THEORY HOUSE"
So, does anyone have any songs or riffs written to start us off with?
JUNE 13TH
PROVOKE
8PM
$3
CAREER
Cheesecake!
CAREER
CASEY
KEVIN
JEFF
SHEILA
SERIOUSLY? C'mon! Any ideas about what kind of band we're going to be or what this project could stand for?

Hey! We should just be a free form psychodelic noise rock band!
BLASPHEMY!
I'M GOING TO THROW UP!!
SIGH.
NEVERMIND.
Thank goodness!
JUNE 13TH
PROVOKE
P
8PM
$3
AxTxHx
Well, we've only got ONE WEEK until our first show with PROVOKE! What are we going to do?!
UP THE PUNX
TO BE CONTINUED...

DIY or DIE!

I wanted to write an article for those of you who read this zine who aren't necessarily immersed in a punk scene and who might not really know what punk rock is outside of Afro-Punk. And just to be clear, every time I reference Afro-Punk in this article, I am not referring to the documentary itself, but to the whole phenomenon that developed after the release of the movie, specifically the online discussion forums, the concerts in NYC and LA and most recently the Afro-Punk tours. I also wanted to remind myself, and other folks who have been at it for a while, why we do what we do.

Right now, more than ever before, punk rock fashion has been co-opted into mainstream popular culture. Everyone has a mohawk now. I complimented this girl on her shirt the other day thinking it was something she or a friend screen printed and she said she got it from Old Navy. Dammit, fooled again! Tattoos & piercings are no longer any kind of big deal. Anyone can get a tattoo if they have the cash. And suddenly in the past few years, hip-hop kids got into punk fashion, sporting tight jeans, Vans and mohawks.

This isn't new. Punk rock looks good and everyone's been wanting a piece of it since 1977. Afro-Punk leads people, especially young people, to misunderstand what punk rock is really about. I also wanted to write about this in a zine that is written to kids who aren't white because, in general, kids who *are* white are more likely to be able to access punk rock and benefit from it than brown kids.

Punk is a slightly different beast depending on what country, city or town yr in and even within the same city, there might be several different punk scenes that are more or less separate. As soon as I start saying things like, "This is what punk rock is really about," I know I'm already getting into trouble because no one gets to say what punk is. No one owns it. And in reality, punk rock ranges from Christian punk to radical queer punk; from drunk white boys annihilating each other in a mosh pit to anarcho-feminist reading groups. The characteristics associated with punk can be found outside of punk rock too, in the lives of activists, artists, hippies and other wingnuts who are not necessarily affiliated with any "scene" per se. Things like communal living; anti-consumerism; DIY music and art making; feminist, anti-capitalist (including but not limited to socialist & Marxist), anarchist, anti-war and environmentalist beliefs.

At the risk of seeming unsupportive to the Afro-Punk phenomenon, I'd like to offer a few critiques of what I see happening. Afro-Punk is important to a lot of people, especially black teenagers and adults who never had a word that encompassed the experience of being the only black kid at a punk show. The documentary focused on black punks who had no choice but to operate within predominantly white scenes if they wanted to be in a DIY/punk community. If you are an Afro-Punk and you love the way the website is run and the way the concerts go down, then you can stop reading now. This isn't for you. If the whole Afro-Punk experience has left you wanting more, then keep reading. If you want to take Afro-Punk into your own hands instead of attending a corporate sponsored concert, keep reading.

Like James Spooner himself said in SS #4, punk rock has to be run by the kids. Right now all of the activity within Afro-Punk seems like it's generated by a few individuals who use corporate money to make things happen. Is the Afro-Punk tour really punk or is it more like Black Lollapalooza? Punk rock is supposed to be a *counterculture*, not a miniature version of mainstream culture painted brown. It is a cultural movement based on *resistance*. Resistance to what? Well, to the status quo and all it entails, the backbone of the status quo in our society being capitalism. Many have argued that capitalism actually supports racism, classism, homophobia and all other forms of oppression because in a capitalist society, there are always winners and losers. Discriminating against people of color, queers, the poor, etc. keeps the white, rich, straight, heterosexual men of the power elite on top, now doesn't it? Rather than corporations controlling and defining our lives, why not take that power into our own hands, because at the end of the day corporations only care about one thing at the expense of all else and that one thing is profit.

This is why it pains me to know that Afro-Punk showcases and tours are corporate sponsored events.

In a day & age where corporations are the most powerful entities in the world, causing environmental and human destruction across the globe, including the town you live in, why make friends with the devil? You may argue that these tours couldn't even happen without corporate money but I know that's not true because right now this second, thousands of bands, including black DIY punk bands, are touring across states and nations without corporate sponsorship. And what's up with expensive Afro-Punk themed Vans sneakers, "limited edition" posters that sell for up to $35 a piece? I can see how Afro-Punk is a very relevant and important thing, but it also seems like it's become a business.

The term DIY is pretty much commonplace now, but if you don't already know, it stands for "Do It Yourself" and this ethic is probably the most important idea behind punk. It tells us that anyone can be in a band, anyone can change their community, anyone can grow their own food, anyone can write a book, etc. DIY is about empowerment and self-actualization--like, realizing your potential instead of feeling held back by feelings of inadequacy or inferiority. In my mind, DIY is automatically feminist, anti-racist and anti-classist because once you learn to think a certain way, you realize that being a woman, or being a person of color or being poor doesn't have to hold you back from fulfilling your potential as a human being. Instead of thinking of reasons why you can't do something, you start to figure out ways that you can.

In our society, historically white middle class and rich men have been given the privilege to do and be whatever they want and till this day, finding historical examples of artists, activists, political figures, writers, scientists, world travelers, cross-country bike riders, business owners, etc. who are women, queer, poor, of color, disabled, etc. is difficult and requires much digging. For me, finding out about Zora Neal Hurston was so important, especially when I realized she wasn't only an author, but also an anthropologist, artist, singer and world traveler. I've never heard of another black woman doing the types of things she did (and all at once!) Historically, as women, we've been told that we aren't as good as men when it comes to playing instruments, or learning math & science, or anything deemed "technical" in our society. The existence of DIY culture is so important for historically marginalized people because it shows you that you don't have to have formal education in something or be an expert to do it well. DIY makes room for everyone to participate, and that means you.

There are plenty of people of color DIY bands across the nation right now, not to mention overseas. They play small shows for their friends at houses and clubs, they go on tour in beat up old cars and vans, they put out their own music, they record themselves, they have little or no formal training being musicians and they're definitely not in it for money or fame. They play great music, raw and straight from the heart and they are not on the Afro-Punk website or on their tours. If you live somewhere and would like one of those bands to play in your town, did you know that you could make it happen? You can contact any of these bands and they will personally respond to you, and as long as you can find them a space (your house, a coffee shop, a book store, a warehouse, a record store, a community center, etc.), depending on where you live, it is likely that they would come play in your town. If you're seriously interested in making something like this happen and you want to know more, get in touch with me.

Black people in this country have a long history of resistance. Over time, things have obviously changed for us for the better and I want us all to be comfortable, but let's not get *too* comfortable just because it's the year 2010. We're living in a strange time when so much has changed from the Jim Crow days of racism, yet so much remains the same. Being black, having a nose ring, wild hair, a bunch of tattoos and listening to Bloc Party isn't really changing the world, ok? And neither is being white, wearing a studded jean vest or having an asymmetrical haircut, by the way. Punk fashion is fun but it's just not very important and doesn't take the place of actual political resistance. In fact, the more we use our fashion to conform to each other inside our tiny groups, be it Afro-Punk or "regular" punk, the more we're just recreating the same standards we thought we were resisting.

Capitalism is black people's #1 worst enemy! Black people in this country don't have shit. We don't own shit. We don't even own the businesses in our own neighborhoods for the most part. Every time we spend money, we make a white person somewhere a little bit richer. Even some prisons (generally the private, for-profit ones) profit from our incarceration.

In my mind, being a musician and an artist goes hand in hand with being a political visionary.

I expect a community of black folks who care about music, art and freedom of expression to also care about changing the system that created the boxes and labels that have been holding us back for too long. Thinking about the fact that black folks aren't expected to be punks or goths or indie rockers or even rockers period is step one. What else are we not expected to be in this society? What *are* we expected to be in this society? How did those ideas come to be? Who benefits from those ideas?

It's cool that Afro-Punk is a celebration of a different type of black identity. Everyone's sick of black culture (as if there is one monolithic black culture) being labeled "hip-hop culture" or "urban." In DIY punk culture, we celebrate something similar: being weird, not doing what's expected of you, rejecting social norms. It's a worthwhile, fun thing to celebrate, but for many of us, it's only the tip of the iceberg. We also wanna change the way people think. We wanna change the way society works. We want things to be more fair, especially when it comes to economics. We want people to feel empowered to make things better for themselves and their communities. We want to challenge ourselves and the ideas we were brought up with, and we want to live these new values in our daily lives so that they spread to other people, making things better for everyone. I think it's time for Afro-Punk to move forward from just being a statement about identity. Why not use it as a political tool?

The people who are really in charge of the Afro-Punk experience are all the people that go to their shows, all the people who fill their website with discussion topics, blog posts, pictures and personality. I'm calling on you, black kids who are interested in punk rock to create your own Afro-Punk scene and remember to use it as a site for critical rebellion. Resist corporate consumer culture. Get in touch with DIY punk bands with black kids in them, read zines by other black kids, become real-mail pen pals with another Afro-Punk kid in a different state, have an art show in your bedroom and invite your friends. Tie your art to political struggle whenever you can. Like I've written in this zine before, we have so much more potential as a people than our potential to consume.

Get Anti-Capitalist.

Until he talked with Lawrence, Burns had believed that the work of a black artist had to be in the nature of protest to qualify as "black." Lawrence assured him that his first obligation was to be true to his vision and to produce the best art he possibly could. "You are born black," he told me, "and whatever you do when you let your emotions go —whatever comes out will be a reflection of your black ex-perience."

Maurice Burns on his relationship with artist Jacob Lawrence from Black Artists of the New Generation.

DEATH is nothing to be afraid of.

by Sean Padilla

The last time I visited Waterloo Records, arguably Austin's most popular record store, I saw the CD reissue of *For the World to See*, an EP recorded in 1974 by the heretofore obscure band Death (not to be confused with the 1980s speed-metal band of the same name), displayed on one of its back walls. A brief written recommendation was taped onto the display, warning listeners to "expect lots of bad comparisons to Bad Brains due to them being Black." Such prescient sarcasm illustrates how easy it is to ignore historical context in the face of sheer novelty.

Although Death and Bad Brains are both all-Black bands that play fast, aggressive rock music, Death preceded the latter band by almost five years, and had an entirely different set of influences. Death didn't incorporate jazz or reggae into its sound; their music is much closer to what most people would consider "classic rock." They weren't afraid of gratuitous unaccompanied solos, a practice most punks would scoff at. The trio's Detroit upbringing ensured distinctly Midwestern influences: the polished R&B of the Motown label, which they imitated as teenagers; and the proto-punk of local heroes the Stooges and MC5, which transformed them as they entered adulthood.

When Death recorded *For the World to See*, they weren't entirely aware of how ahead of their time they were. Only guitarist/songwriter David Hackney believed that they were doing something truly revolutionary. His brothers, bassist/vocalist Bobby and drummer Dannis, could only see the disapproval that the predominantly Black audiences at their shows greeted them with. After allegedly being denied a recording contract from industry mogul Clive Davis, due to a refusal to change its radio-unfriendly name, the band broke up and shelved its recordings. However, David held on to the master tapes, passing them on to Bobby shortly before his death, in the hope that Death would eventually find its audience. This tug-of-war between hope and disillusionment is common to artists struggling to reach their own people through work that defies the stereotypes assigned to them.

When I think of Death playing to an unwelcome audience of fellow Blacks at a garage party in their own neighborhood, I receive flashbacks of getting booed by hundreds of Black classmates at talent shows in my own high school. It took Death 35 years to find its audience, but that audience is comprised mainly of White hipsters and record collectors. I don't know any Black artists who are truly comfortable with having a predominantly non-Black audience. There's a baseline gratitude that we have for anyone who values our art, regardless of race, but there's also something to be said for being accepted by people who look like us, whose experiences parallel our own. Still, I'm sure that this baseline gratitude compelled the living Hackney brothers to resume playing live as Death, with guitarist Bobbie Duncan (who currently plays with the brothers in reggae band Lambsbread) playing David's parts.

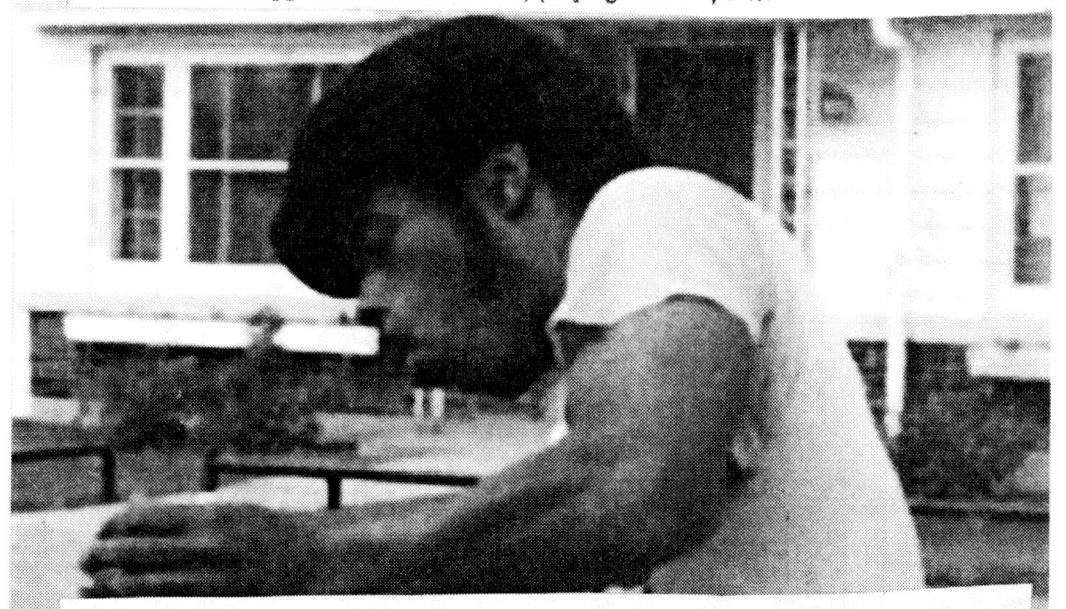

Death's performance at last year's Fun Fun Fun Fest was a must-see. The historical importance of this gig was astounding: it was their first show in more than 30 years, their first time playing Austin AND their first time playing a festival. Part of me expected the band's performance to be compromised by nerves and rustiness, and the overlong sound check did the men no favors. I was surrounded by White dudes who shouted unnecessary history lessons at me ("DUDE, THIS IS REAL PUNK ROCK - EVEN BEFORE BAD BRAINS!"), as if I hadn't done my research, as if they were actually alive to see Death in its prime. I stared at the posters of David that the band hung on both sides of the stage: the sight of a big-haired, well-dressed Black man standing tall and proud, with a guitar resting at his feet and a look on contentment on his face, calmed my nerves.

tym.→

The members of Death walked on stage wearing black hooded robes and stood silently for about 30 seconds, as another tribute to David's memory. When they removed their robes, picked up their instruments, and played the opening chords to "Keep on Knocking," the rest of the audience lost its collective mind. I, on the other hand, cursed my perfect pitch and wished that Bobbie would've spent a bit more time tuning his guitar. It didn't even matter that the band sounded just as fast and tight as it did 35 years ago, or that Bobby's vocals sounded even better live than they do on record. I just wanted Bobbie to tune that one flat string! He eventually did, though, and I was able to enjoy the last three songs of the set, freed from my irrational perfectionism.

I saw the happiness on Bobby's face as he profusely thanked the audience between songs. I pumped my fist, banged my head, and shouted his refrains back to him. I threw myself into the mosh pit during "Politicians in My Eyes," feeling my brain rattle as I knocked around the White guys who earlier annoyed me. Finally, I said a prayer of thanks to David, and to every other deceased Black rocker who planted seeds of revolution by being themselves. Because of them, I can live to find my own audience.

RECORD REVIEWS

Hornet Leg "Ribbon of Fear" (K Records)
Hornet Leg was originally a solo outlet for Christopher Sutton who you may also know from COCO, Dub Narcotic Sound System and most recently the Gossip. Their first 7", "The Bloody Trilogy" was three songs worth of garage rockin' rawness with Sutton on guitar and vocals and Claudia Meza (later of Explode into Colors) on drums. This LP is a more finely recorded 14 song opus, with Bob Desaulniers on bass and Robert Comitz on drums, that is essentially a document of Sutton's love affair with American rock 'n' roll. I mean, I know the guy which is kinda why I'm saying this. Every song on the record captures a different a facet of rock music, from the indie pop number "Wait!" to the garage rocking "Night of the Phantom" (a completely reworked blues over) to the totally psyched out "I'm Leaving You." The songwriting is solid and the delivery is on-point. It seems like Hornet Leg has finally made its way from solo experiment to full-fledged band. The only criticism I'd give is that... Well, the essence of rock 'n' roll is that it's dirty and I feel like the recording could've been more raw, but this is also coming from a punk who likes her music in blown-out, disintegrated, monophonic sound. Plus I got the CD version, so maybe the vinyl sounds better. Overall, I really like it.

The Younger Lovers "Rock Flawless" LP (not yet released)
If you've ever read a past issue of Shotgun Seamstress (or Maximum Rock N Roll), you know who Brontez Purnell is and you know that we're friends. But don't think that I'm not gonna give my own friend an honest review, although I'm obviously gonna be biased because I am *in love* with this kid. Okay, the "Rock Flawless" LP picks up solidly where the California Soul EP and the Newest Romantic LP leave off. The new record is cute, it's poppy and it's rocking. We've got 14 songs about young gay boy crushes, romance and all of the sadness and misery that can go along with that. The thing I loved about The Younger Lovers' earliest songs is the obvious blend of soul that might remind one of some 60s R&B ala "I'm Your Puppet" mixed with some straight-up Cali pop punk. I feel like the soul influence is becoming a little less obvious on "Rock Flawless," and I really would like to hear more of those cute bass lines like we heard previously on "I Dig You Anyway" and "Sha-Boo-Lee." But if this LP were to stand on its own, without being compared to previous Younger Lovers releases, I'd say, "Check it out!" (once it's released.) It's fun, the songs are good, it's makes you wanna dance and the lyrics are clever as fuck. If the Younger Lovers are playing a show anywhere near you, go and dance your socks off.

Trash Kit self-titled LP (Upset the Rhythm)
I love this band and I love this record! Writing these reviews, I realize I'm never gonna be able to do a non-biased record review in this zine of any current releases cuz it's a small black punk world and I have some connection with all of these bands & artists. Oh, well. I loved this band before I made any kind of connection with them, anyway. Trash Kit is an all-girl art punk band from England and the kind of music they make is right up my alley. What we have here is a sonic experiment that doesn't leave you bewildered. You can feel it! Powerful but minimal drumming that steers clear of typical rock beats, very rich vocals with some pretty amazing vocal layering throughout many of the songs, sounds that seem inspired by other art punk bands, but also possibly by some Afro and Carribean sounds, as well. Inventive guitar work and even some violin. Oh, it's too good to be true. The only band I could possibly compare them to is Wet Dog, also from the UK, in the way that they are both minimal, artsy, all-female trios that come up with some pretty unexpected parts, but they don't really sound alike. The connections between Shotgun Seamstress and Trash Kit run deep. Look for an interview with this band in a future issue of this zine.

I Smell a Rat: Early Black Rock 'n Roll #2 1949-1959 (Trikont)
This is a history lesson in the form of a double LP and it delivers hit after hit after hit. These are our forefathers and foremothers: Howlin' Wolf, Big Mama Thornton, Sister Rosetta Tharpe, Etta James, Chuck Berry and some other early black rock 'n' rollers I hadn't heard of till now like Rosco Garden, Billy the Kid Emerson and Sandra Meade. I'm sorry I missed Volume #1 of this amazing compilation. Minor comment: The cover could've been better looking. One of the best things about re-issues are the cool covers. Anyway, if you see this record, buy it. If it's out of print or yr broke, pirate it. I'd call this one essential.

CAZUMBI: AFRICAN SIXTIES GARAGE VOL. 1

I saw this record at Domino Sound Record Shack in New Orleans and I would go on different occasions and hold it and look at the cover but never buy it, probably much to the annoyance of the store owner. But I just couldn't bring myself to spend $27 on a single LP! Can you blame me? So, I downloaded this shit online! Yes, I did! And I think it's out of print by now, so I don't feel bad encouraging you to download it, too. There's also a Vol. 2 of this that I haven't checked out yet. And the reason I wasn't sure that I wanted to buy it was that I didn't know if I was gonna get some tripped-out, weirdo Afro-Beat version of garage rock, or if it was gonna be like Africans trying to emulate Nuggets. Well, ladies and gentlemen, I'm glad I saved my $27 because it most definitely is more the latter than the former. I mean, it's a cool record for sure, especially for the garage rock nerds out there. And there are definitely some really special cuts, my favorite being the delicate and mournful "Rien De Mots" from Mozambique. It's also a really interesting document of African rock 'n' roll because most of the vintage African stuff out there is Afro-Beat, Afro-Funk, highlife, etc. But I really wanted to hear African bands putting their own spin on rock 'n' roll in the same way that Fela Kuti put his own original spin on American funk. Besides the stellar "Muato Wa N'Gingila" from Angola and the aforementioned cut, this is more a record of African bands emulating the 60s American rock 'n' roll sound, even singing in English with fake American accents at times! Check it out, but don't pay thirty bucks for it unless yr way into collecting obscure garage rock records.

Purple Rhinestone Eagle
"The Great Return" (Stankhouse)

    Purple Rhinestone Eagle are the new soldiers of the feminist armageddon. "The Great Return" is the soundtrack generated from the explosion and the beautiful aftermath left in its wake. This Portland, Oregon trio use a cornucopia of psych and metal influences and mix them together in a medieval cauldron, the result being a mastery of the psychedelic craft and a fully realized collection of songs and rhythms celebrating the power and sensuality of woman or more importantly, humanity. The influences of Black Sabbath, Flower Traveling Band, "Phallus Dei" era Amon Duul II, and even sprinklings of Pentagram are represented here but only serve to augment a message that is wholly their own. This writer is not one to overemphasize gender but only a few sister bands like Quix*o*tic, Lozen, and Afrirampo come close to the grandeur that PRE are able to conjure, but the Eagles' spectrum of musicality stretch further than even most of their male counterparts.

    The war begins abruptly with the pounding "No Space Nukes", a reference to the recent mining bombs that were sent to the moon. While this song serves as more of a cautionary warning against such atrocities, "Burn It Down" is exponentially more direct and spiteful quotation, as "The Queen of Rain and Grey" will loudly proclaim from her mighty throne. "Scorpio Moon" and "Thirteen Cycles" both twist and turn under the thunder pomp of drummer Ashley Spungen's tribal warcraft and Morgan's mountainous bass pulse, rhythms that straddle the line between oscillating light and black magic dirges. The beautiful cornerstone of this monolith however is "Her Lady Of Forests", featuring guitarist/singer Andrea Genevieve (a POC, y'all!). This song provides a delicate intermission to heavy proceedings and the ballad brims with lyrics filled with renaissance sexiness and a longing for the deepest of loves. Her guitar is gentle and pretty here, but the fight is not over because "Crown Cobra (The Snake Is Awake)" ends the album with yet another demonstration of Andrea's invention, sonicism, and devout tribute to hard rock's guitar masters.

    Overall "The Great Return" is a solid and epic collection of songs and I've been listening to it constantly while I've been on tour overseas. The live experience is equally as exciting and they tour diligently to broadcast their craft. The first time I ever saw them I was playing a show in Philadelphia. They hit the stage and tore the roof off. Immediately afterward I called my friend back in Olympia and described a trio of sorceress amazons that cast a face-melting spell on me. I'm not sayin', I'm just sayin'.-Chris Sutton

ZINE REVIEWS

Ataxia

I want to use the word "basic" when describe this zine, but not to mean "overly-simple" or "boring." This zine is basic as in it shares with the reader the fundamental experiences and ideas behind the black punk experience. It's like Black Punk Rock 101. That kind of basic. There are a few articles about the experience of being the only black kid at a punk show and some very revealing interviews with white folks about their perspective on having to "share their scene" with people of color, but the bulk of the zine is a re-print of the very important *Roctober* article from 2002 called "Black Punk Time: Blacks in Punk, New Wave and Hardcore 1976-1983 (Part 1)" This was one of the only comprehensive resources about blacks in punk before Afro-Punk came about. It's like an encyclopedia for black freaks. Very important stuff. It seems that this zine was published in the mid to late 2000s, but I ordered the zine fairly recently from Stranger Danger zine distro.
Contact: aidan.aberrant@gmail.com

Borders & Margins

Borders and Margins is a collection of imagery, brief poems and prose that expresses its creator's experience of black genderqueer life in the UK. The author breaks with normative illustration and writing tricks in favor of a more seamless collage. A piece of art in itself, Borders and Margins conveys a sense of longing, possibility, and recognition in a world of categories, physical and imagined boundaries. Contact: too_eclectic@hotmail.com (Alix Chapman)

Basic Blac #1 & 2

In Basic Blac, author Kaos Blac offers a cultural critique, imagery, and his own poetic musings. Basic Blac likens to a black punky version of Interview magazine for the zine world. Whereas Kaos admittedly takes a step back, revealing small glimpses of himself he illuminates up and coming cultural work. Basic Blac's themes are consistent but a bit disjointed in presentation and writing style. Contact: bryan.aj.edwards@gmail.com (Alix Chapman)

Hair Stories

Most black women will be able to relate to Sonrisa's "Hair Stories." If you've ever had to explain to a white person that your dreads aren't braids or that your braids aren't dreads, if you've ever had miserable hair disasters after trying to straighten your hair with a hot comb or a chemical perm, if you've ever had someone try to reach out and pet your head without asking as if you're an animal, you'll whole-heartedly relate to this zine. The zine features journal-style entries and photographs of the author (and her very adorable hair) as a baby, toddler, teenager and adult. Contact: shrimpcrime@gmail.com

All zine & record reviews written by Osa unless otherwise noted!

Cocoa/Puss Zine #3
"The Hoes and Heartbreak Issue"
Fall 2009

Price varies based on dick size and degree of fatness. About $4

"It's for you."

Cocoa/Puss #1-4

I had a good time reading these and I hope we can hang someday. In your writing I tasted various versions of your special black mama sauce: the private everyday thoughts of an exhibitionist who wants to be valued for the possibilities of what she can do with her body, the need to justify the pleasure you receive through your pornographic work, and a sensitivity to the mundane. The first four issues of Cocoa/Puss reveal a sharp, indignant, and a bit perverse sort of black femininity and motherhood that got this homiesexual hot and bothered. Keep it cumming. Contact: lamesha4@hotmail.com (Alix Chapman)

If I Could Live in Hope: Sexual Abuse and Survival

I haven't read a zine like this in quite some time, so it was good to revisit this style of zine, especially one written from a black perspective. In this zine, Kisha (same girl who wrote "Public Hair Announcement") reveals a painful past of sexual abuse at the hands of her mother's boyfriend as a child, and a painful present of dealing with her own emotional reality and her family's denial in the aftermath of her abuse. Zines like this are important because they bravely put words to experiences that often go unmentioned. Writing and reading these stories can help decrease shame about abuse and can empower survivors. "If I Could Live in Hope" is brief, well-written and effective. Obviously, the subject matter is sensitive and potentially triggering for some people, so only read this if you're ready. Contact: todayneverhappened@gmail.com

Scorpion #3-6

I am reviewing these zines purely for historical purposes since they are long out of print. I found out about these zines through Ataxia zine and I sent an e-mail to the writer hoping the address still worked and it did! Scorpion zine was made by a black punk girl named Wilona who lived in Washington, DC. Like any zine, Scorpion is a labor of love, very well done, printed on newsprint. There are tons of interviews with the crème de la crème of punk rock: Exene Cervenkova of X, Ian MacKaye, Mark Robinson (Teen Beat Records), and Jem Cohen, for example. She mentions *Book Your Own Fucking Life* in two different issues of her zine, so one can gather that the book was very influential for her. She's obviously steeped in harDCore and an avid Fugazi fan, being from DC, but also (in issue #5) covers international scenes in Puerto Rico, Brazil, South Africa, Indonesia and more. There are personal writings and contributions from other writers as well. I can't believe I didn't know about this zine when I lived in DC! Why don't people put dates in their zines? It drives me crazy! Judging by the contents, I have to imagine that this zine was made in the late 1990s. I wanted to write about it because it's a long lost publication that no one knows ever existed, leading us to believe that there are "no black punk zines" or "no black punks" or whatever. But there are, there were, there always have been! I hope Wilona doesn't get mad at me for saying so, but she has a few back issues and if yr a black punk interested in black punk history, she'd probably send you one if you pay her for postage.
Contact: creativegeniusdc@gmail.com

Thank you for reading

Shotgun Seamstress #5

Thanks to everyone who contributed to this zine: and to my friends and family, namely Senora, Candice, Takiaya, Mom & Dad and my new rad housemates!

Also thanks to the city of New Orleans, LA for much inspiration.

I write columns each month for Maximum RockN Roll: shotgunseamstress.blogspot.com

shotgunseamstress@gmail.com

SHOTGUN SEAMSTRESS FANZINE

NO. 6

for black PUNK rockerz

Shotgun Seamstress is a zine by, for and about Black punks, queers, feminists, artists, musicians & activists.

::CONTENTS::

1. TRASH KIT interview
2. PUNK through the AFRICAN DIASPORA by Diane Enobabor
3. MANIFESTA by Cocoa/Puss
4. MS. JACCI GRESHAM interview
5. CAMPING
6. POLY STYRENE
7. 80's DC HARCORE
   - Shawn Brown
   - Bubba Dupree
8. Conversation with LEAH LAKSHMI PIEPZNA-SAMARASINHA

comic by Donovan Jim Crony

This image and a few others throughout this zine are from a website called "Reclaiming History: An Archive of Black Hardcore & Punk" by David Ensminger

dear READER,

This is the last issue of Shotgun Seamstress zine. I plan to keep all six issues in print as best I can, and to make them available for free online, but I can't envision myself making new issues after this. I finally feel as though I've said everything I want to say about Black Punk identity and experience. In fact, I said everything I needed to say on the topic by the time Issue #2 came out, but at that point there were still so many other bands and individuals I wanted to have the chance to interview or give exposure to through my zine.

I made Shotgun Seamstress a fanzine because I was sick of personal zines and because I wanted to take feminist and people of color zines in a different direction. The late 1990s and early 2000s feminist/POC zine scene was all about venting your anger—figuring out that even though the white punks you hung out with claimed to be on your side, they could still be racist, sexist assholes. This was a productive phase, but by 2006, I felt ready to wrap up the anger & grieving and start celebrating a little bit. I didn't want to write an "It's hard to be a black punk" zine. I wanted to write a zine about why being a Black Punk is the shit.

The first issue of SS was the most personal and the most angry. Even still, it featured only two pieces of writing by me; the rest was interviews and submissions. I always knew that I could express my feelings and ideas through writing about music, books, art, other musicians and artists, and other times and places, and that it would be more interesting and less self-indulgent that way. But what I am discovering now that I'm working on the final issue is that even though the zine wasn't all about me, making it changed my life.

Whatever hangups I had about identifying strongly as both black and punk are long gone. I've proven to myself through six issues worth of examples of black punk rock queerness and freak power that my identity is absolutely normal and I need not question it. It's made me able to function within a white punk rock scene when I need to without hang ups and it's brought more brown punks into my life so that I'm not as isolated as I was before I started writing the zine. It helped me to just accept myself.

The thing is, I still get so excited about punk rock. I talk to so many other brown ex-punks who don't go to punk shows anymore and listen to hip-hop, reggae, R&B and other stuff, and I know that could never be me. I listen to a little bit of everything, but punk music has my heart. My favorite bands are The Slits and The Ex. There's nothing that can change that. On the last tour I went on, after our show in Salt Lake City, we ended up watching *Another State of Mind* in the living room of the house we were staying at that night. It's a movie that documented the totally macho 80s hardcore scene, but still managed to capture the voices of women and a couple of people of color in the scene at the time. It took me a long time to want to sit down and watch this movie, because previously I couldn't deal with how white-boy-hardcore oriented it is. But like my friend Candice says, it's just an honest portrayal of the scene at the time, for better or for worse, and what those few black punk kids, as well of what a lot of those white

kids, had to say in that movie was so affirming to me, even now. Even at the age of 32, I still have these moments where punk still feels so meaningful and important to me, and I feel in love with it.

Anyone who reads my zine knows I'm a feminist and that my approach to punk and DIY culture is deeply influenced by the existence of riot girl, a movement within punk in the 90s where women started bands and created their own feminist DIY culture. Living in New Orleans, and being 32 years old, I feel like I'm one of a tiny minority of people who thinks of punk rock as this wholesome thing. Since moving here, I've had to remember that for some people, punk rock is about being an underachiever. It's about having lower standards for yourself. It's about being drunk, apathetic and depressed. Punk is supposed to be a reaction to regular society, but regular society is drunk, apathetic and depressed, so what does that mean for us? I was exposed to punk in Washington, DC where the punks were serious and political. Punk there, as I saw it, was about holding yourself to higher standards and Keeping Your Eyes Open, i.e. always thinking critically of the world around you. There were lots of straight edge kids, there was Positive Force (punk activist group), there were benefit shows, there were tables at punk shows with the works of Emma Goldman and Angela Davis, and there was Fugazi. Then I moved to Portland where I got dumped directly into this post-riot girl feminist punk community that was all about lots of girls in bands, making your own clothes, lots of vegan and vegetarian food, starting activist groups or joining community organizations, learning about herbs and gardening, biking a lot, being healthier. Sure, Portland has become a horror to my very eyes since that time, but living there made me who I am today.

I still remain convinced that African Americans have so much to benefit from punk mentality: Not buying into consumer culture, not allowing yourself to be defined by your possessions, not defining yourself only by your job or your career, not letting the pursuit of money control your life, allowing yourself to live free and become an artist if you want even if there's not a lot of money in it, creating the change you want to see in your own communities, letting go of homophobia and fucking whoever you want, letting your body be it's natural self, letting your legs be hairy and your hair be nappy! I believe so much in the power of punk to transform people's lives and liberate people, that I can't just leave it to white people. I have to use it to transform my life, and I want to help make it a viable option for other brown kids, too. I really hope that Shotgun Seamstress does that, even if it's for just a handful of people.

Usually, I try to create a cohesive zine, where everything flows together and makes sense. This time there's no theme, it's just all over the place, but still, as always, representing Black Punk experience and identity from 1977 up to today. Thanks so much for reading.

XO Osa   Sept. 2011

TRASH KIT

Trash Kit are from London, England and they play experimental post-punk songs. Rachel Aggs plays guitar & violin and she sings. Rachel Horwood (who was unable to be a part of the interview) plays drums & sings. Ros Murray plays bass & sings. They formed in 2009, put out an LP on Upset the Rhythm records and even toured with Grass Widow!

SS: I'm your #1 fan! Thinking of touring the U.S. at all?

Rachel: Hopefully, yes! Our main focus right now is to record some more stuff but then it would be really cool to tour the US! W're a VERY disorganised band though...

SS: I've admired so many older British punk bands for making sounds that are inspired by reggae, African music, soul music, etc. as well as by punk itself. Trash Kit really embodies that to me. Is it the multiculturalism of London that does it?

Ros: The Raincoats should definitely get a mention here!

Rachel: Listening to what people call 'world music' is something I've always done... Maybe it's to do with being mixed race, maybe it's not.. but looking to other cultures for inspiration seems pretty normal to me. I think all the best (or okay, my favorite) music is stuff that is very aware of all genres especially roots music from different parts of the world. The Slits, The Raincoats, and The Ex are examples of that. But yeah, London has always been a crazily diverse city so its not surprising that we have a rich history of punk and post-punk that's inspired by reggae and other things here. I think London in 2011 still seems disappointingly segregated in terms of music tho,ugh. There's nothing like the crossover there was in the 1970s with punk and in the 1980s with 2tone and post-punk and I've been to a few LOVE MUSIC HATE RACISM shows recently where there were white indie bands that none of the black kids danced to and vice versa... anyway that's a *whole* 'nother question!

SS: Is Trash Kit involved in any way with Ladyfest Ten? There's a video of you playing an event called Gals Rock in London. Tell us what you know about Gals Rock and how you got asked to play that show.

Ros: Gals Rock is in Paris - it's a shop run by a couple of girls called Pauline and Clémence that stocks music, art and clothes made by women. They put on shows as well, and have loads of amazing things in their shop. They are riot-grrrl inspired, and are doing a really great job, especially in France where the mainstream music scene is still very male-dominated and based on being proficient, like everywhere I guess... Also, it's on a street full of macho music shops with guitars decorated with naked ladies in the windows, the sort of places that you would never go into if you were a teenage girl wanting to get into music, so it's really cool that they have all this feminist/queer stuff in a place like that.

SS: You mentioned Red Monkey in your Maximum RockNRoll interview (July 2010 #326). Did you ever see them play? Was the activity around Slampt! (their record label, run by members of the band) something you were aware of at the time?

Ros: I really love Slampt! records. I got into it when I was a teenager living in Oxford in the late 1990s. The music scene there was kind of rubbish; all the bands wanted to sound like Radiohead. There were a couple of girl bands, but it was a really hostile place to be making scrappy DIY music, which is what we were doing. Boys would actually come up to us and tell us to our face that we were shit but it wasn't our fault because girls can't play guitar. So discovering Slampt was quite a revelation. Bands like Avocado Baby, Red Monkey, Milky Wimpshake and Pussycat Trash (who feature Rachel Holboro and Pete Dale who ran the label) and Golden Starlet, who were British riot-grrrl-inspired bands. I discovered Slampt at the same time as Kill Rock Stars and K Records. Slampt had a lot of the same ethics [as those other labels] and it was really important to them to promote local bands (most of the bands were from Newcastle and around there) and to make releases as cheap as possible. They were against doing 'limited edition' pressings, against all forms of elitism and snobbery, they released a lot of stuff on tape, and they did a really amazing zine called 'Fast Connection'. I bought my first Slampt record (the Avocado Baby "A Million and Nine and Sex and Gum and Stuff" LP) simply because *The Avocado Baby* was one of my favourite books as a kid. It's about a baby who eats lots of avocados, gets really strong, and beats up some bullies. And then the LP became the most important record I ever bought. The Rachels were too young to see Slampt bands, I was only just old enough. I saw Red Monkey once in London, it was a kind of 'reunion' gig I guess, although I'm not sure they ever split up. But by the time I was old enough to move to London they'd pretty much stopped playing (from what I heard this was because Rachel of Red Monkey was working on an organic farm and Pete Dale was having babies and being a teacher). So I was really, really happy to get to see them. That was a really exciting gig. I might be wrong, but I think Chris and Claire from Upset the Rhythm's band, Hands on Heads, supported at that show.

SS: Are there any bands, venues or promoters in London that make you feel at home musically? Who are they?

Our favorite promoters and labels are UPSET THE RHYTHM and CLUB MILK and bands like Peepholes, Woolf and Wetdog who are very close friends of ours. We also love lots of bands from out of town like Corey Orbison who are mostly in Bristol and Bellies who have a tape out on Club Milk now which is incredible... London is kind of bad for venues at the moment though. All the nice places keep closing down! Upset The Rhythm are excellent at moving around the town and creating a really great vibe wherever they are but there definitely isn't a scene that exists because of any single venue.

SS: In your MRR interview, there seemed to be a bit of reluctance or unease on your part to claim the label "punk." What's your relationship to that word as a band?

Ros: I felt like I learned what 'punk' really was from Slampt! and Fast Connection. They said it was not necessarily about a style of music but a politic and a way of doing things. So for me there would be no reluctance at all to claim the label "punk". I guess it depends what you're referring to, because there's a different type of punk that's been appropriated by mainstream fashion. I mean you can buy t-shirts that say "punk" written in sequins in Topshop now... but for me it's about making the personal political and the political personal, and as long as you're doing that then you're a punk.

Rachel: I agree with Ros! there was a question about 'punk cred' in the MRR interview and it was suggesting that if you made tuneful music and had music lessons then you couldn't be punk or it would ruin yr 'cred'. I replied by saying "what punk cred?"...I don't want to belong to any label where you have to prove yourself in some way to be part of it... I think it's the nature of punk to be contradictory and confusing, it's a space for weirdos and rejects and people who don't want to be in a scene. But also i was just trying to be funny but probably ended up sounding like a brat!

SS: I think that the power of feminist art, such as your own, is that it creates an atmosphere that reflects your politics and has the ability to change your local scene and the world. What are the specific images, ideas or emotions you wish to convey through Trash Kit?

Ros: I love Rachel's lyrics because they are political but never crass. They never tell you what you're supposed to think or do but I think they're really poetic and beautiful, because they're often so personal, but you can always take them and apply them to your own experience. I guess they're specific without being too specific. I didn't know what they were for the first 6 months or so when I joined Trash Kit cause I couldn't make out what she was saying...

Rachel: Oh that's nice! Thanks, Ros. I think we try to make music that is fresh and sincere and in turn empowering for people who feel the same frustration and boredom, loneliness or longing that we do, especially if you feel like a minority or a freak living in a world where people don't seem to be shouting about the things that matter to you. To me our music is about communicating a kind of alternative head space that's hopeful and proud, while at the same time acknowledging how drab and annoying real life can be. I like singing about things as sincere as coming out as well as things like riding the bus (I really like singing about buses!) Quite a few of our songs don't have lyrics though, but I hope that it's possible to express all this stuff without using words. I feel like you can communicate and create everything you need to with just some weird noises because sometimes, like Ros said, it's not really that specific. I like what you said about feminist art though, I think that's so true! I love this song called "Favorite Sweater" by Y Pants. The lyrics are just about washing your favorite sweater and looking at it hanging on the line but somehow the song is so epic. I think we're yet to write a song that good!

PUNK through the AFRICAN DIASPORA
by Diane Enobabor

DIANE IN RIO DE JANEIRO!

Last Summer, I traveled with my university to take some courses at the State University of Rio de Janeiro and see what life is like for Black Brazilians. Needless to say, just like the experiences of Black people in the States aren't monolithic, neither are theirs. Throughout my many adventures, my awesome beautiful host sister (who was Black) introduced me to many alternative scenes in Rio, including the anarcho-punk scene. I repeat, a young Afro-Brazilian female introduced me to the scene! She saw me wearing a Bad Brains shirt one day and let me that her friends were going to be throwing a seriously good show in a couple of weeks and she was totally down to take me.

That night, we traveled on bus to a neighborhood of Rio De Janeiro (Praça da Bandeira) that was hosting the show. Little did I know, the bar the show was held at, Rua Ceará, has held punk shows since the offset of punk in Rio since the late 1970's. We walked into the outside bar and I saw groups of punk kids and neighborhood kids hanging out and drinking. My suprise was in just seeing all the different colors of punks there: brown, black, white, all hanging out together. Tt was like the punk version of "We Are the World"! In all seriousness, I have never (or do I think I will ever see again) a more diverse group of kids and adults than I saw that night. Old and young, black and white, gay and straight were all there to support bands their friends and families were in.

Seeing all the kids talking about politics and just day to day life, while trying to incoporate me into the coversation with my limited (almost non-existant) Portuguese, made me feel really accepted. They all knew where Texas was (my home state), and we all hated George Bush. However, what really struck me about this group was how socially conciouss they were, and how open they were about talking about issues. There wasn't a sense of taboo when addressing politics or relationships, or whatever, it was all fair game to talk about as long as it was done respectfully.

Seeing as how I was there to study political movements concerening Afro-descedants in Brazil, many of the people that attened that show would ask what exactly I thought was important politically to them, and why I wanted to know in reality. There was a particular person that was very adamant in making sure I knew about what was important to the state of people that lived in the favelas (a favela is a community of small dwellings that are stacked upon each other). To him and many other favelados (a favelado is someone that lives in the favelas) an important topic to consider was the future of the favelas concerening the World Cup in 2014, and the Summer Olympics in 2016.

While I was there in 2010, there was already an increase in state police surivellaince on the streets of Rio, but they also began to include the UPP (Police Pacifiying Unit) in favelas with high rates of violence. The problem with this is what the state intends to 'clean' these favelas- which means an attack on poor people and people of color who may look 'suspicious' of illegal activity. As of last year, there have been numerous police attacks or 'raids' on what are considered notriously dangerous communities such as Complexo do Alemão. This dude also reminded me of the building of 'eco-barriers' which started in 2009 as a way to protect the biodiversity of the environment from the growth of favelas. These 'eco-barriers' are essentially 10 feet walls put up against certain favelas to keep people from building their homes into the biodiversity - but its really meant to enhance the capablities of police surivellaince in their community. Essentially, in the next couple of years many people believe there will be more direct action between the people and the state.

Another thing thats struck my interest were people's punk patches. I mean, you can go all over the world to different punk scenes and you will see patches of Subhumans, Amebix, and even Dead Kennedys on peoples jackets, but political patches and local band patches outweighted the amount of outside band patches I saw. Rio has many problems, as with other industrial cities, but today it feels like people, especially in alternative scenes, are hard pressed to call problems out and discuss it among different people in their scene. I remember seeing this dope patch that basically said, "Stop discrimination to blacks, native peoples, and people from the north" (who are stereotyped as poor) worn by a black person and a white person. I have yet to see patches like that on punk kids here in the States be so blunt, although our problems (race relations and poverty issues) are so bluntly in our face. However, that doesn't mean that their struggle with race is non-existant.

Part of the program was to figure out how we related to others within the African Diaspora, and I think that its easy to say that Black people of all kinds face some sort of discrimination within any society. In Brazil, race is defined through different means than the United States. In the United States, we constitutionally had the one-drop rule which meant that any mixture of black in you meant you were black. On the flipside in Brazil, with the offset of African slavery and indigineous people building Brazil for the Europeans, there was higher racial mixing. What that means in today's society is that because everyone is mixed, its is impossible to discriminate based on race alone. Thus, a "racial democracy" has been created. Unfortunately, this notion is a facade that the state propogates to make Brazil seem absolved of their history of slavery (which ended in 1888) and to create a sense of unique nationalism. There has not been discriminatory laws against Afro-descdents in Brazil unlike the United States where we expereienced Jim Crow. There is racism against people who are darker, and clearly of African descent, but it is negoiated differently. For example, there are hardly any Black models or actors in mainstream advertisments. And there are lower rates of poverty and educational attaintment particular to Afro-brazilians. In fact, the school I attened in Rio was the first University in the State of Rio to embark on affirmative action in 2003.

BRAZIL

PUNKS AT A PUNK SHOW IN RIO!

And admist all of this, Cariocas (people from Rio) are still super friendly and nice to each other. Speaking to that sentiment, I had never been to an anarcho-punk show were the majority of the people were dressed and acted so casually. Yeah, a bunch of kids had their jackets on (I did!), but a lot more didn't, which kind of just made the space seem really open to everyone. One woman that I did meet there was the wife of the drummer of the band (shout out Jorge Roberto!!!), Falência Cerebral. By introducing me to her friends and family members that were at the show, and talking to me about the attractiveness of Will Smith she showed me a much more communal side to the event. It felt like I was at a down south style barbeque!

In all, my experience in Rio was pretty cool, but not perfect. Brazil's struggle with the facade of a racial democracy, and extremities of socioeconomic disparities created a atmosphere that was in constant negiotation for existance and challeged me as a member of the African Diaspora. As we partied on Rua Ceara I couldn't help but notice the high amount of young kids selling drugs around the street and the ridiculous number of police present. And amongst all this chaos, almost everyone found time to stop what they were doing to sing The Smiths "This Charming Man" together. In these upcoming years Rio will find itself in the spotlight for global capitalist events such as the World Cup and the Olympics, and the currently marginalized will find themselves in direct action against the state as it continues to 'clean up' the city. However, as my friend Jorge, the drummer from Falência Cerebral told me (in refrence to communities or favelas that are being attacked by the state), "They say there is more control and safety down there then up here, but I think things up here make more sense."

Bands from Rio to check out: Repressão Social, Lacrau, Falência Cerebral
Scenes to check out: Anarcho-Funk!!!

Diane interviews Ayná (above)

D: Ayná, when did you start listening to punk? Who introduced you to punk?

A: I began listening to punk when I was fourteen with kids that liked to skate, but didn't have much contact with the punk movement, instead they hung around gangs that called themselves punks. The places I hang out now has led to my taste in punk.

D: What are the different types of scenes within the punk movement in Rio?

A: I think the anarcho-punks and gangs are the most pronounced and they don't get along too well. Mainly because the gangs exude machismo, sexism, and other things in closed groups and they have no experience.

D: So, why do you think your scene is diverse (students, community activists, travelers)?

A: Yeah, for sure it is diverse, but I think the difference in the scene is due to the lack of the bourgeoisie in our space, because we do have some that say they like the sound, but I think the majority of the movement here is made up of the lower class. And having different backgrounds is very good, too!

D: How does it feel to be a Black woman in your scene?

A: Its rare! I also know stories of other women like me that have stuck with the movement too, but we do have black women, but not as much as other scenes that also have music I believe supports militancy. For example, other revolutionary genres—Funk (Baile Funk) was revolutionary, but it was muted for its call to sabotage the government. But I think that any person that has made music against the state, against religious "scientific" observations, I consider that person to be punk. All the same, I don't have a vision or stake within the movement, because that isn't punk. I by chance, also perform anarcho-funk!

D: Do you feel like you are in solidarity with punks outside of Rio?
A: Of course!

D: Where do the best punk shows happen in Rio?
A: There isn't really a best place for shows. I think the best place would be outside of everything, but that really can't happen right?

D: What are your favorite bands in Rio?

A: Well, I don't believe in regional classifications like "Rio" because I don't believe in military borders. But, to answer your question, bands like Mercenaries, Operation 81, Istinto Suicide, and others like that, but I also like playing anarcho-funk. Of course, you have to search the internet to get most of it here, I think that there is more out there. There are other musicians that could be considered punk too, like the psychedelic theater band, Ave Sangria.

D: What are your favorite bands outside Rio?
A: Can't answer that directly because Rio De Janeiro doesn't exist.

D: If there was one thing you could change in your scene what would it be?
A: Everybody could soon be social libertarians (social anarchists) without it we will always have money and, fights, (social) injustices and evil and everything else that sucks.

Diane Enobabor is a Nigerian-American feminist punk who lives in Austin, Texas and attends the University of Texas at Austin. Contact her at odenobabor@gmail.com.

MANIFESTA

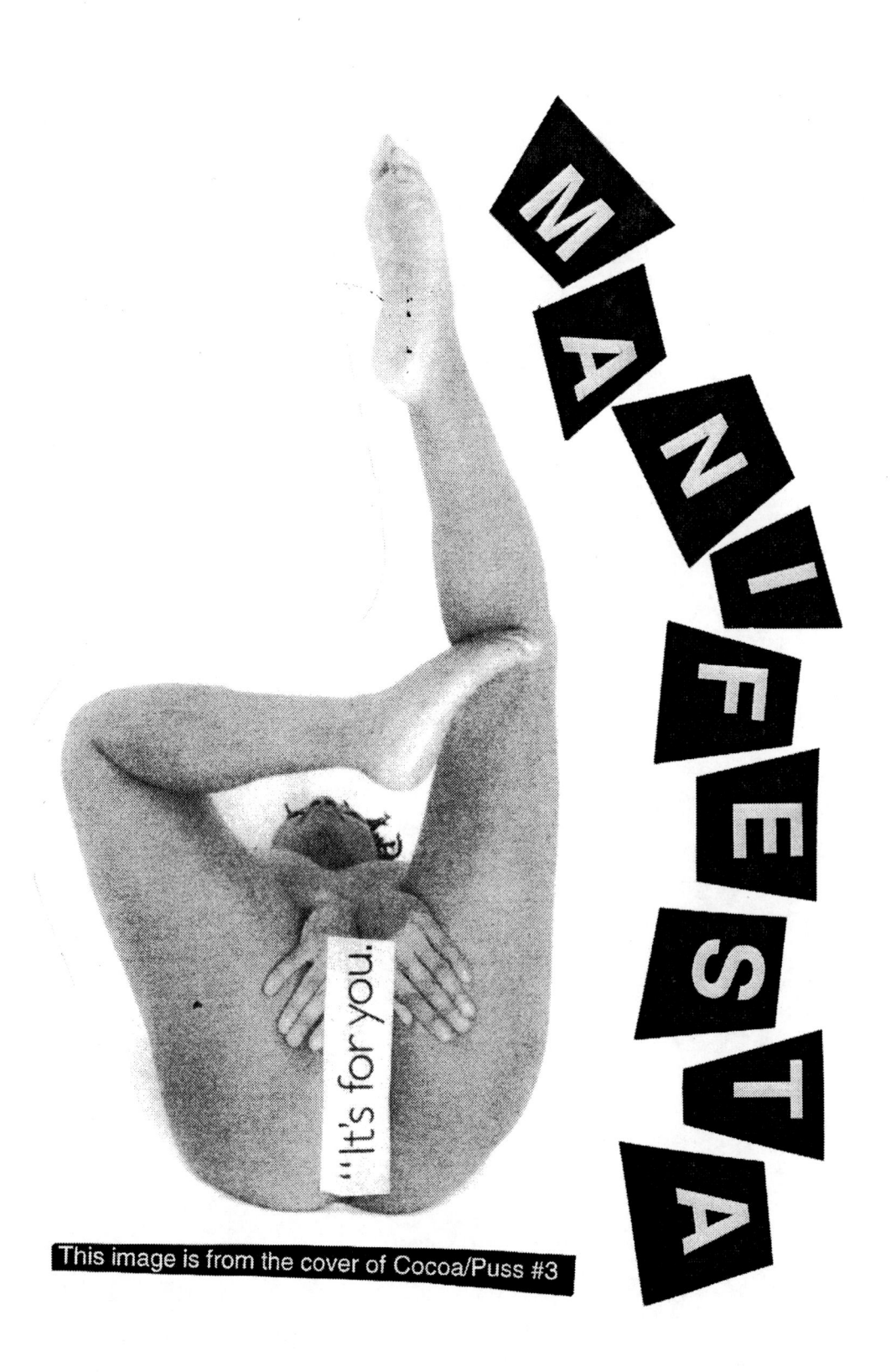

"It's for you.

This image is from the cover of Cocoa/Puss #3

I know you are black like me and you are afraid of being called loud and ghetto and big and black.

I know you were told to put a longer nightgown on when your uncle came over and you had to hold your ear back when you got your hair pressed and your biggest fear is getting your hair wet or swimming but I just want you to know that you can't be afraid to riot. Just because of, and despite all these things, you just have to do it anyway. Don't let your fear or your grandma's fear of you getting pregnant or people not being afraid to pronounce your name or your black skin or your big ass (or anger at not having a big black ass) keep you from being your true self. Even if you are the only black person or black woman or woman or whatever.

Here you are.

You don't have to be a few pages in the feminist book. Demand to be the whole damn book. Write your own. Challenge other feminists. Get loud. Swear. Drink 40s. Dance. Fuck who you want. Get your rent paid. Be mad. BE happy. Be sexy. You do not have national geographic boobs, your baby is not a soldier for the movement, your job is not to make food for pastors and deacons who demand your silence, your dress can be short or long. Hell you can wear pants if you want to. Or you can be naked.

Fuck western beauty standards.

Be proud of your naps. Be proud of your skin. Your rhythm. Question the meaning of "lady like". Have three boyfriends. Fuck two of them in one day, tell the other you are bleeding, or vice versa. Carry your own condoms. Have a favorite flavor. Do every fucking thing you want to do that people told you not to do or warned against because you are female because you are black and because you are both.

Or simply take a nap. You've been trying to live up to the myth of the strong black woman your whole entire life. You must be exhausted. It's a myth you know. You can cry, admit weakness, ask for help or play the damsel in distress role if you want to. Being strong all the time is not something to be proud of. No need to wear it like a badge of honor. It's OK to take a break. Your kids will be fine. Your man will be fine probably but he may whine more than the kids do. And if nobody is fine, too fucking bad. **You are the most important person**. Riot. Rest. Scream. Think. Read. Fuck. Get your pussy ate. Demand chocolate. Kick his sorry ass out. Collect child support. Pass go.

Repeat Repeat Repeat.

Cocoa/Puss has been making zines for about two or three years. She has been on the cover of *Hip Mama* magazine and has written for many other feminist, riot grrrl zines. She is a mother, has an advanced degree, and hates wearing pants. If you say anything bad about Lady Gaga on Facebook she will un-friend you. Contact: Lamesha4@gmail.com Buy zines: www.cocoapuss.etsy.com

Ms. Jacci Gresham

Jacci Gresham just may be the only black woman in the country to own her very own tattoo shop. Certainly, when she got into the tattoo industry in the mid-1970's, she was the only one in the business. This is her story.

SS: I don't have any particular interview questions, I just want you to tell the whole story of how you came to be a tattooist and a shop owner in New Orleans.

JG: What kinda interview is that?!

SS: Well, you can just tell your story, you know, start from the first tattoo shop you opened in New Orleans.

JG: You're gonna have to put all of this together. The first tattoo shop that I started out with was this one right here. It was just one room and there was an apartment in it. And then I stayed here for about two or three years. I think the most interesting thing you wanna know about that is when I first opened up this tattoo shop, I didn't know how to tattoo. I was taught to tattoo and I didn't *have* a tattoo until two or three years out. I feel like everyone should have a tattoo that tattoos. You learn a lot. It's nothing to sacrifice your body to learn to give to thousands of others. But I did not have a tattoo until about 1979, and the first year, all I did was color in tattoos. I didn't actually do a complete tattoo until much later.

SS: Okay, so if you didn't know how to tattoo then how'd you end up owning a tattoo shop?

JG: My business partner had a tattoo shop, and the wages were so low down here, that we wanted to start our own business.

SS: So that was when? 1977?

JG: That was '76. March of '76.

SS: And you said it was this location right here?

JG: Yeah, this same building.

SS: Okay, the reason I'm asking about the location is because when I first met Todd and Christine [*employee & employee's girlfriend, respectively*], they were telling me some story about how maybe you had a shop in the French Quarter...

JG: Well, that was *after*. We started right here, and at that time there were two or three tattoo shops in this whole town. There was one on Dauphine, there was one on St. Claude and there was this one. We had driven down South to look around because both of us had been laid of from General Motors so we were looking for a place to work. He had the skills, but I didn't. I had an architectural background.

SS: Where are you from originally?

JG: I'm from Michigan. [Starts yelling out to a friend or customer she knows.] Check out this tattoo! I just got it! A little ashy, but I just got it.

Customer: You just got it?

JG: Six months ago, but that's a just for me!

Customer: How did it feel getting it on your leg?

JG: Not bad!

Customer: How long did it take?

JG: Six hours. I *am* 64 years old and I was 63 and 9/10 when I got this one.

Customer: Do you have any on your back?

JG: No. I'm not doin' no tattoos where I can't see 'em. Check this one out. That's my tribute to 9-11. See that? The girl giving the world the finger.

Customer: Wow, that had to hurt.

JG: No... That didn't hurt *really*. Check this one out. This is one of my favorites. The little girl with her mom. That reminds me of me. I actually stopped getting tattoos for a while. I got these tattoos from 30 to 40 and then I didn't get any more tattoos till my mid-50s. Young kids are always whining, but I gotta show 'em, old people —we got this. And we can do it right. Okay, back to you. I'm from Flint, Michigan and I moved out here in 1976 and learned to tattoo through my partner who was from Portsmouth, England. He'd had a shop over there, but I didn't realize it until a few years after I'd met him. He'd be drawing pictures for little kids of hearts and eagles and banners and stuff, and I didn't know *why*. In Detroit the economy was bad. We both got laid off around 1970, so we were both on unemployment and so that's how we both got back into the tattoo business. Originally, when we opened this shop, all the flash in there was hand drawn. Not this store-bought garbage that people have now— including me! But, back in the old days everyone had to draw. Nowadays, you can just copy what's on there. But if you just copy what's on most of this flash, it won't hold up. You need to really know how to draw, I think. But so, I was here and left and went to the West Bank and had my own shop on my own for about two years. And then I came back to this shop. I've been in this town since 1976.

SS: So how did all of that drama happen with getting kicked out of the Quarter and all that?

JG: What happened with the Quarter was there was a tattoo shop that was a bike club and somebody fire bombed that bike club.

SS: Do you remember what it was called?

JG: Uh, I can't remember what the name of the shop was...

SS: Do you remember what street it was on?

JG: It was on Dauphine & St. Louis, and it was just a little house. And back then, people didn't sterilize like they sterilize now. I can remember they had a bowl of water and the tattoo gun was on a rubber band, and they'd bring it down and rinse it out, and go like that from one customer to the next.

No alcohol, no nothin'. I remember that. See back then, usually, a little bit of a rougher crowd got tattoos than the people getting them now, you know what I'm saying? I mean, now, everyone gets tattoos. It's almost like a *must*. But the thing was, back then, let me tell you, I was legendary in prison. Half of the people I worked with went to prison. It's not like that now. Now, you get a whole bunch of professional people, you get older people. And I'll tell you, it's more artistic than it was then. Because then... You see, like the work you got...?

SS: Yeah, but this is crazy. I let everyone tattoo me. Even people who don't know how to tattoo. I did these stick and poke...

JG: See, I don't do that. No, I don't do that. A lot of people do that. I wanna write a book on why people do that because I ain't figured that out. Because I figure, I *need* the best, especially since I've gotten older.

SS: Well, that also makes sense since you're in the business...

JG: But like I'm saying back then, tattooing wasn't as artistic. Stuff like that, back in the day, you could get it, but you couldn't get it all of the time. Especially, back then, I could count the number of black people who got tattoos *in a year* on one hand. But people like Aaron Neville and folks like that always had hand-stuck tattoos. In the South, black people have always had tattoos.

SS: What kind of style did they like back then?

JG: In New Orleans, what I notice most is names. Like it proves something. And let me know tell you, names have paid for that car, paid for a truck, paid for 40 acres out there in Mississippi. Names. Nothing else. And I don't think people even think about it because that name of your boyfriend will be there forever, but the relationship probably won't be. But I'm telling you, that's what's paid me. We used to have a name day on St. Claude and there were so many people trying to get names, you had to take a number. That was probably 90% of the work we did. But the good thing is, if they come to you to get that name, they'll probably come right back to you to get the coverup. [*We laugh.*] People are so naïve they think you can just remove a tattoo, and you can but it'll leave a scar. So, which do you want? The tattoo or the scar? I mean, like this piece is a very nice piece. [*Touching the Afro pick tattoo on my forearm.*] I don't know who did it, but it's a nice piece.

SS: This woman named Annie Danger who lives in the Bay Area.

JG: They did a good piece.

SS: Thanks, so back to the bike club on Dauphine.

JG: Okay, so you're talking about in the early 1980s when all of that got fire bombed. And that is still, to my knowledge, illegal to open up a tattoo shop in the Quarter, per se.

SS: Well, that was what I've been trying to get at, because people like to say that your shop was the reason for that. Is that true?

JG: Mmm mm. In the old days, the center of that street [*pointing to Rampart*] was the edge of the Quarter and I was never in the Quarter. No, I don't have any moratorium or any pull or anything like that.

SS: So, how'd that story get started?

JG: I don't know. 'Cause people are too young to know, I imagine.

SS: Did they ever figure out the cause of the fire or why it happened?

JG: No, everything is hearsay.

SS: So, one fire happened at one tattoo shop and they banned tattoo shops in the Quarter? A fire just happened at Verti Mart and they're not trying to ban corner stores in the Quarter.

JG: Right. I don't know what the reasoning is, but we can't be inside the French Quarter. We can be on the edge, but not in the center of it.

SS: Alright, well let me show you this real quick. *[I pull out a copy of* Bodies of Subversion: A Secret History of Women and Tattoo *by Margot Mifflin.]*

JG: I've seen that. That's an old book.

SS: Yeah. Remember this lady? *[Laura Lee, more on her next page.]*

JG: Yeah, of course. I did all this work on her. This girl killed her self, with her stupid ass.

SS: Really?

JG: Her mother was a doctor. I did *[she's pointing at the Laura's tattoos in the picture]* this, this... uh, Jack Rudy did this. I did one like it, but it couldn't touch Jack Rudy's. I did quite a bit of work on her. This girl was strange and I'ma tell you why I say she was strange. When I started working on her, all she wanted was skulls.

SS: Yeah. She's quoted in this book as saying that she wanted to get a skull tattooed for every person who died in the trans-Atlantic slave trade.

JG: Uh huh. She's a good lookin' girl to me. A good lookin' little gay girl and what would blow me away about her the most was she got upset when people stared at her. Now, come on...

SS: Well, this was in the 80s, right?

JG: Yes it was, mid-80s.

SS: Well, a lot of people look like this now, but not back then.

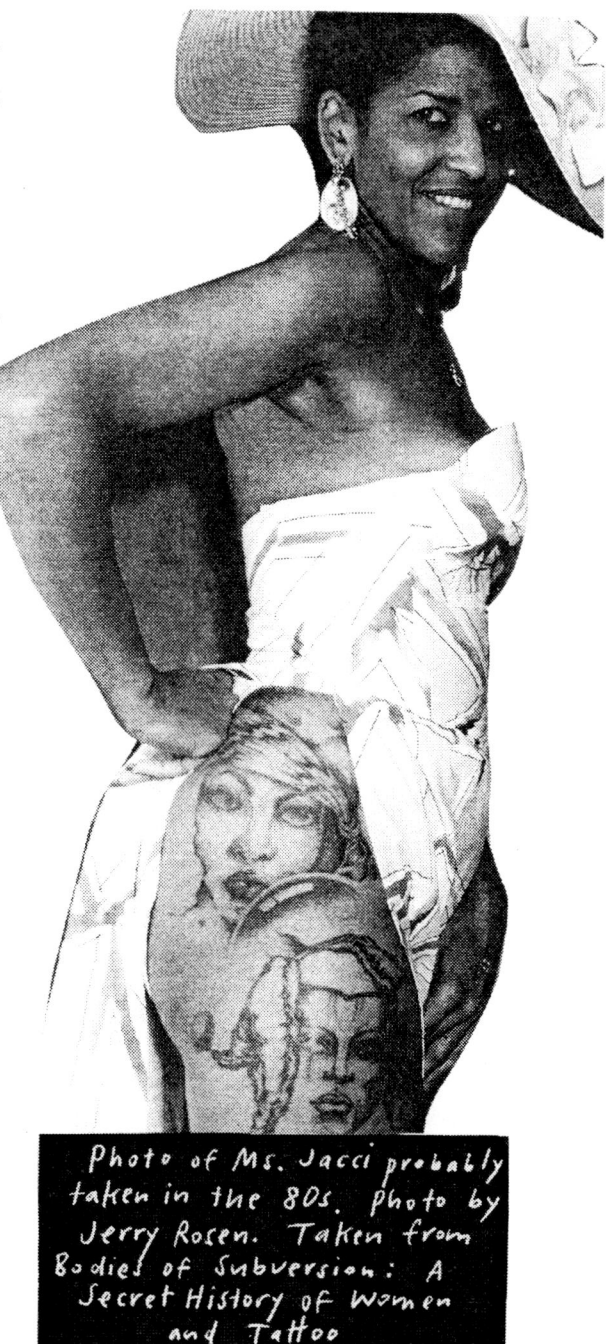

Photo of Ms. Jacci probably taken in the 80s. Photo by Jerry Rosen. Taken from Bodies of Subversion: A Secret History of Women and Tattoo

JG: And see how she had her hair shaved and bleached out? You know... you know, when I do stuff like that, part of it is so I'm talking to people. So people will come up to you. But she didn't like that at all. I still got the sweater her mother knitted for me. They were from Detroit and her mother got busted for writing [*false prescriptions for*] pills or something and then when they put her in jail—Laura was mad at her for going to jail. [*She laughs.*] But I used to let her trade and barter for tattoo work. But, like I said, the thing to me that was strangest about her was she just didn't like people—come on, now, back in the mid-70s if you walked around looking like this, everybody's gonna stare at you, you know? I must've been 35-40 when I did her work and we would do it late nights so nobody would disturb me. We'd do it twelve till 6 o'clock in the morning.

SS: **Do you know where she worked?**

JG: She didn't work.

SS: **So how could she afford to get tattooed?**

JG: Her mother was a doctor! But, when I worked on her, a lot of the stuff I did was bartering, like big expensive cameras. She was into photography and stuff like that. She obviously got depressed at times. I had a house on St. Claude in the 9th ward and she would come down to New Orleans—have you ever come to New Orleans and not left the house?

SS: **No. It's all about being outside here, you know.**

JG: Right. She was relatively shy as far as talking to people, but to me, to get a tattoo is because you *are* gonna talk to people.

SS: **Yeah, but I guess I can relate. I don't want people always asking me questions or strangers touching me because I have tattoos, but sometimes it's fine. Just depends on the situation. Not everyone likes that.**

JG: Well, then don't get a tattoo. [*We're laughing.*] Don't look like this. [*She points to Laura Lee's picture.*] I have youngsters stop me in the store, "Man, I love your tattoos. What're old people doing with tattoos like that?" No problem, let me give you a card! If you get tattoos like this, normally, you want people to talk to you. For sure, like you with this piece [*my Afro-pick*]. To me, this would be a conversation piece.

SS: **Yeah, people ask me about it and I don't mind.**

JG: And it's flattering. I would think that you chose the right thing, you know what I mean? But this litter girl—oh, she'd be so pissed if people were staring at her! But I couldn't care less; I do everything for people to stare at me.

SS: **How old was she right here, do you think?**

JG: She was probably in her late 20s, I think. I couldn't believe she killed herself. That was not too smart.

SS: **Do you think it had to do with being gay?**

JG: I think it had to do with a lot of things. Being depressed. Her mother had her spoiled, but when she went to prison, it was a different story. Laura felt it was very selfish of her mother.

SS: **Was her dad around?**

JG: She never mentioned her dad, but she always talked about her mother and she talked about how selfish it was that her mother went to prison and left her, and stuff like that. And maybe she's got a point, but she was grown when it happened. And she was almost one of these little punk rock kids? You could *see* it. But she definitely loved tattoos.

> Until her death in the early '90s, Laura Lee was the only well-known black woman collector to travel the convention circuit. Lee got much of her work from Gresham, including one of two Malcolm X portraits she wore on her leg (the other was by portraitist Jack Rudy). "She was ahead of her time," says Gresham. "She was getting total coverage before other women did, especially black women. I tattooed most of her body and talked he into getting the African-American pride stuff." Lee also wore an ever-increasing collection of skulls; she said she ultimately wanted to have a skull for every victim of the black holocaust, in which untold numbers of Africans died on slave journeys from Africa to America.
>
> BODIES OF SUBVERSION

SS: She found you through just coming by the shop?

JG: No, she found me through a tattoo convention down here.

SS: You used to go to a lot of those conventions, right? You still do?

JG: I'm getting ready to go back. Mainly 'cause everyone thinks I'm dead, or they're hoping I'm dead. One of the two, you know. Let me tell you, as far as a *black person* in the industry, I think that people resent this. Tattooing has been a white industry for*ever*.

SS: And predominantly male, too.

JG: Predominantly male, but the women are doing a good job coming in. What I like about women working more is that the care about what they do. They're more sensitive. I met so many people who all they talk about is the dollar—get 'em in and get 'em out. They don't care. I see people right here and they get on my nerves. I was trying to have a Happy Hour where you can come in and get a free little design. But what was happening was people

211

stencil the free design! You oughta be able to free hand that. I want it to be an art design. But most of the time, I'm working with men, and like I said, when I'm working with women, they seem to put a little more into it. At the time when I came along, what made me as successful as I have been is caring about what it is I'm doing. That people feel that extra mile. Other people just do it. Also, I'll tell you another thing. When I'm working, I'm working with these people I like to critique their work. They say I like to complain, but you can call it what you want. I want you to do the best job you can do. You have to adapt your work to your client. With the variety of different clients we have today and the variety of skin tones, you can't just pull something off a wall. You have to adapt to your client. A lot of people don't see that. I feel that a lot of these youngsters, they just work from the time they come in till the time they leave, meaning they don't draw, they don't try to promote themselves, they're not enthusiastic. Well, if you draw something that you're excited about, I want you to get to get paid something, but you don't have to get paid what it's worth because you're excited about it, you drew it and you want to see it on skin. It kills me when people come in here and pick something off the wall. With me being older, I can still tattoo, but I have to have an interest in it. I need to see that there's an artistic concept to your design.

SS: So, is it a policy that you hire people who can draw original stuff?

JG: No, that's not a policy. I hire people who are trying to do better, you know, because I can always stick people in certain time slots. You can do the little lick 'em stick 'em tattoos and then I got someone over here than can do the artistic ones.

SS: Do you have any female tattooists right now?

JG: No, I do not.

SS: How many women applicants do you get?

JG: Not many. And I don't know why that is. There's a black girl on Broad Ave. who's tattooing right now. She might be about 28 or 29. She's a bit arrogant for me, and her work is just so-so. She's young. But let me tell you, her lettering and her graffiti is bad ass. But with some of the other stuff, she could apply herself and be better as an artist and I imagine she will get there. But I'm trying to think of women tattooists in this town. If there's ten women who tattoo in this town, I'd be surprised.

SS: What about at the conventions?

JG: Yeah, they have an all-women's convention in Florida in January, but I noticed that the last time I went, which was about three years ago, they also had men there. See, that's what I'm talking about

—that old *dollar,* you know what I'm talking about? The dollar is the rule. I was kind of disgusted because the all women's convention had been that way for years, but obviously not enough women had applied, and so they let men in.

SS: Was it still majority women, at least?

JG: Yes. Yes, it was. When I first came into the scene, you could count women tattooists nationally on one hand. And the only way you got in was you had to be someone's old lady. And they were training *you* to work with *them* so they didn't have to hire anybody else. A lot of women now are on their own. After this shop, I opened a couple of shops on my own, but then again, I'm back at this one, you see? [*Her phone starts ringing.*] Let me see who this is. Mammogram. You know, when you get older you get all these tits! You don't know yet, but you will. [*Raises voice to a yell.*] I was flat chested when I was here! I used to jog to Broad with no bra on, all the way to City Park. When I turned 30 I used to jog. If I tried to do that now, I'd kill myself within the first block. Anyway, I did get a mammogram and it's okay, they said. I was kinda concerned and they made me take it twice.

SS: That's good.

JG: Yeah, for today. But it is good... today.

SS: So, how long do you see yourself staying in the tattoo business?

JG: I see myself promoting tattoos for life. Normally, my car has tattoos on the side of it. My job at this point is to promote people getting good work. I know a lot of people get tattoos and they practice on themselves. I could never do that. I flew all over the country to get this leg done, to the best artist in the business at the time. But then again, I was learning. And because I was a woman, to tell you the truth, they gave me a break. That had to be it, because back then, black people weren't tattooing. You didn't see black people come into tattooing until the mid 1990s.

SS: What changed in the 90s?

JG: What I think what's gotten more people to get tattoos is more black entertainers and athletes getting them.

SS: What about gang tattoos?

JG: That may have been part of it, but I know so little about gangs.

SS: I was just talking to this guy today who told me he was a gang banger and he had one of those little tear drop tattoos on his face.

JG: The teardrop, back when I knew it, was from when someone had killed somebody. But I think that athletes and entertainers have made tattoos more acceptable to black people in general. But these days, you know, black people want to be as good as any other race, so people see it as a status thing.

SS: If that's true, that's a strange flip because before tattooing maybe took away from a person's status instead of adding to it.

JG: Yeah, you were like a stripper or a street person. But now, it's like somethin' ain't right if you *don't* have a tattoo. Everybody has one.

SS: At least you know you'll always be in business.

JG: We thought years ago that tattooing was going to die out. But black people, Latin people started getting tattoos, so it accelerated business back up. And women started getting tattooed. For a long time women would just get a little something on the ankle, something subtle. And now, it's accepted more as an artform. I can't get over how many people nowadays have full sleeves.

SS: Oh, I was going to ask you if you do other kinds of art, like if you paint or anything.

JG: I have, but I don't do it now. I used to do it. I've got airbrushes and stuff like that. But tattooing is my main focus now. Reason number one is that I live 50 miles from here. I have to do two hours of driving to come to work. Back in the old days, I lived three miles up this road. It does make a difference. And I've gotten older. Eventually, I'd like to write a book. Because I feel that they're not giving black people the recognition we should have within the tattooing industry. There's a lot of great work out there that's not being shown. See, and then there's tattoo artists that just don't understand tattooing black skin. Like this piece right here [*she points to her own tattoo*] is an Ed Hardy piece from 1979. But the problem with it is that there's too much detail in a small amount of space. On brown people, big and simple is the best.

SS: But that's a thirty year old tattoo. You can still see the detail. That's not bad. Did being a tattoo artist make it possible for you to travel a lot?

JG: No, I just like to travel. I've been to Italy, India, China. I haven't been traveling like I used to, though.

SS: How serious are you about this book?

JG: I'm gonna get serious about it because I want to see people get better tattoos. You do have to be concerned about the price, but I would really like to see people being more particular about what's going on their bodies.

* Go find Ms. Jacci at her shop **Aart Accent** on Rampart! *

had plans to make a feminism themed issue of SS, but I never did. I asked Vaginal Creme Davis to write something for it & she sent me this.

Winter, 2009
11:30 Berlin

Dearest

When my mother died in 2000 my elder sister Teresa Ray, casually mentioned that in the late 1960s and early 1970s my mother was involved in a gang of women who robbed banks in order to establish a feminist enclave somewhere in Palestine.
Thy mother, Mary Magdalene Duplantier

was the youngest woman child in Creole Louisiana family. My mother had dark curly hair and captain blue eyes but almost would turn violet in certain light. She hated her eye-color and never allowed any one to take a photo of her. I have absolutely no photos of my mother. I have nine years since she died and I'm beginning to forget what she looked like. Her old sister, my Aunt Florence is still alive and

lives in Jersey City, New Jersey. She is almost 100 years old and has bright green eyes. My Aunt helped Lavender some of the bank robbery loot. It was too young to be aware I say of this activity. It is I think of my mother as a revenge agent. She would clean houses in a dress, high heels and a string of pearls. From what I have learned through my sister, my mother was a barracuda femme top who ruled an army of proper butch women who were committed to creating a feminist separatist state.

Vaginal Davis

CAMPING #3
remember tonight
created by donovan vim crony

FYI, I'm singing about heartache...
I'LL LAUGH WITH YOU WHEN I GET HOME, BUT YOU'RE NOT THERE. NO, YOU'RE NOT THERE.
SO REAL
We played ten songs in ten minutes.
Fuck, I was so scared...

Hey, Casey!
CRUCIAL MOMENT
Huh? Lydia! How are you? Thanks for coming out tonight.
I wouldn't have missed your show for anything in the world! I'm so proud of you.
CRUCIAL MOMENT
That's the first time I've heard you sing. You're so awesome!
CRUCIAL
Really? Thanks. I was so nervous singing in front of *everyone.*
C'mon, I think **PROVOKE** is about to start. This is a night that no one will *ever* forget.
You think so?

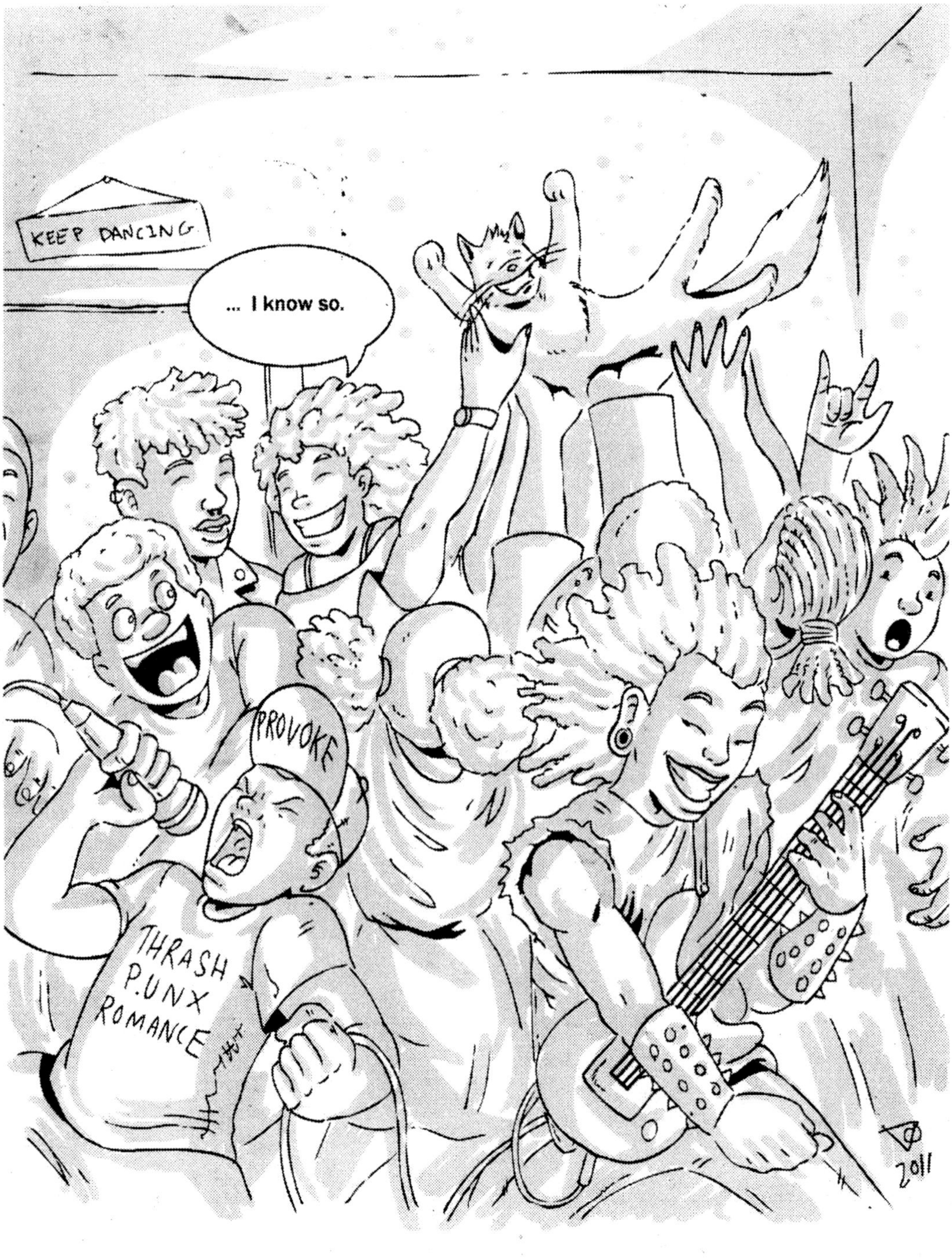
KEEP DANCING
... I know so.
PROVOKE
THRASH
P.UNX
ROMANCE
2011

ROCK against RACISM with

POLY STYRENE

X-Ray Spex

You already know all about her. She started a legendary punk rock band in the late 1970s in London when she was a teenager and inspired generations of vocalists—from Kathleen Hanna to Beth Ditto—with her powerful voice and timeless lyrics. She was indeed the Captain of the Brown Underground, and I feel lucky to have gotten the chance to interview her before she died earlier this year.

SS: Briefly, what were the political circumstances in society, in the music industry and in punk rock that lead to the creation of the first Rock Against Racism concert in 1976?

PS: In 1976 Punk Rock was considered outrageous and a dangerous youth movement by the Establishment, the music industry was shaken up by Punk Rock Music & racism was rearing it's ugly head with fascist right wing political groups calling for the repatriation of all foreigners. Rock Against Racism came along as a breath of fresh air and many Punk Rock bands played at their events including X-ray Spex.

SS: Did you or any friends of yours suffer any attacks as a punk or person of color during that time?

PS: Some of my friends were attacked for being Punk Rockers I never was physically but I got some negative press as a punk rocker and some verbal abuse on the street for my skin tone.

SS: Who were the main organizers of Rock Against Racism and are they the same group that organized Rock Against Racism's 30th Anniversary show?

PS: I remember a guy called Red Saunders as being one of the main organisers and was still involved with the Anniversary show 30 years later.

SS: How did it feel to be a part of this event? What was the audience like? Any favorite moments?

PS: It was a great historical event it felt really great to be up there fighting with music against racism. I remember revealing a shaved head to the audience I shaved my hair off in sympathy for Jewish women who were raped in concentration camps during the second world war.

SS: What was your involvement in punk outside of X-Ray Spex?

PS: I just hung out at most early Punk Rock shows and met lots of other Punk band members.

SS: What was your social life like at the time that X-Ray Spex started? What types of people did you hang around, or were you mostly a loner? Where, if it all, did you find community?

PS: I had a great social life I was invited to lots of party's and gigs I hung out with a girl called Mad Mary and we lived just off the Kings Road in Chelsea we knew lots of people in the neighbourhood.

SS: I'm assuming the punk scene then was predominantly white, just like most punk scenes are now. Did that ever bother you at the time? Did you ever feel isolated on the basis of race? Why or why not?

PS: Yes, that is true, but I never felt isolated because of race as I had grown up in a mostly white family, I was aware that I looked a bit different but I thought that made me more exotic and I grew up in a predominately Afro-Caribean neighbourhood so felt at home in any racial situation.

SS: How did you find out about punk rock in the first place?

PS: Through a friend called Jon Savage who latter wrote the book England's Dreaming. Jon took me to the Roxy and to see the Clash in my local Town Hall.

SS: It can be easy for girls and young women to fall prey to all of the marketing geared toward us. What made you so critical of consumerism at such a young age?

PS: I don't think I was that critical but just wrote songs about consumerism as I felt society expected girls to look and behave in a certain way that seemed a bit corny especially in marketing girl orientated products.

SS: People often confuse fashion with consumerism, but you can definitely be fashionable in a DIY sense without being a rabid shopper. What inspired the one-of-a-kind fashion you sported as the lead singer of X-Ray Spex?

When you look in the mirror, do you see yourself, do you see yourself on the TV screen? Do you see yourself in the magazine? When you see yourself does it make you scream?

PS: I think I was inspired to be creative with clothes and fashion due to having a low budget available to me. I also used to make jewelery out of sink chain and plastic tubing from the DIY store as I thought it was a fun thing to do and it looked quite futuristic.

SS: What personal experiences inspired the lyrics in the song "Identity"?

PS: I was inspired to write Identity after seeing a teenage girl called Tracey who was a sales assistant for Vivienne Westwood slashing her wrist in the Ladies toilets at the Roxy Club in Covent Garden. Sadly Tracey later died of a drug overdose.

SS: I always assumed the song was about your own experience as a woman or mixed race person in society or in punk rock. What do you think the issue of identity had to do with Tracey's attempted suicide?

PS: No, Identity wasn't a personal angst song, but Tracey brought it home to me as a young woman trying to be cool playing around with drugs and identifying with the dark side of life rather than the positives that she could have identified with. I thought it was a tragedy that here was this beautiful young girl who was so desperate to be a punk and fit into a sub culture that she would go to any lengths and even public displays of self harm.

SS: "Oh Bondage, Up Yours" has become somewhat of a feminist punk rock anthem. Did you identify as a feminist at the time the song was written? Do you now? Why or why not?

PS: At the time of Oh Bondage Up Yours I didn't think I was a feminist I didn't think it mattered what sex you were, but as I have got older I realise there are a lot of injustices in society and women bare the brunt of some of them. I wouldn't call myself an active feminist but I do believe in equal rights for women as women still earn less money in the work place than their male counterparts here in the UK.

SS: I was a bit surprised at the way you were portrayed in Don Letts' book Culture Clash: Dread Meets Punk Rockers. Have you read his book? If so, I wanted to give you a chance to respond to that portrayal if you wish.

PS: I haven't read Don's book so have no idea how I was portrayed.

SS: How did it feel to be part of Rock Against Racism's 30th anniversary concert, especially having been a part of the first one?

PS: It was great to be part of the 30th anniversary of Rock Against Racism, I was very surprised how many people knew the words to Oh Bondage Up Yours I really wasn't expecting that as I sang it so long ago.

SS: How do you feel about the way racism has changed since 1976, or do you think it has? You can speak from personal experience, or about society in general, or both.

PS: I think it has changed tremendously you have a dual heritage President of the United States for one thing and we have a Afro-Carribean female running for leadership of the Labour Party here in the UK. This would have been unimaginable in 1976. However, there are still racists that want all the immigrants to go back to their Countries of origin so there is still a way to go.

SS: What are your current musical or artistic projects?

PS: I have just finished a new album called Generation Indigo I was collaborating with Youth from Killing Joke who was the producer and arranger he was great to work with it is a solo album as if I had done it as X-ray Spex would have had to stick to a certain sound. I have also been co-writing a screenplay that is going to be sent a well known producer in Hollywood.

Is there anything BRONTEZ PURNELL can't do?

Brontez Purnell, who you ought to be familiar with either through this zine, his monthly Maximum RockNRoll columns, his zine *Fag School* or his band The Younger Lovers has yet another thing going on. His newest project is the Brontez Purnell Dance Company and their debut performance happened this past winter at the Berkeley Art Museum. Brontez has been holding dance classes at the warehouse he lives at in Oakland and he makes it clear that you don't have to be a trained dancer to attend. You just have to want to move your body. He's enlisted the people he sees at punk shows to be a part of his dance company and with his idea, he takes the DIY and punk modus operandi into a whole new realm. Look for his video FREE JAZZ on Youtube and be inspired to move your body, too.

80's DC

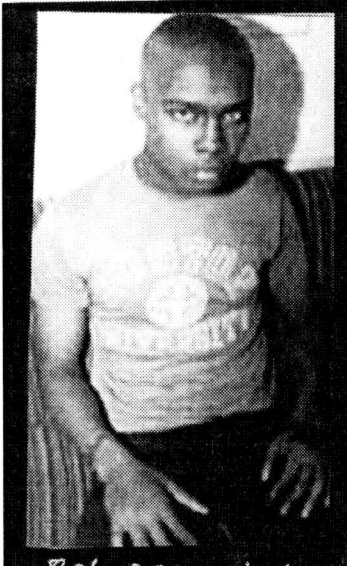

SHAWN BROWN

I never did write about Bad Brains, but it is also my general tendency to ignore the obvious. By now, I've pretty much worn out my copy of Banned In DC, this book by Sharon Cheslow & Cynthia Connolly, that documents the 80's DC punk/hardcore scene. That book illustrates that the scene back then was peppered with black punk rockers, from Toni Young to Skeeter Thompson, from Bad Brains to Beefeater. To be fixated on just Bad Brains as the legacy of Black Punk Rock is to be LAZY! Plus with the internet and with Dischord being nice enough to reissue all their old releases, you can actually still check this stuff out if you never did before.

I've been a **VOID** fan for a long time now, but I have to admit that my fandom is directed mostly at the three songs on the Flex Your Head Dischord compilation that came out in 1982. "My Rules," "Dehumanized" and "Authority" blew me away at first listen because it all sounded like a disaster — like a haphazard accident captured on tape. I love the sound of a band almost falling apart, but at full speed! Their sound is much the opposite of the tight hardcore of Minor

HARDCORE ✯✯✯

BUBBA DUPREE

Threat & Bad Brains. Bubba Dupree was their guitar player and he shreds like a maniac. Their next release was the FAITH/VOID split LP which features DCHC classics like "Organized Sports" and "Who Are You?" They also have an unreleased LP from 1983 called Potion for Bad Dreams that I've only heard once. It kinda sends VOID in a more metal direction, which ain't really my thing. I read that later, Mr. Dupree ended up playing guitar with the likes of Moby & Soundgarden!

This brings us to Shawn Brown. Look how angsty & pouty he's being in his photo. Mr. Brown had the good fortune of singing for **Dag Nasty** before Dave Smalley became the singer. When Shawn sang — or more like shouted — in Dag Nasty, the year was 1985 and the band had this early melodic hardcore sound that makes you wanna pump yr fist, but with a lil tear in your eye. Then Shawn got kicked out and there was some drama. There's an interview online where he talks about how the new D.N. singer used his lyrics without giving Shawn credit & blah, blah, blah. Anyway, he later joined **SWIZ** in 1987 and they released an LP on Sammich Records a year later, and they endured till the early 1990's. Shawn Brown still resides in the nation's capital & works as a tattoo artist.

A Conversation with Leah Lakshmi Piepzna-Samarasinha

This conversation has been a long time coming. In 2009, I wrote that "Where are they now?" column in Maximum RockNRoll about people of color (POC) punks and it made me want to catch up with the brown punks I found out about through the late 1990s and early 2000s feminist punk zine scene to see what riot girl and punk meant for y'all and where it took you. First, I want readers to know your background and where you came from and then from there you can talk about how you found punk and where it took you.

Well, I lived in Worcester, Massachusetts from 1997 to 2007 and it's kind of where I grew up, came of age and found myself. So, yeah, one of those places. The first place I found punk was as a terminally weird brown nerdy kid who was living in a pretty violent family in a rust belt city in Massachusetts in the early '90s. I was a scholarship kid to a two-bit private school my mom had sweated blood to get me into with the goal of Getting Out Of Worcester, and I also lived with parents who had me on super lock down. So due to both these situations, I was seriously isolated. I found Patti Smith through the Ladyslipper catalog. Ladyslipper is this "women's music" catalog that I'd found through reading feminist theory in the library when I was 15. They had a tiny punk rock section and she was in it.

I was primarily a super disassociated, nerdy, crazy, deeply depressed mixed brown queer girl who lived in books and was just trying to survive to get out of the house through college. However, I had this idea I should try and find other freaks and weirdos, and punk was one way of doing it. But my first relationship to punk was through listening to music alone in my room and reading zines. I had zero social skills and could barely get out of the house. My mom called the cops when I was five minutes late coming back from walking to the mailbox that was a block and a half away.

I tried to reach out socially to the local scene, and had some formative experiences, but mostly, in Massachusetts, the punk scene was super racist and sexist. Worcester is a racially mixed and blue collar, but it's super segregated, and the local punk scene was mostly white, broke kids. Black and brown kids in Worcester were into hip hop in 1993. And for a minute, groups like Aryan Youth Front were recruiting in Worcester--I mean, it was a town of white, broke kids who were angry. Of course they would recruit there.

I tried to reach out socially to the local scene, and had some formative experiences, but mostly, in Massachusetts, the punk scene was super racist and sexist. Worcester is a racially mixed, blue collar white/people of color (POC) town, but it's super segregated, and the local punk scene was mostly white, broke kids. Black and brown kids in Worcester were into hip hop in 1993. And for a minute, groups like Aryan Youth Front were recruiting in Worcester—I mean it was a town of white, broke kids who were angry. Of course they would recruit there.

So, all this to say that, while I was glad I made it out to Worcester Artist Group to see shows with other freaks, the mass of boys moshing to Slapshot or Poison Idea wasn't so awesome, and it wasn't a super friendly scene to my nerdy light brown slutty self. However, I did connect through zines and pen pal networks to other baby queers, and I related and was saved a lot by the raw truth of early 90s riot grrl zines, esp. those about surviving incest, sexual assault and family violence.

I kept holding out hope that when I moved, I would find the 'real punks/anarchists' who were political. I applied to 14 schools and my mom was like, "You're going to wherever gives you the biggest financial aid package."

That turned out to be NYU, with a full ride. So in 1993, I finally got out of the parental lockdown and moved from Worcester to New York, right in time for riot grrl, SLAM, ACT UP, the Clit Club, baby women of color feminism, and finding other brown girls. New York in the 90s was a really formative, intense and hard time. I had so much riding on getting out of the house, and I'd been surviving by thinking that once I did, everything would be cool. Reality was more complicated.

So, I did seek out the punk/anarchist scene in the Lower East Side (LES), volunteered at Food Not Bombs, volunteered at Blackout Books, did stuff at ABC NO RIO, was arrested at the 13th Street Squat eviction but I was also this brown girl, from a blue collar city, who had to maintain the scholarship my mom had sweated blood and worked 3 jobs and pushed me int getting. there was no way I could just drop out.

I started figuring out a lot of things about race, class and gender within punk/anarchist stuff and at the same time, I was really getting involved in student organizing against Guiliani's budget cuts, going to a lot of meetings that weren't just punk rock/anarcho stuff, that were organized predominantly by POC. I wasn't fitting into or finding the community I was really longing for in the LES anarcho-punk scene for a lot of reasons. And I started realizing that a bunch of them were about racism, sexism, classism, sexuality, femmephobia, the works. So it's weird. I have these punk rock roots and past, but I never fit in, really, while I was in the thick of it.

I should say, the stories of the New York years are really huge and would take a long time to complete fully, but what I do want to say is that I was really excited by the idea that we could do things ourselves, for free, take over abandoned buildings and parking lots, feed folks for free. I was in love with the idea of the LES as a liberated zone. However, those were also the years where I dated this older, street involved, white tattooed/pierced crazy queer daddy type- who I was attracted to cause he was also queer and talked about abuse, but was also a very violent person- and when he started calling me 40 times a day threatening to kill me from the Blackout Books free phone, no one would intervene. These were the years where I can remember, as a 19 year old, trying to bring up the fact that Blackout was a majority white space (like 3 volunteers of color) and we should talk about how we were contributing to the gentrification of the neighborhood, and being told, literally, "We're anarchists, Leah, of course we're against racism!"

I moved to Toronto in 1997 for a lot of reasons—there were Sri Lankans and radical, queer South Asians, and this giant queer women of color community, and the living was a lot easier, and I was mad in love with someone. And the crew of folks I first started working with were POC punks who had been working in anarchism and punk for years, but were all now, in 1997, deciding to leave it. We had huge conversations about 'going back home', and just giving up on having the same old fights about racism with defensive-ass white people all the time. And by and large, we did it.

From 1997-1999, I didn't even talk to most white folks. I mean, one or two who I did anti-prison stuff with, but my life totally changed. It was like a white person master cleanse! I did a huge amount of prison justice, police brutality, and psych survivor organizing. And for the most part, me, my partner at the time and our friends all turned our backs on punk rock. We went back to, or started to, listening to hip-hop and Bhangra and dancehall and Nina Simone, decided to look less weird because we didn't want to be green-haired brown kids anymore. We wanted to just be brown or Black, and work within our communities. A lot more happened- that relationship turned abusive, and my partner was pretty obsessed with becoming pretty heteronormative because "Queerness was a white thing," etc. The usual bullshit. I was rooting myself in queer of color and feminist of color writing, organizing and art in Toronto and even though I didn't have pink hair anymore, I was still super attracted to zines and the DIY ethos I was a writer who wanted to self publish, and I saw this connection between zines and small, independent publishing and culture lead by queer people of color and feminists of color, like Sister Vision and Kitchen Table press.

So by the time you saw me connected to Mimi and Lauren, that's where I was at. I feel like I was part of a crew of ex-punks of color who left white Punk Rock Landia and gave up on trying to make it be less fucked up, and took the tools and strategies we'd learned from it, like self-publishing and throwing shows, to POC communities we were a part of, or were building. We didn't always claim it, but sometimes we did. Some of those early 2000s zines, like Race Riot or Lauren's zines, were still obviously trying to talk about racism within punk and riot grrl.

So, one thing about your story so far that strikes me is the fact that you were even able to find enough other brown, ex-punk, politically minded people to start projects with. So many brown kids in punk, even today, remain racially isolated. Do you think it was all about being in the right place at the right time?

Yeah, I do. I think Toronto was really unique... And I should say, it was like five of us. But Toronto was interesting. It's Anti-Racist Action (ARA) chapter was majority POC for a minute and worked with POC-lead anti-cop brutality and indigenous organizing, which is very, very different from other ARAs. There were still mad white vegan children, but the fact that there was leadership by a Sri Lankan, a Chilean, a Native guy and a Vietnamese punk rock girl was really different. It made it so that both things happened, like the ARA chapter would work with dudes of color who were selling dope in the market and getting hassled by cops and Nazis *and* that when arguments with the vegan white suburban 14 year olds got really annoying, we left. Toronto is a majority POC city and the activism is very vibrant and cross-racial, especially back then. It made it easier to split. There was someplace to go.

So, that brings me back to your original questions about where all those women POC zinesters went. I remember when you originally posed it, I was like, Helen Luu (former editor of "How to Stage a Coup" zine) is a DJ, taiko drummer and organizer who helped organize a women of color lead response to 9/11 that was the big response meeting immediately after it happened. There are so many ex-punk rock queer women and gender non-conforming POC I know who are in INCITE (Women of Color Against Violence), who I organize with around queer & trans people of color art. I feel like with the work me and Cherry Galette did forming (queer people of color performance group) Mangoes with Chili, we both drew on our punk rock and also broke women of color roots in putting together this DIY queer & trans people of color art tour. I mean, somewhere in my genome, I had the experience of knowing that you could book a DIY tour in my head. We just weren't gonna play Gilman! We were gonna queer POC it, you know?

Leah Lakshmi Piepzna-Samarasinha is a queer mixed Sri Lankan disabled femme writer, performer, teacher and cultural worker. The author of *Consensual Genocide*, her work has been widely anthologized. With Ching-In Chen and Jai Dulani, she co-edited *The Revolution Starts At Home: Confronting Intimate Violence in Activist Communities*. Her second book of poetry, *Love Cake*, is forthcoming in fall 2011. She co-founded Mangos With Chili and Toronto's Asian Arts Freedom School, has taught with UC Berkeley's June Jordan's Poetry for the People and is a lead artist with Sins Invalid. In 2010 she was named one of the Feminist Press' 40 Feminists Under 40 Shaping the Future and nominated for a Pushcart Prize. She comes from a long line of queers, crips, border jumpers, Sri Lankan feminists, full scholarship winners, storytellers and survivors. Born in Worcester, Mass, she currently divides her time between her families in the Bay Area and Toronto. www.brownstargirl.org

hello...

I've got an extra page here to ramble to you about whatever I want, so here we go. I've been at the copy shop all day making the master for this zine fueled only by coffee and trail mix. My deadline for getting this done is tonight because I'm leaving town tomorrow to go see the RAINCOATS in Washington, DC and I wanted to make sure I had enough time to send my zine to London in time for Trash Kit's last two shows on Sept 23 and 25 before they go on an indefinite hiatus.

Hopefully I didn't rush it too much and make too many mistakes & typos.

xo osa

RU PAUL!!!

THANKS FOR READING...

SHOTGUN SEAMSTRESS NO. 6

↓ ↓ ↓

Please write me!
Shotgun Seamstress zine
PO BOX 792372
New Orleans, LA 70179
shotgunseamstress@gmail.com
Read past issues in full at
www.issuu.com/shotgunseamstress

Shotgun Seamstress would like to give credit to the creators of Banned In DC: <u>Photos & Anecdotes from the DC Punk Underground (79-85)</u>, namely Cynthia Connolly, Leslie Clague and Sharon Cheslow. The photographs in that book document black people's involvement in punk better than any other punk book I've ever seen. Every single issue of Shotgun Seamstress except for issue #4 contains photographs from <u>Banned in DC</u>. Check this book out if you haven't already; it's still in print...

About the Author

Osa Atoe is a musician who lives in New Orleans, Louisiana. She started making Shotgun Seamstress zine in 2006 while living in Portland, Oregon. She has been a columnist for Maximum RockNRoll and was a recipient of the Printed Matter Award for Artists in 2009. Currently the drummer for VHS, her former bands include New Bloods and Firebrand.